Devil In The Details

Hex After 40 Book 3

Shelley Dorey

ISBN: 978-1-988913-31-5
072921docx
Cover Design Juan Padron
https://www.juanjpadron.com/
Editing by Paula Grundy
https://paulaproofreader.wixsite.com/home

DEDICATION

To the women
Worn out or blind-sided,
Who rebuilt their lives
The Happiness and Joy
Does come back
With a richness and depth
That will surprise you!

CONTENTS

ONE

My heart catapulted into my throat when I stepped into Mary-Jane's restaurant. Oh my good goddess! He was there in all his *GQ* glory.

Alone at a table by the window, Devon Booker sat with his tablet propped up, reading as he had lunch. A lock of dark-blonde hair brushed the smooth skin of his forehead, while the chiseled features of his nose and jaw once more took my breath away. He was drop-dead gorgeous.

Maybe it's in our genes or something, but I knew instinctively all the things I could do to get his attention, despite having spent twenty years married. It's like falling off a bicycle, I guess. I could call out his name (we've already met, right?) and flash him a smile. Or I could just "brush" past him on the way to my seat or something...you know, those little tactics we girls employ to get a guy to notice us.

But no... I actually took a faltering step back, seriously considering escape before he noticed me. That's because Devon is pretty much convinced I'm a complete psycho, and I really don't blame him for that.

Besides thinking I'm out of my mind, he's kinda—okay, totally—pissed off at me. Getting shot really takes the bloom off attraction, don't you think? Not that *I* shot him: no, that was Steve Murphy. But it was on my property, and Devon kinda blames me.

So hot guy I know, public space, and I was trying to figure out how to blow this joint. But that plan was blown to bits when Ray called to me from his usual spot behind the bar.

"Shannon! It's good to see you. MJ didn't mention you were coming in for lunch today."

I really didn't want to look over at Devon, but I couldn't help stealing glances his way. And, yeah, I got busted when he looked up straight at me. When our eyes locked, I'll admit my heart went pitter-patter. But when that now familiar scowl appeared, darkening his absurdly handsome face, my pitter-patters fell into my stomach. He shifted in his seat and turned away from me as he studied the screen before him.

Damn.

I pasted on a fake smile and headed over to the bar. "Hey, Ray. I just finished a meeting with Wayne Silver about that article he wants me to write. Since I was in the neighborhood, I thought I'd stop by for some lunch." My voice only squeaked a little bit. Just a tad.

As I spoke, half of my mind deliberated on what to do about Devon. I'd tried so many times to apologize, but he wouldn't take my calls or texts. When I stopped by his office, he'd threatened to physically throw me out, if that was what it took to get rid of me.

"Take a seat wherever you want, Shannon. Can I get you a drink?" Ray leaned closer and lowered his voice. "If you'd prefer to visit with Mary-Jane in the kitchen to avoid Devon, I totally get that."

From the concern in Ray's eyes, Mary-Jane must have filled him in on everything between Devon and me. Plus, he probably wasn't keen on a nasty scene going down in his restaurant.

Ray's cautionary kindness, coupled with Devon's rudeness, had the opposite effect on me. It was like a switch was flipped, and I went from scuttling skulker to assertive broad. Instead of slinking away with my tail between my legs, I decided to deal with the situation head-on.

For decades in my life, I had backed off "for the sake of peace." Don't ruffle feathers; don't make a stink; just shut up, and take it with a smile. I kept that façade until I became a doormat. Terrified of being classified as a "bitch," I became the world's bitch. Well, that version of Shannon is long gone. It took my divorce to learn that if I didn't stick up for myself, how could I expect anyone else to?

I hitched my hip onto one of the barstools. "Thanks, Ray, but I'll sit out here. I'll pop into the kitchen to see MJ before I leave. Would you pour me a shot of Jack Daniels on the rocks?" There was *barely* a tremble in my knees, so that was something.

Ray's eyes widened for a second before he turned to get the bottle and pour me a generous shot.

I stared at the drink for a second, working up my nerve. I didn't say sticking up for myself was easy, just that it was the right thing to do. I took a deep breath and strode over to Devon's table. If Devon had his way, I'd never get the chance to see him face-to-face again, so I might as well go for it while I had the chance.

Not looking up or acknowledging my presence in any way, Devon casually took a sip of his drink, his gaze focused on the tablet's screen. My eyes narrowed as I stood there like some afterthought. Ha! Deliberately ignoring me? Well, we'd see about that! Adding gas to the fire, I sat down in the chair across from him and flipped his tablet over.

"Devon. You have every right to be pissed, but I want you to know that I'm *sorry*. I'm sorry for jumping to conclusions about you and your intentions with the land. I'm sorry that you got caught up in the battle that day between Steve and me. I'm sorry you got *shot*."

As I spoke, his steely blue eyes bore a hole through me, while the muscle in his jaw twitched. Dressed in a navy blazer with a crisp button-down shirt, it looked like he'd just come from his office. It didn't help my frayed nerves that he was so freaking attractive, a fact that I'd made known to him countless times when MJ hexed me with her spell. The spell was now lifted, and I could control my mouth around him, but the feelings for him still smoldered.

When I finished speaking, he dabbed his mouth with his napkin and then picked up the tablet, making ready to leave.

I grabbed his arm. "Wait! Don't you have anything to say? I apologized and you're going to *ignore* me? Come on, Devon! That's not fair."

He plucked my hand from his arm like it was a piece of lint. Scowling, his tone was terse. "I'll tell you what's not *fair*, Shannon! Trying to make peace with you but walking into some weird shit going down between you and that idiot, Steve Murphy! And in the process, I take some buckshot in my shoulder!"

I sat back, hunching lower from the verbal assault. Not that I didn't deserve it, but still... "I *said* I was *sorry*. You weren't the only one who got shot, y'know. My bobcat got hit too, and I haven't seen him since!"

I swallowed the lump in my throat thinking of Robert, my "familiar." The very last thing I wanted to do was to break down in tears in front of Devon and the other customers scattered throughout the dining room.

His eyes became so round I thought they'd pop out onto his cheekbones. "Do you even hear yourself? Comparing a human being getting shot, to an animal? Me?" He shook his head. "You're something else; you know that?"

He gritted his teeth so hard I could hear them grind from across the table. "You lead me on, making me believe you're hot for me and I buy into that BS. All the while, you're sticking the knife in my back, spreading rumors, and generally maligning my character. And that's not bad enough, but I end up in the goddamn hospital for trying to prevent your bobcat getting shot by your mouth-breathing *boyfriend*."

All the breath left me as I sat there totally gobsmacked at the venom in his words. Accusations that held a hint of truth, sure, but far from the complete story. I jerked forward to defend myself, but Ray arrived with my drink and set it down before me.

"Everything okay, here? Can I get you anything else?" Ray's gaze ping-ponged between Devon and me.

"Just the bill, Ray." Devon shot a pointed look at me. "I've totally lost my appetite."

When Ray hurried off, Devon slipped his overcoat on. "I've said this before, but it bears repeating, Shannon. You are dangerously psycho. You've gone from hurting my reputation to *physically* harming me."

I stood up, blocking his way. "It's true I said some outrageously flirty things to you. Things that were all true, by the way. I also jumped to conclusions about your business dealings, so that's fair. But it wasn't me who shot you, you know. It was Steve. And if you think that Steve Murphy's my boyfriend, you're dead wrong. He's anything but!"

Devon stepped to the side, avoiding getting anywhere near me, like I was contagious or something. His words were coldly officious when he spoke. "If you come within twenty feet of me again, I'll have you arrested, Shannon. Are we clear?"

"I wish you'd just try to listen to me, Devon. Even if we could just be friends. Hear me out; that's all I ask." It came out all whiny, something I hated but was powerless to stop. And dammit, tears welled up in my eyes. I'd hurt him so bad, and now he wanted nothing more to do with me. There was truth to that saying *"You don't know what you've got till it's gone."*

Devon leaned closer, rapping the table with his knuckle before he hissed. "We could have been so much more than friends, Shannon. No doubt if we ever got together, it would be an awesome wild night of amazing sex. We both know the attraction is there for both of us. But in the morning, I'd wake up, and you'd still be the whack-job that you are. No, thanks." With that, he turned and left me sitting there.

TWO

I swiped at the tear rolling down my cheek as I rushed across the dining room. As soon as I stepped into the kitchen, Mary-Jane looked over from the stove, where she was sautéing something in a frying pan.

"Shannon!" She signaled to Debbie, her assistant, to take over before she rounded the counter. Instead of asking me what was wrong, her arms folded around me in a hug. Normally, I would resist her "reading" me with her psychometric gift, but not this time. I wouldn't have been able to get the words out anyway, not without blubbering. Great. Not a doormat, just a freaking blubbering schoolgirl. Argh!

Mary-Jane eased back and steered me to the back of the kitchen, where we could talk without Debbie hearing everything. We sank into the chairs at a small table, and her head tipped to the side as she gazed at me.

"I'm sorry he's being such a jerk to you, Shannon. I'm no fan of Devon Booker, but I can see that this is hurting you. And then there's also Robert. Still no sign of the bobcat?"

I grabbed a tissue from my purse and dabbed my eyes. "No. I've searched every square inch of the forest, but there's no sign of him. Even Libby came out yesterday to help. She let that raccoon she fostered go free and asked him to keep an eye out for Robert."

Mary-Jane smiled. "Well, that's got to help! You know what raccoons are like. They're the busybodies of the woods, poking their noses in everywhere. And with Libby now able to talk to animals, I'd say that the prospects of finding Robert just got better."

I nodded. "Yeah, she uncovered a warren of rabbits to ask about the bobcat, but they hadn't seen him. I've been putting wild salmon and even free-range chicken meat on my verandah for Robert, but nothing's working. Nada. Maybe the wound was worse than I thought, and he died."

Her eyebrows rose high and she snorted. "That eccentric little bugger is tough, Shannon. Hell! He lost an ear in another battle. Don't write Robert off. Not yet."

"Unless he's given up on *me*. You know how critical he was of my witch skills when he talked to Libby. Maybe he's found a more worthy witch." I slumped over the table. "Robert deserts me, and Devon can't stand me. The only guy who hasn't given up on me is Steve Murphy. Although, I seriously wish he'd take a hike."

Mary-Jane winked. "I can make that happen. Say the word." When MJ saw the shock in my face at her offer, she held her palms up. "Don't worry. I'm not going to try another spell, not where you're concerned, Shannon. I learned my lesson after what happened with Devon."

"Good. Although I won't mind if you cast a spell on *Robert* to make him come back. I miss the little shit." There was an ache in my chest thinking of the evenings the bobcat and I sat in my living room next to the fire. Although he was prickly, and I wasn't able to have conversations with him like Libby could, he was my *friend* and my familiar. Feeling him purring as I absently pet him was such a peaceful, comforting sensation. He was the first pet (although he'd be insulted to hear me use that term) I ever had.

Mary-Jane scowled. "I still can't believe that Steve would show up at your house to shoot Robert! What the *hell* was he thinking! You know something? It kinda makes you wonder about his marriage breakdown. Maybe Amy had more reasons to leave him than meeting and falling in love with Suzanne."

I thought of the times I'd argued with Steve. "He's definitely a control freak. And I've definitely had enough of guys *mansplaining* and trying to make decisions for me. But this? He totally went too far this time. He was lucky to get off with a fine when Devon was injured. Steve's never setting foot on my land again. Thanks to him, Robert's gone, and any chance I had with Devon got shot to smithereens. Literally."

"Which brings us back to Devon. I feel like I'm partly to blame for what happened between you. If I hadn't hexed you, removing the filter between your brain and your mouth, the two of you would be friends at least. Do you want me to touch Devon? Maybe give him a hug to try to figure out how to fix things between you?"

I sat there silently, mulling over her idea. Technically, it wasn't a spell she'd be doing. I had enough of her spells on me to last a lifetime. This would be using Mary-Jane's *gift*—the ability to read into a person and find the truth of their feelings and actions. So, technically, we weren't breaking any rules with this.

"Okay. If you could accidentally bump into him, grab his hand and read him, then sure! Why not? Things are terrible now, so it couldn't hurt to try it. I hate it that I can't even be *friends* with him."

Which was only half true. I hadn't had a romp in the sack in far, far too long, and Devon was... well, yummy. I wondered what it would be like with Devon. He even said that sex between us would have been crazy wild, and who am I to argue? I mean...the number of men I slept with in my entire life I could count on one hand and have fingers left over.

Stop it, Shannon! I came back to MJ. She was looking at me oddly, so I said, "What's the matter?"

She rolled her eyes. "You're forgetting who you're talking to, Shannon. C'mon! *Friends with benefits* is more like it! I picked up on that when I hugged you." She stood up. "But, I'm not judging you. Go for it, if that's what you want. Get laid. Just don't *marry* him."

There it was again. Anytime Devon was mentioned in a conversation, there was always a negative remark. It was a conditioned response that everyone in Wesley seemed to share. But I didn't see it. He'd been decent with me. Even that episode of telling me my septic system needed replacement had been the plumbing guy trying to pull a fast one, not any shenanigans by Devon. So, no, it was my actions that had hurt him, not the other way around. But I wasn't there to argue the point with MJ.

"I'm not marrying anyone, not any time soon."

"Good." Mary-Jane glanced over at the cooking area before she stood up. "I'll see what I can do with Devon. I'd better get back to work."

I rose as well. "Thanks, Mary-Jane. I think I'll take a pass on lunch, but I'm glad we talked. I'm going to buy some steaks and try my luck with Robert again."

She looked over at me as we walked back to the main area. "We'll make Robert the focal point of our Esbat on Monday. In the meantime, leave Devon to me."

THREE

As I stood at the counter waiting for the butcher to finish wrapping the sirloins I'd picked out, someone tapped me on the shoulder. Turning and seeing Cynthia grinning at me made me smile in return. As usual, she was dressed to the nines in a green leather coat that made the glints of red in her auburn hair more pronounced.

"Hi, Shannon. I was going to call you tonight, but here you are! We need to start planning what we're doing for Beltane."

Beltane? I'd heard the term, but I drew a total blank. "Sure." I took the package of meat from the butcher and turned to her. "Remind me again what that is. I should know it, but..."

Her eyebrows arched. "I keep forgetting how new you are to all this stuff." She grabbed a package of pork chops and tossed it into her basket. When she turned to me again, her eyes practically glinted. "It's kind of like May Day, celebrating summer's arrival. But it's also an ancient festival seeking fertility for the coming year."

"Fertility? As in good crops and harvest?" I let out a chuckle as we started walking away from the meat counter. "It's certainly not fertility as in *babies,* not for me. Mary-Jane, Libby, and I are well past that and..." My voice trailed off as it hit me. Cynthia was only in her mid-thirties.

She actually giggled, seeing the surprise on my face. "Yeah, ME! I've been giving this a lot of thought, Shannon. I want to have a baby before it's too late. Specifically, a daughter."

My mouth fell open, and I literally gaped at her. "You're getting married or...who's the *guy*?" Cynthia had dated practically every guy in town who was single. But I'd never thought she was serious about any of them. As far as I knew the closest had been Steve. But she'd only dated him for a few months before breaking it off.

"I'm not getting *married*!" Her face tightened, looking at me like I was an alien or something. "And as for"—finger quoting in the air—'the guy,' I haven't the faintest idea. I'm going to a fertility clinic to get the deed done."

"Oh, my good goddess! I had *no* idea how badly you wanted this!" But as I gazed at her, it made perfect sense! Cynthia was so independent. No doubt there'd been guys who had wanted to get close to her, marry her even, but she'd chosen her freedom. I shook my head in wonder. "When? When are you doing this?"

She grabbed my hand and squeezed it excitedly. "Next month! That's why I want to celebrate Beltane! Now that I've made this decision, I want to do the spring festival in glorious style." Shrugging, she continued, "Usually I do a small ceremony, but now that I'm part of a coven, and wanting to have a baby, I *really* want to go all out! You know, have the big bonfire, and the maypole. I want this to be *perfect*."

"And it will be!" Her enthusiasm was contagious. "We're going to do everything we can to help you with this." I was still gobsmacked by her decision. "I'm excited for you, Cynthia! Wow."

As we walked to the cash register to check out, she gave me a side eye. "I've always envied the fact that each of you has a daughter. Nothing against boys, but they grow up and marry, and then you kind of lose them. But a daughter...You *always* have your daughter."

I thought of how close I was to Jessica, even though she was away in college. We still called or texted each other every day, but my son, Thomas... A week could go by without contact unless I called him.

"It's true what you say about daughters, but you *could* have a boy. What then?" My forehead furrowed as I peered at her closely. Surely she wouldn't do anything to end a pregnancy if it was the wrong sex.

She smiled. "I'd still love a son. Nothing is guaranteed in life. But the technology is there to favor the odds of a girl. Something tells me it's going to be a daughter. And especially if we do Beltane up right! We've got a couple of weeks to plan it."

As we stood in line waiting for the cashier to be free, she made a small gasp and leaned in close, peering at me. "I'm sorry. I've been so excited about my plans that I haven't asked about Robert. He hasn't come back, has he."

It wasn't a question. Cynthia was as good as MJ in reading people, often not even needing to touch them physically to pick up thoughts and energy. "Nope. That's why I'm here getting steaks. I'm still hoping he'll turn up. MJ offered to make this week's Esbat about invoking the Mother to bring him back to me. You're coming Monday night, right?"

"Of course. I think she's right. If all four of us focus our intention, it will work." Her eyes narrowed when she looked at me. "I saw Steve Murphy at the coffee shop today. He tried to get me to listen to his explanation about bringing a gun to your house. There was no way I was buying his BS. I blew him off with just a look. Imagine! Trying to justify shooting Robert!"

I snorted. "He's sent me flowers every day since. As if that's going to make any difference. Just more crap to add to my compost pile. To think at one time I really liked Steve. I sure called that one wrong." I stopped myself from adding anything about Devon, another one I'd gotten wrong.

Cynthia nodded. "I hear you. I dated Steve for a few months. At first it was fun but then the *real Steve*, the master manipulator, emerged. That doesn't work for me. At. All."

As she started putting her few items on the conveyor, she brightened. "Don't tell Libby or MJ about my pregnancy plans. I want to be the one to tell them. Maybe at Esbat."

My fingers mimicked closing a zipper across my lips. "It's your tale to tell, Cynthia. I really hope this works out for you." As I watched her turn to pay the cashier, I thought again of my own children. I couldn't imagine my life without either of them. Summer was around the corner, and I was pretty sure that Jessica would spend it with me, in Wesley. Thomas... well, I was still working on him.

FOUR

That same day...

Libby

See you tomorrow, Libby."

My head turned at Dr. Hawley's voice, and I smiled at seeing the elderly physician. "Have a good evening, Doctor." I continued on, walking past the nurses' station where Janine and Beverly sat. I sighed inwardly. My days manning that station as a nurse were gone now that I'd been promoted to the head nurse position. Like everything in life, there was good and bad in the new job. The regular hours—even with constant calls at home—were good, but it was *sterile*, lacking the warmth and challenge of patient care.

When I stepped out into the early April sunshine, I took a deep breath to clear my head. A car horn let out a quick toot before Stan Jones's truck pulled up to the curb. The passenger door swung open, and he leaned across the seat, grinning at me. The worries and stress of the day melted as I hurried to get into the truck to be with him.

Things had been going great between us, and the kids had warmed up to the fact that there was a man in my life. Stan was the first (and probably last) man I've dated since that drunk driver killed Hank over six years ago. I suppressed a snort as I settled into my seat. The kids were as nuts about Stan as I was, if not more so.

There. I said it. I was nuts about the guy. And... it felt *good* to feel that way. Again. Sure, I'm a jerk; I'm pushing fifty, and just like when I was sixteen, *I got a boyfriend!* Do they even use that phrase these days? I'll have to check with Cynthia.

"Hey, Libs!" When I was seated, he leaned over and gave me a quick kiss. "Straight home, or do you need to stop to get something? Either way is good with me." The lines creasing the corners of his gray eyes deepened, and one side of his mouth rose higher in his lopsided smile. Pushing fifty, he still had a boyish, open quality about him that tugged at my heart. Not to mention that as a firefighter, he was in amazing physical shape!

"You know what, Stan? I'd really like to go for a hike today. Take me home so I can get changed, and let's go to that old logging road. You know, the one with that little spring where we first went." I looked up at the sky. There was another two solid hours of light, and getting outside to shed the worries of scheduling and administration work was just what I needed.

He reached over and took my hand in his. "How could I forget? It was practically our first date. And it's a gorgeous day for a walk. We can order pizza for dinner. I'm sure the kids won't mind that."

I looked over at him. 'The kids.' The easy way he'd referred to my children was like he was already part of the family. Somehow, I knew in my bones that if Hank were looking down from wherever he was, he'd approve. Life goes on. A fact that until a short while ago, I had desperately tried to deny.

"Are you kidding? They'd have pizza every meal if I'd let them. How was your day?"

"Not as uneventful as it normally is." He glanced over, and the smile fell from his lips. "There was a bonfire that got a little outta hand. You know Amy and Suzanne Smith, right? It was at their house. No one was hurt, and we got it out straight away though."

"Amy Smith. That's Steve Murphy's ex. What the heck was she doing setting up an outdoor fire? I mean, it's nice out, but not exactly bonfire weather and especially not during the day." I pictured the pretty woman who had been married to Steve but was now living with Suzanne Smith. I knew Suzanne from the health food store where I went for local honey. It was always fun to see what color her hair would be next.

Stan's eyebrows rose. "She must have had a little spring fever, I guess. Getting the jump on burning leaves from the fall and getting their gardens ready. I told her to get a burn barrel and let her off with a warning. Her son, Byron, was there, so I didn't want to make too big a thing about it."

I squeezed his hand. "You're a softie. You know that? But it's part of your irresistible charm." I reached for the door handle when he wheeled the big beast of a truck into my drive. "You coming in or are you waiting here?"

"I'll fill a couple water bottles while you get changed. Besides, I'd like to say hi to Dahlia and see how she made out with the poster I helped her with." He killed the truck's engine and opened the door.

We were hardly inside the house, slipping our shoes off, when Dahlia came racing out from the kitchen. She had a stray cat in her arms, cuddling it to her chest.

"Look who followed me home!" Her fingers fluttered in a wave above the multicolored fur of the cat. "Hi, Stan."

Back to nuzzling her nose next to the cat's ear, her eyes met mine. "Isn't she precious! I've always wanted a calico. Can I keep her? You let Rascal my raccoon go, Mom, so it's only fair!" Her long blonde hair almost completely covered the cat's face as she snuggled it closer.

Stan nudged me. "You set Rascal free? I'm going to miss him." He stepped closer to Dahlia and scratched behind the cat's ear. His hand drifted down over the cat's stomach. "Uh-oh. I think this cat's going to have a litter soon."

Argh! I had hardly taken my coat off to hang it up. Shaking my head, I turned to Dahlia. "Someone might be missing that cat, kiddo. You should put up some posters in the neighborhood before you lay claim to *another* animal. Let me see her."

I locked eyes with the cat as Dahlia handed her to me. "Stan wants to see how you made out with the poster for school. Maybe he'll help you with one for the cat." As I watched them leave to go to the den where the computer was, I whispered to the cat, "Okay, we're alone, now. What's your story?"

The cat rubbed her cheek against my fingers, purring softly. *"I heard about you. I had a home, but when the old lady I lived with went to a nursing home. I got kicked to the curb. Seeing your daughter today was a lifeline. I knew this was the place for me."*

Walking past the opening to the den, I saw Dahlia at the computer, talking to Stan. They looked like they'd be busy for a few moments, but just in case, I walked up the stairs to go to my bedroom to change. All the while, I held the cat in my arms.

"What do you mean, you *heard* about me?" I whispered. My heart skipped a beat when a picture of Robert flashed in my head. Could it have been Robert? But why would a domestic cat talk to a wild bobcat instead of running away as fast as she could?

The cat blinked slowly as she looked up at me sending me her thoughts. *"It's all over town! I thought I'd beat the crowd and get here first. Some raccoon bragged about living with the witch who could talk to animals. You know what raccoons are like. Never tell a secret to those blabbermouths."*

I sank down onto my bed and set the cat on the soft coverlet. "Wait! I'm *known* around town? What do you mean, you beat the crowd?" I watched the cat casually lick its paw before she deigned to answer. "What's your name?"

"The old lady called me Fluffy, but I don't like that name. It's trite and a little common. I prefer what my mother called me—Puuurdy. Get it? It's a play on words."

Stars and moons! A cat who was a comedian? And a pregnant one to boot!

Puuurdy or Fluffy or whatever, stood up and rubbed her side against my arm. *"Let me stay, and I'll put the word out to quash these stories. Otherwise, there's at least a dozen strays planning on moving into your back shed. Not to mention...ugh, dogs."*

"Listen, Purdy or Fluffy or whatever...you can't *stay*! Especially not with a belly full of kittens. I'm not a shelter! You have to find another old lady to move in with."

The cat hissed, swishing its tail. *"Your daughter thinks otherwise. Dahlia promised me I could stay."* Its nails sunk into the satin of my pink duvet.

As I locked into a staring match with the stubborn feline, my mouth fell open. "Wait. You understood her? Was she...I mean, did you two *talk*?"

"RELAX! I totally understood Dahlia, but she has no idea that she communicates with animals, if that's what's got your back up. She's probably more gifted than you. It wouldn't take much to nudge that gift along, if you know what I mean. And then when she hears about YOU—"

"You're trying to *blackmail* me! You think I care if my daughter knows I can—"

"*I KNOW you care!*" The cat sat down and preened again, now licking her forearm. *"Come on. Do we have a deal or not?"*

Before I could answer, Dahlia burst into the room. There was a sly grin on her face as she sidled over to the bed. "She's a sweet cat, isn't she, Mom? I'll put up the posters, but if no one claims her, I can keep her, right?"

I looked over at the cat who positively gloated, rolling on her back, leaving a handful of hair all over my duvet. The lumps inside her—the kittens—rumbled and rolled under the taut skin of her belly. Even though the weather was getting milder, I couldn't see myself putting the mother cat out in the street to have her babies.

Turning to my daughter, I nodded. "Put up the posters to be on the safe side. If no one claims her, she can stay. But when the kittens are old enough, they go to other homes. Understood?"

Dahlia scooped the cat up and nuzzled it again. "I've even got a name for her, Mom. Mrs. Purdy! Because she's perfectly pretty."

As she raced from my room, she took all the air with her. She'd called the cat by the name the cat had chosen for herself. Oh my goddess. My daughter was following in my footsteps. She hadn't been to the well and had no clue that I was a witch, but she was showing signs of this supernatural gift.

Maybe I'd have to have the "talk" with her. And it wouldn't be about the birds and the bees.

But first I had to let my friends in the coven know.

FIVE

The next morning, 7:20 to be exact...

Mary-Jane

I finished stretching my quads and started off at a brisk pace of walking. Above me, the sun shone in an azure sky, while the grass in my neighbors' lawns was showing the first signs of spring with a carpet of green. Even the birds had returned, filling the air with their chirps and song. It was a glorious day to be alive and out for a run.

It felt like forever since I'd been clear of Shannon's spell. Now my morning runs were a workout for my muscles and not my hormones. I didn't miss the sprints that turned me into a molten ball of lust. It had been fun at first, but no way could Ray and I keep that pace up.

I'd never been a big fan of exercising, but now it was not only ingrained, it was a high point of my day. And the added bonus was finally ditching the Spanx and still fitting into a size eight! I'd never thought I'd shop from the petite rack again, but it was my go-to now.

But there was another reason I'd gotten up a half hour earlier than normal, leaving Ray sawing logs in the nest of bedclothes. I had often seen Devon Booker out at this time of the morning, his route overlapping my usual trek. After seeing how miserable Shannon was the day before, I HAD to do something to mend fences between her and Devon.

"Hey, MJ! You're out early!"

At the male voice, I turned and saw Steve Murphy getting out of his truck. Shit. He was early in opening Mountain Hardware today. Shielding his eyes from the sun, his other hand rose to wave at me, a tentative smile on his face.

I picked up the pace, stepping a little closer to where he stood. "Hi! I could say the same to you. Gotta go! Have a good day!" There was no way I was going to stop and pass the time of day with Steve, not after what he'd done to Robert. But I couldn't be as curt as Shannon either. Steve had done a lot to help us after the restaurant fire.

Turning off the main drag, I headed for the high school and the churchyard. If I was going to see Devon, that would be the most likely spot. Sure enough, when I emerged on the quiet backstreet, I saw him on the next block, the soles of his sneakers flying fast ahead of me. This was going to take an all-out run to catch him.

When I was about ten feet behind, his head turned to see who was trailing him. He smiled and eased up, so I could catch up. "I thought that might be you out here! It's been a few weeks since you've been out. It's good to see you back into the swing of it, Mary-Jane!"

"Yeah!" Gulping air, I managed to return a smile. "I'm trying to get back into it. The first morning's a killer though." Which wasn't entirely true. I might be winded, but I was hitting my groove again. Now for the real drama that I'd rehearsed in my head as soon as I'd woken up.

Lurching to the side, I let out a loud yelp! "OW! OW! OW!" I almost went to my knees, squeezing my eyes shut as I came to an abrupt halt.

Devon was at my side immediately. "Mary-Jane! What's wrong?" He bent over, breathing hard as he peered at me. His hands were on his hips while his feet continued to walk in place.

"This blasted ankle! Sometimes it just gives out on me! Ever since that accident, it's been tricky." I sank down onto the sidewalk, rubbing my foot with my hands. A side glance showed Devon still standing there with a sympathetic but confused look on his face. I held my leg out, rotating my foot and grimacing the whole while.

Finally, he squatted down, placing his hand on my shoulder. "Are you going to be able to get home with that? Should I call Ray or a cab or something?"

I shook my head, pretending to be caught up in the pain. As soon as he touched me, I started probing his mind, looking for any chink in the armor he'd built up against Shannon. The first thoughts in his brain were confusion and awkwardness at seeing me injured.

My hand rose to grip his arm, and I muttered, "Just help me up, please. Ray is busy, but if you could call Shannon for me, she'll give me a lift."

There! No point in beating around the bush when I could press his hot buttons, homing in on where I wanted to go. My fingers were tentacles threading into his thoughts and emotions, but my efforts were unnecessary. As soon as I'd said Shannon's name, he was an open book.

Oh my goodness! Too much information! He *fantasized* about her? And he definitely had some weird kink going on. What the hell was with him and Jell-O? Yuck.

After I got past the X-rated scene, what came through loud and clear was anger! Anger, disappointment, and yet he was still *thinking* about her. Some of that anger was self-directed that he wasn't getting past his feelings for her. And jealousy. Suspicion there was something still going on between her and Steve. That scene at Shannon's house where Steve had showed up...Shit! He was more upset about Steve casually dropping by than getting shot!

His head pulled back, and his expression morphed from concern to coldness in a nanosecond. "I'll call a cab or an Uber. I don't have Shannon's number on my phone." He pulled his cell phone from the pocket of his windbreaker.

I squeezed his arm. "No! Wait." I grabbed my cell phone from my armband. "She's on mine, Devon." Wincing in feigned pain, I added, "Can you call her? I need to massage my ankle."

His eyes narrowed and he stood up. "No. What are you up to, Mary-Jane? Did Shannon put you up to this? You're not even hurt, are you?"

Oh shit! Busted. I held out my hand, offering my phone. "No! I'm in pain here, Devon! Come on! It's just one phone call. Please."

He shook his head, scowling at me. "This is *her* doing. I won't play into her crazy scheme." He started to walk away, but then he stopped.

For a few seconds, I thought he might have changed his mind. But he didn't turn, kept standing there. But not *just* standing there. He actually wavered from side to side. His hands flew up to his head, and he bent at the waist. Oh my God! Was *he* having problems? It looked like he might fall over in a heap!

"Devon! Are you okay?"

It seemed like minutes that he stayed there still swaying slightly. But then he turned and smiled. "I'll call her if you want me to, Mary-Jane." He took my phone and scrolled through until he found her in my "Contacts."

Holding my phone to his chest before he placed the call, his gaze thawed as he looked at me. "I don't mind walking you back to your house. It might be faster than waiting for

Shannon to get here. Or I can jog home and get MY car. I'll get you home safe and sound."

My forehead tightened as I stared at him. There was something odd in the way he was smiling at me. Even his tone had changed...becoming tender and friendlier? What was he up to? If I didn't know any better, I'd swear he was flirting with me!

"No, that's okay. On second thought, I think my ankle's better. I'll be okay walking home, Devon." I pushed myself to my feet and reached for the phone.

When my fingertips brushed his, I felt my gut sink to the ground below me. What the hell?

Now he's thinking of *me* and Jell-O? What the hell?

Crap.

SIX

That same morning, 7:20 to be exact

Shannon

I looked around the living room one final time before sitting on the floor. No sign of Aunt Maeve. Good. Normally, I love to see her ghostly specter pop in for a visit but not this morning. Nope. She'd give me proper shit if she saw what I was about to do.

Hell! She wasn't the only one! Libby, Mary-Jane, and Cynthia would yell at me too! I didn't care. I'd had enough sleepless nights, enough tears shed over the mess I'd made of things with Devon. I couldn't even think about the tears I'd cried for Robert!

Taking the white chalk in hand, I drew the pentacle on the hardwood floor. As I placed the small white tea lights on the first point, I murmured, "White light on the northern."

Then taking the second candle, placing it on another point. "White to bind the eastern."

I followed with the last two tea lights, setting them on the southern and western points that corresponded with the physical directions. "Casting all to set the spell, I place this candle in the well." I set the larger pink candle in the very center of the circle and reached for the lighter to set all candles afire.

For a few moments, I sat there with my eyes closed, focusing on my breathing to bring my intention into clear focus. I pictured Devon as I'd seen him at ease in his office, the two of us flirting and laughing. That was the easy relationship I wished to return to, albeit without MJ's spell or my suspicions about Devon's business plans. There was yearning underneath the spark of attraction in his dark-blue eyes. I felt a tingle in my body, the attraction flowing between us like a magnet.

Opening my eyes, I reached for the small pot of honey. Letting it drip from my finger into the bowl containing the pink candle, I spoke:

"Nectar of nature
So sweet and pure
Let him find me
I cast the allure."

I finished this part by popping my finger into my mouth to taste the sweetness of the honey.

Taking the petals of dried roses, I held my hand next to the pink candle, letting them fall from my fingers as I spoke:

"One petal to open his heart
One petal to clear his mind
One petal for forgiveness
A petal for friendship
A petal for pleasure."

I closed my eyes again and pictured Devon's face. If nothing else, I wanted us to be friends. If the goddess and the Mother were willing, an *intimate* friendship. I smiled. At one time, it was what Devon and I both had wanted, so it wasn't like I was screwing with his free will or anything. It was more like just cleaning the slate to get back to where we were.

Right?

And it wasn't technically a *love spell.* Although my friends and my aunt wouldn't see it that way. I wasn't looking for "true love" or marriage or anything complicated. Hell! Who was I kidding? It was *attraction*! Sex! We were both single, so why not?

Thud!

My eyes flew open, yanked out of my daydreams about Devon and me with a start! I saw my Grimoire laying on the floor just outside my circle before the air changed, shimmering. In no time at all, my aunt's form became clearer, her mouth set in a hard line as she stared at me.

"Shannon Burke! You don't have enough experience to cast a love spell! This can backfire and cause all kinds of problems." She floated through the air with her gaze centered on the pink candle. "We have to stop this!"

I jumped to my feet, holding my hand out and halting her before she could reach my pentagram. "No! It isn't what you think it is. It's friendship! All I'm asking for is a second chance, to open Devon's mind! Is that so bad?"

The old spirit drew herself up in a huffy snoot, tilting her nose high. "Yes. I hate to tell you this, especially after all you've gone through with spells going awry. This is something you really should have left alone. Sometimes problems are best solved when you allow time to take care of them. Magic is...well, as you know, it's ornery at times."

I picked up my Grimoire and the chalk, leaving the candles to burn out on their own. "My intentions were *pure,* Aunt Maeve. And if I have the same luck as the spells I've cast to bring Robert back, then you have nothing to worry about. I had to give it a try though."

She followed me into the kitchen, nattering at me the whole way. "I love you to pieces, Shannon, but you have become a *headstrong* woman! After all you've been through with spells going sideways, you TRY this... *a love spell!*"

As I poured my coffee, I looked over at her, wrinkling my nose. "Not a love spell, a *sex spell* is much more accurate! Don't tell me you never did anything like this when you were alive! I was here for many summers, growing up. I know you had gentlemen callers! *Booty calls!*"

"Booty calls! Whatever THAT means, although I've got a pretty good idea!" She hovered over me when I took a seat at the table, wagging her finger. "You should focus your intention on Robert! He's your FAMILIAR! I have a feeling that you're going to need his help, sooner rather than later, especially if you keep playing around like this with magic."

My shoulders dropped as I glared at her. "I'm not playing, Aunt Maeve! How the hell am I going to master this if I don't practice? And as for Robert, we're dedicating Esbat this week to his safe return. We're even going to the Witching Well for that!"

As I held the mug of coffee up, I added, "You should be happy that I'm not trying to hex Steve Murphy after what he did to Robert! A little credit here, huh?"

Her expression changed as she looked down at the floor. "I don't know what Steve was thinking. He was always such a good kid. That was before he bought the place next door and fixed it up. I wonder if it was his wife that changed him?"

I shrugged. "I wouldn't know. I've only seen her and her partner once since I've moved here. But their son is a sweetie." As I got up to rinse my mug, I mused, "Who was in that house before Steve? It's strange that I never met them in all the summers I spent here."

She rolled her eyes. "With good reason. I never cared for Alan Thornton. It was just him there, no family. I always suspected he was some kind of criminal on the run; he was so secretive. The one time one of my guest's kids ventured onto his property, he threw a fit. Scared the dickens out of the poor tyke."

"Sounds like a peach, all right. I'm glad I never ran into him."

I sighed. "I still have four cabins to fix before summer so I can rent them. I hate the thought of going into Mountain Hardware for supplies and seeing Steve there. I may have to travel to Ellsboro to get what I need, even though it's fifty miles away."

"I don't blame you for how you feel about Steve. I just wish I knew what prompted him to shoot Robert." She moved to the window scanning the yard for the bobcat. "I might try my other sources to see if I can locate him."

She smiled when she turned to me. "We're both in a learning curve, Shannon. You with magic and me with being a spirit. When I figure out how to break the tether that keeps me in my old home, there's some people I'd like to shake up a bit. It'd be perfect if I knew by All Souls day. What fun we could have!"

"But you visited me when I first came here. Hell! If you hadn't, I might have run Robert over with my truck." I remembered that day like it was yesterday. The bobcat had suddenly jumped into the path of my truck, and if not for Aunt Maeve showing up and wrenching the steering wheel, it would have been a disaster. "You've done it before, yet now you think you're limited to just this house? Why could you visit me then, Aunt Maeve?"

"I know. I WAS there helping you when you first drove here. But how the hell did I do that? I wish I knew what I did back then to do that." She floated over to me, and her hand on my cheek was like the touch of a spider's web on my face. "I'm glad it worked out though. Give me time. I'll figure it out, and maybe then I'll be of more help to you."

My chest filled with love for my old aunt. "You already are, Aunt Maeve, even if we butt heads sometimes."

SEVEN

The next evening...

Shannon

I adjusted the rearview mirror in my truck to dab on another bit of lip gloss and check my mascara. Everything was as perfect as it was ever going to get for my night out with Cynthia, Libby, and Stan at Mary-Jane's restaurant. As I walked across the street, my high heels tapped on the pavement, while a gust of wind flirted with the bouncy ruffles on my skirt.

"Hey! Wait for me, Shannon!"

Turning my head, I smiled seeing Cynthia coming down the sidewalk, waving her hand at me, making the bangles on her wrist sparkle. Her hair was swept up in a messy bun, with reddish-brown tendrils curling over the shoulders of the tight blue dress. But unlike me, she was wearing her signature footwear, a pair of thigh-high leather boots.

When she caught up to me, I looped my arm through hers. "Awesome dress, Cynthia! Look at us! If we don't get asked to dance, there's something seriously wrong with the men in this town."

"This was a great idea, Shannon! If everything goes according to plan, it might be a year before I go out dancing. Or maybe not. Baby bump or not, I could still bust a move." She pulled the door open for me.

As I slipped by her, I muttered, "True. It's the after part that's going to be rough. You won't have the energy to go out much. Not with midnight feedings and sleep deprivation. You have no idea how your life will change, doll."

"Probably not, but I can't wait." Cynthia followed me into the foyer of the low-lit building. She nudged me and signaled with her chin. "I see them! They've got a table next to the dance floor."

Before I could make out where she indicated, Chloe, MJ's daughter, stepped up to us. The white blouse with a small bow tie above the dark pants she wore, was a cute touch. I'd have to mention that to MJ.

"Hi, Shannon. Cool dress." Smiling at Cynthia. "If you ever get tired of those boots, I'll take them off your hands. You guys look awesome. Libby and Stan are already here. Just follow me."

She turned to lead the way, threading through tables in the packed restaurant. A young woman and two guys were on the small stage next to us, tuning up their instruments, so it looked like our timing was perfect.

Cynthia tapped my waist, leaning over to whisper, "Don't look, but Steve Murphy is parked at the bar. I should have put a glamor on us so that he wouldn't see us to ask us to dance. My bad." Her fingers prodded me harder, making me jerk. "Oh crap. Devon's at a table near the kitchen door. Can you feel the daggers from his eyes?"

At the mention of Devon's name, my heart did a flip-flop. But right after that the smile on my lips faded. He was shooting daggers at *me* with his eyes? That didn't sound right. What about the love spell I'd cast? Don't tell me, I'd gone to all the trouble of dolling up in my sexiest dress, scorching my hair with a curling iron and layering the war paint on, just to be ignored by Devon. That damned spell hadn't worked. Shit.

But I carried on, keeping my eyes directed at Stan and Libby as we walked. Cynthia was like my personal bloodhound scouting out everyone in the restaurant. I saw the firefighter, the one I'd privately nicknamed *Studly LaMarre*, sitting next to Stan. But, of course, Cynthia had also spotted him, practically jostling me out of the way to sit next to him.

Libby was resplendent in a red dress, the pearl-drop earring jittering as she laughed at something Stan said to her. She looked up at Cynthia and me. "Wow! You two look amazing." Her gaze swept to the firefighter before she added, "Have you met, Eric?"

I smiled at him as I took a seat. "I saw you at the firehouse, but we haven't been introduced. I'm Shannon, and this is—"

"Cynthia Granger!" Eric jumped up to hold Cynthia's chair for her, all the while his eyes never left hers. "I've seen you around town. When Stan suggested I join him and Libby, and told me you'd be here, it was a done deal!"

I looked over at Libby. From the expression on her face, it was clear we were thinking the same thing. As usual, Cynthia was stealing the show but considering that Eric looked to be in his mid-thirties, that made sense. They were about the same age after all. Yeah. That was it. Sure. Nothing to do with the fact that she could easily have stepped off the cover of *Cosmo.*

"Have you ordered dinner yet?" I smiled at Stan and Libby. Beside me, Cynthia was already engaged in some joke with Eric, the two of them laughing.

"We were waiting for you." When the band started playing, Libby leaned closer. "Mary-Jane is *supervising* in the kitchen tonight, rather than cooking. I think she's going to join us off and on. That's a pleasant change for her."

The waiter who magically appeared at our table was a total shock. I grinned seeing Kevin, Libby's son, dressed in the same outfit as Chloe wore, the white shirt, bow tie, and dark pants. "Hi, Shannon. What would you like to drink?"

I glanced at Cynthia, but her attention was on Eric Studly LaMarre, the dark Adonis. Turning back to Kevin, I said, "Can you get Cynthia and me Jack Daniels on the rocks? But make mine a double, please." I'd need more liquor fortification to get through the night, since it was looking like my spell was a bust.

After he nodded and left to get our drinks, I immediately turned to Libby. "Kevin's working here? When did that happen?"

"This is his first night. He's trying to earn some extra cash for college." Leaning even closer she added, "Dahlia and Jack are working in the kitchen. It's becoming a family affair here." Her eyes rose to a spot behind me, and the smile fell from her lips like a stone.

Even before the light touch on my shoulder, I knew it was Steve standing behind me. His breath was warm on my ear when he asked, "Care to dance, Shannon?"

I turned my head, looking up into his dark eyes. I had to give him credit for persistence, but that was all I'd allow. What. A. Jerk. As if I'd give him the time of day after he shot my familiar? "No." I spun back around, not even waiting to catch the look on his face at my rebuttal. Who cared? No, actually, I hope it stung.

My gaze wandered over to the table by the kitchen door. Devon was watching the band, his fingers tapping on the table to the beat. The casual button-down, white shirt and gray blazer he wore was perfect, adding to his handsome features. The sharp creases and flat planes of his shirt perfectly complemented his sculpted face. My mouth pulled to the side as I watched him. Why wasn't *he* asking me to dance instead of Steve Murphy? I'd had as much luck with my love spell as the one to get the bobcat to come back.

I noticed Libby's gaze drift behind me and across the room. It seemed that Steve had gotten the message. Before she could comment, Stan took her hand, rising to ask her to dance. And he wasn't the only one. Eric led Cynthia onto the floor as well, leaving me sitting alone at the table.

Kevin once again appeared and set the drinks down. On a whim, I decided to try something to help my cause with Devon. "Kevin, would you bring a double Jack Daniels to Devon Booker? You can tell him it's from me."

He nodded, giving me a curious look before he left again. I eased my chair back from the table, turning to watch the performers and tapping my hand to the beat, but giving a serious side-eye to where Devon sat. If my spell didn't work, maybe I could ply him with booze. The attraction was still there between both of us! Dammit!

Planting a smile on my face, I looked around the room, nodding to familiar faces, and watching Libby's son Kevin get the drink and make his way over to Devon's table. The young server set the drink in front of Devon and then leaned in, speaking close to Devon's ear. My heart was in my throat as I watched him telling Devon that I had bought the drink.

Devon sat back and picked up the glass of Jack Daniels and set it on Kevin's tray like it was a hot coal or something. Kevin straightened, and looking over at me, he shrugged before turning to another table who had signaled for him. Devon never even looked my way to acknowledge the drink offer at all. It was like I didn't even exist. Damn! I couldn't even ply him with liquor to soften him up.

The door to the kitchen opened and Mary-Jane, wearing a smart, little black dress emerged. Her strawberry-blonde curls flowed freely over her shoulders, and she was even wearing high heels, accentuating her now slender legs. The weight loss and exercise she'd started six month ago had really paid off.

At least one of my spells had worked.

My hand rose to wave her over, but my fingers did a freeze-frame when Devon stood up, blocking her way. As he led Mary-Jane to the dance floor, my jaw dropped onto my chest. But even stranger than seeing him whisk her to the dance floor was the look on his face. He gazed at MJ as if she were the only woman in the place. And Mary-Jane? She looked like she was in shock, like she'd been taken hostage. What the hell was going on with Devon?

A glance at Libby and Cynthia showed their surprise as well, their eyes also bulging in surprise watching Devon with MJ. He held her close, his cheek resting against her hair as they swayed to the music. It reminded me of something.

Yeah! Pepé Le Pew with that poor cat he was so smitten with. That was the way Devon was holding Mary-Jane in his arms. Like Pepé! All snuggly and close, while she looked like the dance couldn't end soon enough.

What the hell? Was he doing this to hurt me even more? To make me jealous? Shit! If he was, it sure as hell was working!

EIGHT

After we had eaten, and the band was on a break, I noticed Mary-Jane standing with Ray at the bar. From the grim look on Ray's face, talking to MJ, it was clear that he was tense, if not downright angry. No doubt he had caught the close dances between MJ and Devon as well.

Cynthia leaned closer and whispered, "I'm going out for a breath of air. Why don't you join me? We need to talk about that train wreck that just happened."

I nodded. I felt like a pressure cooker building up steam while both she and Libby had been carrying on conversations with Eric and Stan. Finally, that valve would be tripped and I could let off some steam with her outside before I blew a gasket of my own. To be honest, the degree of jealousy over MJ & Devon cavorting surprised me, but that's how it is.

When I stood up, I saw Libby rising from her seat too. Ha! It looked like some impromptu coven meeting was about to happen.

As we walked across the room, I was conscious of us being watched, but I wasn't the center of attention. A quick sideways glance confirmed it. Devon was watching Mary-Jane like a hawk from his seat at the bar. What the hell?

When we reached the doorway, Mary-Jane came over to join us. The look on her face when our gazes locked was...*sheepish*? I pulled myself up straighter, lifting my chin in the air. She had some explaining to do. I'd asked her to "read" Devon, not *bewitch* him.

We eased past the group of smokers standing on the sidewalk until we were at the end of the building, alone. I didn't get a chance to even ask, before MJ blurted, "I don't know what the hell is up with Devon Booker! He's been hitting on me since our jog together yesterday morning! Ray is pissed with a capital P." Her gaze focused on me, but when Cynthia spoke, she turned to her.

"Why do I get the feeling that there's magic afoot? What have you done *this time*, Mary-Jane? But instead of turning Shannon into the flirty come-on queen, you've managed to cast a spell on Devon—flirting with you!"

MJ's hands flew up, and her foot wobbled as she took a step back. "It wasn't like that! I promised Shannon I'd read Devon! She wanted to know if there was any way they could be friends again! That's all I did! I swear!" Her wide-eyed gaze pinged between all of us.

"You did WHAT?" Libby took a deep breath, turning away for a second before she barked, "After all the crap you went through, casting that stupid spell on Shannon, and now you do this?"

But she wasn't through, not by a long shot, when she fixed me with an icy glare. "And you!" she snapped. "You asked Mary-Jane to *help* with this? Honestly! I don't know who is worse, you or her!" She folded her arms across her chest, tapping her toe, waiting for my response.

But I was more concerned with getting the details from MJ! What the hell had she *done*? Was it intentional or just another screwup? "Mary-Jane. If you were only reading him, how did he suddenly fall head over heels for you? Is that even for real? You're MARRIED!"

"Tell me something I don't know!" She looked down at the pavement before answering. "I pretended to be hurt so that I could get him to touch me when he helped me out. Everything was cool. It was working."

Her face brightened slightly. "You'll be happy to know that I found out about his obsession with YOU, Shannon. He's still thinking about you, a *lot*. Well, that plus a bunch of X-rated crap involving Jell-O and you on a swing, but I'm not going there."

"JELL-O?" The rest of us were in unison, a chorus in a crazy song.

Mary-Jane rolled her eyes. "Is there an echo in here? Yeah, *Jell-O*. Yuck. I'll never make Jell-O again, especially not *cherry*! Look! The point is, he's angry, and disappointed in you, Shannon, but he's still *really interested*." She held up her hand, silencing us before we could say anything.

"Devon started to walk away, but then he stopped. He looked like he was going to faint, wavering on his feet for a few minutes. When he came back, he'd *changed*! The way he looked at me, and even his voice was friendlier."

Libby snorted, "Just like that? One minute he's fantasizing about Shannon and the next he's sidling up to you? You must have hit him with more than just a 'touch,' reading him. You've been down this road before with your magic, MJ."

Mary-Jane flicked her hand across Libby's arm. "You think I'd do a spell to make Devon Booker hit on me? Get real." Her gaze drifted to the sidewalk, slowly shaking her head. "It shocked me to my core when I touched his hand again." She shuddered. "Now *I'm* his Jell-O fantasy girl! I have no clue what happened! I've been trying to avoid him but..."

All the while that Mary-Jane had been talking, a coldness seeped into my core. There was no doubt in my mind that she was telling the truth, but magic was definitely involved. But whose magic?

My stomach fell to the pavement at my next thought. "What *time* did you see him yesterday morning, MJ?"

Libby gave me a poke with her elbow. "Devon Booker is hitting on MJ, making trouble between her and Ray, and you're asking about the *time*?"

Cynthia shushed Libby with a wave of her hand. "I've got the feeling there's more to this, Libby." She fastened her green eyes on me, asking coldly, "*You* did something, didn't you? Shannon?" Her gaze locked on my eyes for a moment before her nostrils flared, and she spun around on her heel and yelled at the sky, "Oh shit! I *knew* it!"

As I watched her outburst, it was clear that she'd seen into me. That was one of the drawbacks to knowing a psychic who was also a witch. She'd pried my memories loose and knew about the love spell. And unlike MJ, Cynthia could do that with just a look when she wanted to.

I clutched at Cynthia's hand. "I followed the instructions in one of my books! The wording and my intentions were perfect! I swear, Cynthia! This should have worked!"

Libby shook her head. "Oh, my goddess! Stars and moons! Am I hearing this right? You did some kind of spell to make Devon be attracted to you? This is beyond crazy!"

Mary-Jane practically yelled, "You did what? You caused Devon to fall in love with meeeee? Oh shit!" She took a step closer, getting right in my face, "REVERSE it! Immediately! Ray is having a shit-fit over this!"

At the tug on my arm, I turned to Cynthia. Her eyes were narrow slits, inspecting my face when she commanded. "Tell me everything you did. Don't leave out a damn thing! We've got to figure out why your spells screw up. That's the only way you'll ever get better. Plus, we need to know so we can reverse this before Ray divorces MJ."

Feeling all of their eyes spearing me, I shrank into myself, rubbing my upper arms with my hands. Shit. *I'd* done this, not MJ. It took me a few minutes to bring them up to speed on the exact details of the spell I'd cast, even to the rose petals and the rhyming verses.

Cynthia scratched her head with a long, glossy fingernail. "Weird. And you said your aunt caught you, and only scolded you for not using your magic to find Robert." She looked at Libby and Mary-Jane. "I don't know, ladies. It sounds correct to me. I don't know why it pinged off to affect MJ and not Shannon."

Libby muttered, "These silly spells always go sideways. I would think you'd know better."

At the sound of the band starting up, MJ snarled at me, "Fix it! I'm going to have to stay in the kitchen for the rest of the night to avoid Devon! The *first* time ever that I get to leave the kitchen and socialize and *this* happens!"

"I'm sorry, MJ. I'll reverse it, I promise." I joined the others in walking back to the entrance. How exactly I'd do that reversal was another question! Tapping Cynthia's arm to get her attention, I whispered, "Will you help me?"

"Of course." But her gaze was elsewhere, staring behind me and then across the street. "Does something feel *off* to you, Shannon? It's like someone's watching us. But there's no one there. Everyone's already gone back inside."

A shudder gripped my shoulders as I peered into the darkness. "No, sorry. But my attention was totally on MJ."

"Hmmm..." Cynthia cast one more glance across the street. "I hope it's just my imagination. I hate that feeling, like ants crawling up my spine. Plus, it's freezing out here. Let's go inside."

Hooking my arm in hers, I smiled. "When you come out to my place to help me do this spell reversal, I want to hear all about your night with Eric the stud."

"I usually don't do the whole kiss-and-tell thing, Shannon. But I might make an exception if you include dinner tomorrow. I'm not a big fan of cooking." She held the door, and we went back inside.

As I passed the bar, I noticed Steve had left, which didn't break my heart. Devon was still sitting at the table next to the kitchen, following MJ with his eyes as she walked by.

Crap. That look would have been aimed at me if that spell hadn't gone sideways.

NINE

Sunday, the next day...

Mary-Jane

The light tap on the bedroom door was followed by Chloe's whine, "Are you two ever getting up, Mom? You promised to take me out driving. I need more practice if I'm ever going to get my driver's license."

I rolled over, listening to Ray murdalize "Black Magic Woman" as he crooned in the shower. My body was still tingly from our passionate morning romp. Ray had been an animal, claiming and dominating me. He jumped me as soon as we got home last night, and again this morning. I don't care that it was because of Devon's infatuation. My hubby-doo took control and I loved it!

Sex with him hadn't been that good since Shannon had put that weird spell on me, making exercise an aphrodisiac. But this time was different!

"Mo...om! Come on!"

I shut my eyes and sighed. "I'll be down in ten minutes, Chloe! Is the coffee made?" The one morning I get to sleep in, enjoy being with Ray, and bask in the afterglow was being cut short. I heard Chloe's feet thud quickly down the stairs and tossed the comforter aside.

But as I sat on the edge of the bed, listening to Ray, I let out a long sigh of relief. At least he wasn't still angry, ranting and raving about Devon hitting on me. But, if this was the result of Ray's jealousy, it had been totally worth it.

I probably shouldn't be so hard on Shannon. As I slipped my housecoat on and shoved my feet into my slippers, I considered calling her to see if she would postpone the spell reversal for another day or two. Shannon. That crazy woman had really thrown a can of gas on Ray and my sex life. Yeah. I really shouldn't be so hard on her.

The door to our ensuite bath opened, and Ray stepped out, the sides of the towel flapping open as he strode over to plant a kiss on my cheek. "We should encourage Chloe to do more sleepovers at Janie's. Especially on Saturday nights."

My finger drifted along his damp, stubbly cheek. "We could go away for a weekend, you know. When's the last time we took a holiday?"

His head turned and he kissed my palm. "If last night is any indication, the staff are able to handle things. There's nothing I'd like better than a weekend in the Big Apple with you. Just the two of us."

I tried not to fall to the floor. Was this MY Ray? The guy who pinched pennies until old Abe Lincoln howled in pain? Mr. Careful, planning everything down to the last detail? I definitely HAD to talk to Shannon about holding off on that spell reversal.

He gazed into my eyes. "How does the first weekend in May sound? That's only a couple weeks away. By then, we'd be absolutely sure that the staff could handle things."

My stomach fell. That was Beltane! Shannon and Cynthia had mentioned they were getting together to plan it out. It was a pretty big deal and our first Beltane as a coven.

"Maybe next weekend would work out better, or even the one three weeks out? That first weekend in May... well, I'm getting together with Shannon and the girls. She's already planning it."

Ray's face tightened with puzzlement. "You'd pass up a weekend in New York for a night with your gal pals? Shopping? Dinners out?" His eyebrows bobbed up and down. "A king-sized bed with all the time and imagination in the world?"

But as quick as his face had lit up, a shadow darkened his eyes. "You're sure you're getting together with Shannon? Not *Devon*?"

My arms went around him and I snuggled close. "Definitely not Devon! It's you I want, Ray. I don't know what Devon Booker's problem is, but I'm not interested." As I stepped away, I murmured, "Devon would have more luck with Shannon if he could get past his anger."

Ray plucked clothes from his drawer and started getting dressed. "From what I heard about that day, it was *Shannon* who shot Devon. So I can't blame the guy for being pissed with her."

I was about to go out of the room to join Chloe, but what Ray said made me pause. "What? Who told you that? That's not what happened." And then it hit me, the only other person there had been... "Steve told you that, didn't he?"

"Yeah. When you were up cavorting around with Devon on the dance floor, Steve and I had a little chat at the bar. And for what it's worth, I don't blame Steve for trying to shoot that wild bobcat. He was trying to *help* Shannon. Too bad she grabbed the gun and ended up shooting Devon. But, of course, it was Steve who got blamed."

"That's not what happened at all, Ray. It was all on Steve. She and Devon lunged at him, trying to stop him, but it went off, shooting Devon and the cat." I stared at Ray wondering how many other people Steve was selling that story to. He'd been charged with trespassing, and Devon was trying to sue him, but that wasn't stopping Steve from spinning it to make himself look like the victim.

Ray slipped his shirt on and walked over to me. "So technically she and Devon *were* responsible for Devon getting shot. If they hadn't interfered, only the cat would have been hit. But Steve gets the blame."

Only the cat? My eyes opened wider upon hearing that. But, of course, Ray didn't know how special the bobcat was. To him, the cat was a wild animal acting odd coming around people.

His hand rested on my shoulder. "Look, Shannon is your friend, and she helped us when we thought Devon was going to buy the building out from under us. I *get* your loyalty to her. But we've known Steve all our lives. He's been a good friend too. I think you should cut him some slack, Mary-Jane."

Well, maybe he had a point. I mean, I never really liked Devon Booker anyway. In fact, most people I know in Wesley didn't care for him at all either. But Shannon was stuck on him now, and that was that.

My forehead knotted as I followed Ray down the stairs. As well as being ignorant of the cat's place in Shannon's life as her familiar, Ray also knew nothing about me delving into magic. When he'd touched me, I sensed his resentment of Shannon and our weekly girls' night. Ray liked things the way they were before Shannon had moved to Wesley.

Chloe slumped at the kitchen table, her eyes glued to her phone, when Ray and I entered the room. She was making sure that we knew how annoyed she was, having to wait for us to take her for her driving lesson.

Ray mussed her hair on his way to pour coffee for us, getting a foul look from her for his trouble. He smiled at Chloe. "So while you and your mom are driving all over town, I'm taking Steve up on his offer to go fishing at his place."

Chloe looked up from her phone, shooting a puzzled look at her father. "Fishing? That's a first. You're actually taking the morning off?"

I watched him as he walked over with my coffee. I had to agree with Chloe. What was up with Ray? Normally, on Sunday mornings he'd putter in the garage or yard before going into the restaurant to work on the books.

He set the mug down in front of me. "Your mother has her friends that she sees regularly. I think it's time for me to do more male bonding. Steve asked and I thought... why not?"

As Ray took a seat, he continued, "Steve wants to show me what's happening on the land bordering his, you know, that parcel that Devon Booker scooped up after Ed Cousins died? There's been surveyors and trucks coming and going for the last few weeks. I want to find out what he's up to. So does Steve."

It looked like Steve now had an ally in Ray, both of them suspicious of Devon. After how Devon had hit on me the night before, in front of practically the whole town, I could understand why Ray would join forces with Steve. But considering that Ray never hung out with friends, it would be good for him to spend some time with Steve.

As I stirred sugar into my mug of coffee, I looked across the table at Ray. "As for that land that Devon bought, Shannon mentioned she's doing a piece about that in the *Wesley Weekly*. She's going to interview Devon to find out what he's got planned. That is, if he'll ever agree to meet with her."

Ray snorted. "Yeah, Steve mentioned she was writing a piece about that. But considering how Shannon feels about Devon, I think I'd like to see for myself what's going on out there."

Chloe rolled her eyes. "That whole situation with Devon is whack. I was there that day in the restaurant when Shannon said some pretty outrageous things, hitting on Devon. But, instead of taking her up on it, he calls her a crazy psycho. Then he gets shot by Steve at her house."

She looked over at me. "I know she's your friend, Mom, but I have to agree with Dad on this one. When it comes to Devon, Shannon's totally messed up."

As I looked at both of them, I couldn't argue the point. Looking at it from the outside, Shannon had acted pretty outlandishly. But neither Chloe nor Ray knew about the spells—spells that I had cast which made Shannon act that way! If they knew, they'd lump me right in next to Shannon.

Arching my eyebrows, I shot a look at Ray and Chloe. "Shannon's gone through some pretty massive changes in her life—first the divorce, her kids leaving the nest for college, and then moving here. It hasn't been easy for her. I think we should cut *her* some slack."

Ray smiled. "Exactly what I said regarding Steve, MJ. Cut him some slack. I'm looking forward to spending the next few hours with the guy. It'll be fun."

"Yeah. Getting outside hanging with him will be good for you, Ray."

But if it was such a healthy thing for Ray to do, why was there a knot in my belly? And my spidey sense had started to tingle. I wasn't entirely comfortable with Ray taking Steve's side and dismissing Shannon.

My mug thudded onto the table at my next thought. Wait! How had Steve known that Shannon was trying to set up an interview with Devon? The newspaper editor had *just* asked her to do a write up a couple days ago. For sure Shannon hadn't told Steve—she's not even *speaking* to him!

It was possible that Steve had talked to the editor, Wayne Silver. But was it likely? It would be odd for the wily old guy to confide that information during a casual encounter.

But this was Wesley, and some strange things had happened here over the last six months. Like finding a magical well and being able to read into people's thoughts and emotions.

Still, I'd make a point of running into Wayne Silver to find out if he'd told Steve about Shannon writing that article.

TEN

That same day...

Shannon

The loam on the forest floor was squishy as I walked my land, shouting for Robert. The trees swayed in the slight breeze, rustling the few stubborn leaves still clinging to the branches from the previous season. The chirp of a chickadee sounded overhead, but that was all. No loud snarling answer from my bobcat, my mystical familiar.

My chest sank as I plodded on. How many times had I been out here in the last few weeks, scouring my property for any sign of him? It had become practically a daily ritual for me to comb the five acres and around back to the house, following the shoreline. But it always ended with the same result. The cat was nowhere to be found.

At least the weather had warmed enough that I didn't need winter gear weighing me down. The warm weather had sparked the wildlife to venture out, with squirrels chattering and scurrying up the thick trunks of maple and oak. Birds preened on branches pregnant with budding leaves. I took a seat on a jutting rock, gazing up at the clear blue sky above.

My fingers closed over the rose quartz crystal that my daughter had given me for Christmas. It was supposed to bring me luck and good fortune... love even. I'd never been much of a jewelry person, but the rough stone hanging from a black leather cord felt perfect. Jessica claimed that it practically jumped from the shelf when she'd been out shopping for my gift.

I could use a bit of luck in finding Robert and getting past this thing with Devon. To say nothing of good fortune in keeping the job at the newspaper. If I couldn't get Devon to even meet with me for an interview, how was I ever going to write that piece?

I fished my phone from my pocket to check the time. Cynthia would be at my place in an hour. Just enough time to get home and make a salad to have with the lasagna. As I headed for the water, I heard the murmur of voices and a man's hearty laugh. Steve Murphy's property bordered mine, but that outburst didn't sound like him. I crept from tree to tree until I could see the water.

A red rowboat with a small outboard attached, floated on the smooth surface of the water with two men holding fishing rods. One of the guys was Steve. I squinted, trying to get a better look, and my mouth fell open. Ray? Since when had Ray become so buddy-buddy with Steve? The voices became clearer the closer I inched to the shoreline.

As they neared I was able to make out their conversation. "...yeah, and now that damned cat's not only missing an ear, he's got a chest full of buckshot! Too bad Devon didn't get the same. He certainly wouldn't be flirting with your wife if he had."

My mouth fell open as I clung to the trunk of the willow. That bastard! Steve was actually *bragging* about shooting Robert! And goading Ray about Devon hitting on MJ! I inched out, zeroing my eye on Ray. Nope. From the look on his face, his eyes narrow, he wasn't finding Steve's joke all that funny either.

"I'm not worried about Shannon. She'll come around. She might be pissed now, but I dated her a few times. I had to practically fight her off, she wanted it so bad." Steve's slimy chuckle followed this.

My fingernails dug into the bark of the tree. Now he was boasting about having sex with me? As. If. It had never gone that far and never would!

Damn. My forehead dropped onto the hard trunk of the tree a few times. If he was spreading these rumors to Ray, who else had he talked to? Was that why Devon was so angry with me? He'd heard about Steve's bullshit conquest? It wasn't bad enough that he'd shot Robert, but he was trying to ruin any chance I had with Devon? When he laughed again, it grated my last nerve red raw.

"How about you, bro?" Steve asked Ray. "You and the missus gettin' any?"

Ray shrugged, and I could hear over the water his reply, "It's married life, bud; I'm not complaining."

"Yeah...especially with all the weight she's dropped. No wonder Devon's making a play for her." He held up a hand. "I'm just complimenting your woman, bro. I know she's not a pig like Shannon." When Ray grunted, he added, with a snort, "The slut's not that great in bed anyway, just another piece of ass, y'know? Screw 'em an' lose 'em kinda bitch, that's all."

Pig? Slut? Piece of ass?

Bitch?

My hands gripped the tree with white knuckles. Rage coursed through my body as I stood there. The pounding pulse eclipsed Steve's words in my ears. It was all I could do to hold back the scream that threatened to erupt. White-hot fury throbbed in my gut, rippling out to my arms and legs.

The air around me darkened, and a stiff wind lifted my hair up and around, whipping it across my face. Above me, through the long, twisting branches of the tree, a dark cloud scuttled across the sky, blocking the sun. Eddies of leaves swirled at my feet, rising higher. When I turned toward the lake, waves rolled across, what seconds before, was a glassy surface. The boat pitched high at one end before crashing down. The whites of Steve's eyes showed as he yanked the pull cord of the small outboard motor, starting the small engine.

Ray's bellow was lost in the wind's whistle, shrieking through the trees. The fishing rods were forgotten as both men clung to the sides of the boat, now battling the waves. A plume of smoke from the motor catching faded, sucked into the storm as the boat turned, heading back to Steve's.

I watched until it rounded a bend of the shore. My body shook from the wind but also from adrenaline coursing through my veins. My legs gave out, and I barely caught myself from falling, gripping the tree once more. I clung to it while my eyes widened, staring at nothing.

Holy shit...

I'd done that! It was like that day when Robert was shot. The rage inside me had jolted out in a wave of power. That day, it had been a bolt of lightning knocking the gun from Steve's grip. Today, it was a thundercloud and wind, like a tornado had touched down!

I looked up at the sky again. The black cloud raced across the sky. The sun's rays, freed from its shadow, almost blinded me! The wind let out a final slough and faded. Oh my good goddess! As quick as it started, it was now over.

And I'd caused it.

***

There was a tap at the door before Cynthia called out. "Shannon?"

Her voice yanked me out of my reverie. I was barely aware of walking home as I sat at the kitchen table, my glass of Jack Daniels not even touched. "In here."

When she stepped into the kitchen, she jerked back. "What's wrong? Oh my God! What's happened?"

I watched her hurry to my side and felt her hands on my head. It was just as well to let her read me. I don't think I could have ever described what had just happened. It took her about ten seconds before her hands arced back from my head.

Her eyes bulged as she stared at me. "You did THAT? You caused the dark cloud and the burst of wind earlier? I thought it would rain but... but..." She practically fell into the chair across from me. Her mouth opened and closed a few times before she could speak again.

It was kind of humorous in a dark way. Cynthia had always been so assured and competent when it came to magic. Hell! She'd been doing it a lot longer than any of us! But what I'd just done totally shocked her. Left her speechless even. I reached for the glass of whiskey and downed half of it. The smooth burn in my throat felt real, grounding me again.

"Frankly, I'm *amazed*, Shannon. I've read about witches who can affect the weather, but I've never seen it! It's rare. Elemental." Her hand rose to cup her chin as she stared at me. "Rage. Both times you influenced the weather, rage was the spark."

My voice was barely a whisper when I looked at her. "It happened so fast. I was so angry listening to Steve brag about hurting Robert. But then, it boiled over. It was scary, Cynthia." And foreign. Always in the past I'd been in control of my anger. Even when cheating Ass-Hat had dropped his bombshell on me that he was leaving, I'd been angry but had managed that feeling. I had to for the kids' sakes. But what had happened today had been explosive.

Cynthia reached over, rubbing my arm. "Of course it was scary. That kind of power—

"I never want to feel that again, Cynthia! It was so wild and out of control. The darkness and the windstorm just blew in.

Even when I caused a bolt of lightning to shatter Steve's gun, it wasn't as scary as this."

"Or maybe it was, but you didn't have time to process it. You were trying to help Robert and Devon." She stood up, and her hand drifted to my shoulder. "It *should* scare you, Shannon. If it didn't, *I'd* be scared."

She grabbed the bottle of Jack Daniels and a glass from the cabinet. "But it happened. Now we need to figure out how to *control* this power. If we can't, we're going to have to dope you up on a ton of meds to keep you emotionally level."

"Or maybe I could get a job as a rainmaker? Does that pay very much, I wonder? Enough to finish paying off that land-tax bill I got hit with?" This whole thing was insane! A chuckle bubbled out but I clamped my mouth shut. To start laughing might mean I'd never be able to stop, if I didn't give into tears first. I finished the whiskey and held my glass out for more.

She scoffed as she poured me another. "Hell, I could take care of that tax bill. It's as simple as a tiny computer entry. No magic involved at all."

I wagged my finger at her, scowling. "So why didn't you do that before? I twist myself in knots trying to find a job, and all this time—"

"You didn't scare me back then. *Now* you do." She took a seat again. "Seriously. You need to practice using this power." She jerked a finger at me. "With intention, though. Both times you did this, it *erupted* out of you, Shannon. You weren't controlling it."

I shrugged. "Like how my other spells work out? They usually go sideways in all kinds of weird and wonderful ways. Well, not so wonderful, I guess, but definitely weird."

But at the chastising look in Cynthia's eyes, I snapped back to the seriousness of this. "So, how do I control this? I tried to summon Aunt Maeve to talk about this, but she's off somewhere in the ether doing ghostly things, I guess."

"Maybe she's trying to figure this out, too. This is way beyond anything she or my grandmother ever did, Shannon.

And me, as well. As long as I've been practicing magic, I've never been able to affect the weather."

Cynthia was silent for a few beats before she continued. "Start small is what I always say. Use your mind and intention to cause a little whirlpool in the air around you. You've seen the wind make eddies of leaves and dirt. Try to make that happen. And after you accomplish that, we get you focused on something bigger."

Her face was serious and earnest as she gazed at me. "This is important, Shannon. You could hurt yourself or someone else if you don't get a handle on this."

I nodded. For a moment when it was happening, I'd wondered if that boat would capsize. Not that I cared so much about Steve, but Ray had been there. If anything had happened to him...

I nodded. "You're right. I promise I'll try."

This time it was her finger in my face. "No. You'll *do* it. There's no room for trying, only *doing*! And I'm going to be checking up on you." Her eyebrows rose high, "This kind of makes reversing that love spell seem like child's play. But, we might as well get it over with before Mary-Jane gets in more trouble with Ray." She shook her head. "And for it to be with Devon Booker, of all people. That really takes the cake." She shuddered a little. "Devon Booker...ewww..." She glanced up quickly at me. "No offense, hon. He's just super not my type. At. All."

I rolled my eyes. "Whatev. You're not the only one. MJ can barely stand him either. But let's fix this mess, huh?" I stood up and gestured for her to follow me. "Everything is set up in the living room. After what happened at the restaurant, we'd better do it. Maybe that was why Ray was with Steve today. Maybe he and MJ had a horrible fight after that stupid thing with Devon."

We settled across from each other on the floor with the pentagram between us. As I cast the circle and lit the candles, Cynthia murmured. "It's important to say the exact things you said when you cast the spell, even if the words are just in your mind."

Frowning, I stared into the flame of the pink candle. How was I supposed to remember that when my brain was still mush from what I'd done with the weather?

Okay. Time to focus. I took a deep breath, to a count of four and let it out slowly also counting to four. Gradually as I continued measured breathing, a heavy warm feeling seeped into my arms and legs and my mind quieted. The words bubbled up and I whispered,

"The petal to open Devon's heart,
return to the start,
The petal clearing his mind
Put thee behind,
A petal for forgiveness."

I paused. Forgiveness? Did that even apply to his feelings regarding Mary-Jane? No, that was all on me. I'd skip that one in the reversal.

"A petal for friendship
Bend back to the source
A petal for pleasure."

I took another deep breath picturing Devon as clearly in my mind as I could. This was the meat of my previous spell. I had to take Mary-Jane out of the equation, but was there a way of slipping ME into it?

"Shannon? Continue."

My gut sank lower at Cynthia's command. Damn it! She was right. I had to clear all of this spell away from Mary-Jane. That was why I was doing this. Again, trying to clean up the mess I'd made.

"The petal for pleasure
Recoil from Mary-Jane
Reverse and return
The love spell invoked

So be it now
This is no joke."

My hand drifted slowly over the flame of the pink candle, pulling the air toward me. All the while "return to me" was a mantra sounding in my mind.

Cynthia murmured:

"By the power of the Mother, her
earth, air, and water.
Use this small fire, the love spell to
alter.
So mote it be."

"So mote it be." My eyes opened, and I noticed Cynthia's lips twitching, trying to suppress a giggle. "What?"

"This is no joke? Sometimes when you try to make the words of your spell rhyme, it just sounds... weird." She smiled as she shook her head. "You don't always need the words to rhyme, Shannon. But you got the point across, so that's okay."

I could feel my face grow warmer. "Okay, so I'm no poet. Sue me."

She raised her hand, edging back a little. "Hey! Don't get mad! I don't want any thunderbolts raining down on my head! I'm *teasing*, Shannon. What you did is fine."

Her forehead knotted as she gazed into the flame of the pink candle. "I've never done a love spell. Never needed to. But from what I know of them, what you did when you cast that spell on Devon *should* have worked." Her gaze lifted to meet mine. "Even as ornery as magic can sometimes be, this is weird, especially when you consider that your power has grown so much."

Her eyes narrowed in thought. "Unless..."

"Unless, what? Why do you think my spell went off the rails, if I did everything right?"

"Bad juju. Something interfering?" She held up a finger. "I've got an idea." She reached for the bundle of sage that had burned out and held it over the flame. When it caught she blew on it, dousing the fire but making the smoldering ends of the twigs to flash a bright orange.

Making a circular sweep, covering all points of the pentagram, she whispered,

"Cleanse this sacred space. Only good, pure intention, white energy will prevail here. Anything else, bad or mischievous, is not welcome. I banish it. So mote it be by the Mother's great goodness."

This time it was me shooting puzzled looks at her. "But I always cleanse myself and the altar before I do spell work. I read that in my book."

"I believe you."

She smiled as she set the smudge back in the bowl. "It's just a hunch, Shannon. But when I get even a niggle, I act on it. It doesn't hurt to make doubly sure that no other forces are screwing with us. We practice white magic, but that doesn't mean there isn't dark energy trying to get a foothold here."

Her words sent a shiver up my spine. "You're talking about evil and the devil? I can't believe that anyone would want to practice it. You'd have to be bat shit crazy to try that."

She huffed. "Yup. But they're out there. We just have to be aware and protect ourselves."

I nodded and leaned over to get the sage smudge to make sure it was doused in the fine sand of the bowl. When I did, the rose quartz crystal escaped my shirt, swinging free.

Cynthia's fingers closed around the quartz, holding it higher as she gazed at it. "I've never noticed this before. The pink is more vivid than normal, even though it's layered. It's beautiful, Shannon."

I smiled at her. "Thanks. My daughter gave it to me at Christmas. It's supposed to promote healing and harmony, right?" Taking it from her, I tucked it back inside my shirt.

She winked before she stood up. "And love, Shannon. There might be hope for you with Devon yet. Make sure you wear it when you interview him. But heels and a low-cut top wouldn't hurt either." She bobbed her eyebrows. "You got a push-up bra? Those are practically magic themselves!" she added with a snicker.

Hmmm...I didn't think I needed one when I was married...but now? Well, being single does kind of change things. "I'll see what I can do," I replied.

Riiiight. If I could manage to GET an interview! Oh, to have Cynthia's confidence and appeal. And speaking of which...

"Speaking of push-up bras, you got to give me the dirt on the hot fireman. C'mon. Let's have dinner while you tell me all about your night."

ELEVEN

The next morning...

Shannon

I checked the time on my phone as I sat waiting in the Bear Claw café for Mary-Jane. It was almost eleven, and she'd said she'd be here at ten thirty! I'd finally gotten the nerve up to just barge into Devon's office to get that interview when Mary-Jane called, asking me to meet her at the coffee shop. What was so important that it couldn't wait until later or that she couldn't tell me over the phone?

Sylvie, the usual server, came over to my table with a coffeepot in hand. "More coffee, Shannon?"

I nodded, even though I was on my fourth cup that morning. It was no Jack Daniels, giving me liquid courage, but it would have to do. I thanked her, and she moved on to the table behind me.

The doorbell over the entrance chimed, and I looked up, hoping it was finally MJ.

Shit. When I saw Steve enter, my neck muscles knotted into tight cables. Dressed in jeans with the familiar green shirt with the Mountain Hardware logo stitched on the breast pocket, it was a reminder that I'd have to plan a trip to Albany or Ellsboro to get supplies for the cabin renovations.

I scanned my phone, trying to ignore his hearty greeting to Mary and a few other people in the café. Ugh. They might not see through him, but I sure as hell could! My teeth ground at the sight of him. Slut? Piece of ass? When my thoughts turned to what he did to Robert, the silverware on my table vibrated for a second.

Take a breath, Shannon. I drew in and exhaled slowly, following my own advice for once. Still...

I'll close my eyes, and take another breath. Not here, not now...

From the edge of my vision I could see him walking toward me with a pastry in his hand. I huddled over my mug of coffee, turning slightly to the side as I peered at the small screen.

"Hey, Shannon. Mind if I join you?" His voice dripped with saccharine sweetness, and despite the urge to ignore him, I looked up. A smile twitched the corner of his lips, while his blue eyes fastened on mine. "I'd like to talk to you. I owe you an apology."

Go screw yourself was my first thought. But as I looked into his eyes, my resolve softened. Curiosity? It was weird even to my own ears when I murmured, "Okay. I'm listening."

I gestured for him to take a seat. Try as I might, I couldn't break my gaze from his. There was something *different* about him, his eyes held an intensity that I'd never noticed before. The dark blue held a glint of silver, like the blue fissures of ice on a lake.

"I'm really sorry about coming to your house that day. I had no business doing what I did. You were right. It's your house and your rules." He looked down at the table for a moment.

My eyes narrowed in a flash of anger. "You're damned right!"

As soon as the words were out of my mouth, his gaze darted again to my face, taking my breath away as a sense of regret for snapping at him came over me.

I mean, his heart was in the right place when he shot Robert, right? And he didn't kill the poor thing, right? And him in the boat with Ray—that was just guys' locker room talk after all.

I mean, he's a good guy; he runs a business in town; he's a good father... Maybe it's hormones, but when I peered into his eyes, I couldn't feel angry with him.

In response to my bitchy remark, Steve just nodded slowly and said, "I deserved that. If it's any consolation, I've been looking all over my property for that bobcat. If for no other reason than to let you know it's still alive. I hope it is."

That lying sack of shit! I'd heard what he said the day before. But nodding, I whispered, "Yeah. I hope so too."

His hand inched closer to mine, and he leaned over the table. "I've missed talking to you, Shannon. I'd like us to try to get back to the way things used to be—the way we were before. There's nothing I'd like better than to be close with you again."

Yeah! Close like he was bragging all over town about? *Sleeping with me!* Those words blared in my head, but I muttered, falling into his eyes. "That's a start, I guess. I accept your apology, Steve." Even the downward slant of his lips showed that he was trying to make it up to me, to get along.

The doorbell chimed again, and my gaze darted to the entry. I breathed a fast sigh of relief seeing Mary-Jane step into the café. Her head turned, and her eyebrows arched, seeing me sitting there with Steve. Not even waiting to get a pastry, she marched down to my table.

"Sorry, I'm late, Shannon." Her gaze drifted to Steve. "Hey, Steve. I see you survived the fishing trip with Ray. He told me a storm blew up, and you barely made it back to your dock."

As soon as Steve looked up at Mary-Jane, I sat back, blinking fast. What the hell had just happened here? Instead of tearing a strip off Steve like he deserved, I'd accepted his apology? At Mary-Jane's mention of the storm I'd brewed, my being decent with Steve put that in stark display. I'd been so angry with him, I'd affected the *weather*! What was going on here?

He edged out of the booth and stood up. "Yeah, that was scary how fast the weather turned on us. Up until then we were having a great time. I hope Ray and I can try fishing again." He slid across the booth and stood up. "I'd better get going."

He looked down at me again with that strange intensity and the most beautiful smile. "I'll see you later, Shannon. It was nice talking to you."

Mary-Jane's gaze pinged between Steve and me before she stepped back, letting him pass to go to another empty table. As soon as he left, she plopped down onto the vacant seat across from me, hunching closer.

"What the hell? You *talked* to Steve instead of throwing hot coffee in his face? What's up with that, Shannon?" She eased back when Mary appeared with a mug and pot of coffee, pouring it for her.

"Thanks, Mary." When the woman left, Mary-Jane once more peered at me like I was some kind of alien. "What's going on? Did you two bury the hatchet?"

For a few moments, all I could do was stare at her, blinking quickly. What *had* just happened?

"I don't know! I wanted to throttle him, but instead I was nice to him! My mind was cursing him, but what came out of my mouth was... it was friendly! Friendly*!* Can you believe that? After what he did to Robert and all the slut talk he did about me!"

Mary-Jane leaned to the side, looking past me to where Steve was probably seated. "He's lucky you didn't gouge his eyes out." She turned back to me. "This is weird. You were nice to him? Why? Why, all of a sudden?"

As I looked at her, my eyes opened wider. Oh my good goddess! Was Mary-Jane responsible? I tried to read her face. Was that *guilt* or confusion? The other time when I hadn't been able to censor what came out of my mouth was when she cast that spell on me, making me say sexy things to Devon.

"You didn't do this to me, did you, Mary-Jane?" I leaned closer and lowered my voice. "Did you cast some kind of friendship spell on me so I'd be nicer to Steve? I know you don't hate him like the rest of us do."

She jerked back, and her eyes were wide as dinner plates. "No! I've learned my lesson about casting spells on you. How could you even say that?"

"Easy. Actually as easy as telling Steve I accepted his apology. But how could I do what I just did—be *nice* to him?"

I cupped the mug, and looking down, my mind scrambled to figure this out. When MJ had cast that ridiculous spell, the filter between my brain and mouth vanished. Every lecherous thought I'd had about Devon just popped out! But this time...my mind screamed anger at Steve, but my mouth dripped sweetness. They were totally at odds with each other. And even my inner attitude had changed for a bit while he was in front of me.

Mary-Jane sat back. "Look, I don't know why you were nice to Steve. A moment of weakness? But before I get into why I asked to meet with you... you reversed that ridiculous spell with Devon and me, right?"

I had to give my head a little shake to zap back to reality. I was still appalled by how nice I'd been to Steve. I nodded. "Of course. Cynthia came out and we took care of that. Now, what was so important that you needed to see me? I want to catch Devon and try to interview him for that article. Wayne expects it on his desk by Thursday."

It was bad enough that she'd been late, thus giving Steve Murphy the opening to sit with me, but now, I'd miss seeing Devon if she didn't hurry it up.

"Something Ray said yesterday before he left to go fishing with Steve didn't sit right with me, Shannon. Steve *knew* that you had the assignment to interview Devon about the land he bought."

"Okay. So what?" I wished she'd get around to the point of all this.

"I just spoke with Wayne Silver, and *he* didn't tell him. I'm pretty sure *you* never told him! So how'd he know?" Mary-Jane's eyes were round circles as she stared at me.

My eyebrows bunched together as I thought about that. "Well, it isn't that big a town, MJ. Everyone knows everyone else's business. And considering the parcel of land involved, and that it once belonged to the town's founder, people are sure to speculate. That's why I need to go to the source to find out what his plans are."

I slipped my phone into my purse and finished the last of the coffee. "It's just coincidence, that's all. But considering it's Steve, I can understand why you'd question it. I got to go, MJ. I'll call you later and let you know how I made out."

When I looked over at her, she looked deflated when she spoke. "Maybe you're right. It could be nothing. But just so you know, he told Ray that it was you who shot Devon."

"You're kidding."

"No." She shrugged adding. "Well, that day was pretty bizarre with a lightning bolt blasting the gun away. I can understand why he'd think that."

I could have burst out laughing. If she thought that day was an event, if she only knew what had happened yesterday on the lake. But I didn't have time to get into that right now. I shook my head as I stood up. "Steve's spreading lies, trying to make himself look good." Lies, like what I'd heard yesterday, that I'd *slept* with him! My eyes narrowed as I pictured the windstorm and the boat pitching in the water.

When I glanced at MJ, my chest tightened. I'd have to tell her about my part in causing that squall that had freaked Ray out. Yeah, that was a conversation I wasn't looking forward to.

But I could leave it to later when we met for Esbat. She would not like what I'd done, even if it had "erupted" out of me.

Her smile was wan when she looked up at me. "Good luck with the interview, Shannon. I'll see you tonight?"

"For sure. I'll talk to you later."

I took a few deep breaths, steeling myself to face Devon as I walked up the sidewalk, heading for his office. Would he actually agree to give me even five minutes so I could write this article? Surely he'd want to put a good spin on whatever plans he had in the works and end any negative speculation. And after what I'd written about the historic building where MJ's restaurant was housed, resulting in them getting it bequeathed to them, I had a pretty good record writing articles. Yeah, I'd be sure to mention *that* to Devon, if I had to.

I squared my shoulders as I opened the door and went inside. Everything was exactly as I remembered it from my short stint working there. The reception area with the leather sofa, and chairs, the magazines on architecture, and business magazines, scattered on the low coffee table.

"Hello?" Devon followed this, appearing in the doorway of his office. As soon as he saw me, his face hardened, the smile falling like a brick. "Oh. You shouldn't be—"

"I'm here in an official capacity, Devon. I want to interview you about your plans for the Cousins' property you bought. There're all kinds of rumors flying around and—"

"Rumors *you* started, Shannon! So now you think I'll drop everything and agree to an interview for the newspaper? Anything I have to say, I'll email to Wayne Silver, myself."

All the coffee I'd drank swished and gurgled in my stomach as I stood there, listening to him. Crap! I probably should have stopped at two. If MJ hadn't called, diverting me, I would have. I also wouldn't have had that strange encounter with Steve, and my stomach wouldn't be queasy like it was right then.

I took a deep breath, determined to state my case. "Wayne asked me to write this. It won't take long. Just five or ten minutes of your time." I pulled my cell phone from my purse. "I'll even record it so you'll be quoted accurately." My fingers trembled as I held the small phone up before me. But it wasn't nerves. The longer I stood there looking at him, the more my gut swished back and forth.

Grimacing, he extended his arm, inviting me into his office. "Fine. I'll give you five minutes. No more."

I took a step forward and stopped. The queasiness was now a gut-wrenching pain in my gut. My hand flew to my stomach as a pain spiked through me. "I... I'm afraid that I'm..." My mouth watered, and it felt like all that coffee churned in the back of my throat.

"What's wrong?"

I glanced over at him and had to look away quickly. Shit! Was it my eyes? What the hell had happened to his face? His eyes had seemed like golf balls while his mouth had become rubbery, elongating from ear to ear across his face. It was like that weird phone app that my daughter had shown me, distorting people's features making them cartoonish. My vision and my gut were seriously wonky.

I turned and retreated to the door. "I'm sorry. I'll call, and we can set—" My stomach heaved, but I managed to hold everything down until I was out the door at least. I staggered, and my hand reached out to stop myself from falling. Gulping air, I used sheer willpower to force my stomach to settle as I leaned against the wall. The very last thing in the world I needed was to throw up in public and against Devon's building, of all places!

The door to his office opened, and I turned away. Talk about wanting the sidewalk to open up and swallow me! Please.

"Are you okay?" His voice sounded concerned.

I bit my tongue, holding back the sharp retort: *Do I look okay?* Instead, I waved my arm for him to leave me. "I'll call you later. I need to go home right now." Pushing myself off from the brick building, I hurried on wobbly legs down the sidewalk to where I was parked. The effort was so consuming that I didn't have time to think about my stomach. I just needed to get to my truck and get out of there.

As my hand gripped the handle to open the door, I took a last gasp. Again, I paused. As quickly as the nausea had come on, it had subsided. My gut was calm again. I climbed into the truck and sat there with my hands on the steering wheel, once more taking stock of my stomach. No crippling cramps. My stomach was... It was FINE!

What the hell?

I shook my head. Had I been so keyed up over that interview with Devon that my nerves had taken over, making me ill? It was the only thing that made sense. For a second, I deliberated on whether to go back into his office to get the interview done, but quickly dismissed it. I'd better not press my luck. The next time I'd skip the coffee and do some deep breathing before I sat down with him.

As if Devon Booker didn't think I was crazy enough, *this* had happened! No doubt he'd think I was being theatrical, trying to garner some sympathy from him. I pulled my phone out and saw his number in my contacts. My fingers flew, sending a text.

I'm sorry I had to leave suddenly. Either something I ate didn't agree with me or I'm coming down with a flu bug. Can I call you tomorrow to set up a time for this?

His answer was almost immediate.

It's probably best that I email a write-up to Wayne. Take care.

Dammit! I flung the cell phone onto the passenger seat. I'd been so close to sitting down with him! I'd hoped that this interview would also be an icebreaker between us. Even worse, with him sending the information to Wayne directly, it undercut my effectiveness as a journalist.

But maybe all wasn't lost. I'd drive out to that property he'd bought and maybe take some photos. At least I'd have something to give to Wayne. As I looked out the windshield of the truck, getting ready to start it, I saw Steve Murphy step out of his store.

His hand rose to wave to me while there was a friendly smile on his lips. It was hard not to scowl at him, but instead I turned and backed out of the parking spot. I had no idea why I'd let him sit with me, let alone be decent to him. But that shit was over.

TWELVE

That evening...

Mary-Jane

"Shannon was sitting with Steve at the coffee shop? I can't believe she'd do that!" Libby's face twisted in a confused knot when she looked over at me.

From the backseat of the car, Cynthia also weighed in, "After what Shannon did yesterday, I can't believe it either! You said she was even nice to him?"

My forehead tightened as I stared out the windshield, driving out to Shannon's for Esbat. With a glance in the rearview mirror at her, I asked, "What do you mean 'after what she did yesterday'? I thought you two got together to reverse that spell on Devon—which worked, by the way."

"How do you know? Did you see Devon today?" Cynthia's hand grasped the backrest of my seat when she leaned forward.

I smiled. "He came into the restaurant after the lunch rush. Ray even called me out from the kitchen to hear Devon's apology. Of course I knew why he'd been flirting with me, but Ray didn't. Devon said he was taking some allergy meds that he had a strange reaction to."

Libby smirked. "That's almost as good as Shannon claiming dental problems making her say outrageous things." She looked over at me. "But the spell reversal worked? He wasn't hitting on you or—"

"Worked like a charm! Although I have to say, a little jealousy on Ray's part wasn't all bad. After some awesome sex Saturday night, he offered to take me away for a mini-vacay." I murmured, "I almost called you and Shannon to hold off on the reversal for a few days."

"Of course you would," Libby muttered. "Always about sex with you, MJ." She turned her head slightly, looking at Cynthia. "So that was it, I guess. It worked. That still doesn't explain why Shannon was okay with Steve sitting with her. What else happened yesterday?"

I heard Cynthia take a deep breath before she spoke. "Shannon was out walking in the forest, looking for Robert. When she got close to the lake, she overheard Steve and Ray talking. They were out fishing. When Steve started bragging about shooting the bobcat, and a bunch of crap about sleeping with Shannon, she blew a gasket."

"Can't blame her. That jerk," Libby muttered. "But that can't be all of it. What else happened?"

Cynthia continued, "She did that thing with the weather again. You remember how that bolt of lightning knocked the gun from Steve's hands? Well, when she overheard Steve laughing about shooting Robert, she just blew! Literally. She caused a windstorm to suddenly happen. That's why her being decent with Steve today makes no sense. She was so pissed with him!"

As she spoke, my fingers clutched the steering wheel harder. Ray had been with Steve when that storm had happened! He'd come home white as a ghost after that boat almost capsized.

Glaring at her from the rearview mirror, I snapped, "Shannon almost drowned MY HUSBAND! What does she think Ray is? Just collateral damage? I'm going to throttle her!"

"She didn't do it on purpose, MJ! Steve was bragging about sleeping with her and hurting Robert! The anger burst from Shannon, causing the storm. She didn't mean to do that anyone, most of all not to Ray." Cynthia sat back, her teeth pressing down on her upper lip in worry. "I should have let her tell you."

My jaw clenched and I blew out an angry snort. Seeing the end of her driveway just up ahead, I flipped the turn signal on. "I'm still gonna throttle her!"

Libby spoke, placing her hand on my arm. "At least she stopped the spell on Devon, MJ. There's that. And Ray can swim. He might not be Aquaman, but he's no slouch in the water. I remember that from when we were younger."

As we drove down the driveway, Cynthia once more tried to calm me down. "I made her promise to get this under control, MJ. In the meantime, maybe Ray should stop hanging out with Steve."

When I parked the car, I slammed the gearshift into park and looked at each of them. "You know, Ray doesn't have many friends. He finally goes out with Steve, doing this male-bonding shit, and Shannon almost drowns him. You might not like what I'm going to say next, but I'm going to say it, anyway. Steve Murphy has always been a friend to Ray and to me."

When Libby's eyes went wide and she started to argue, I shushed her with a wave of my hand. "I know he shot Robert. And that wasn't right. But I'm not turning my back on Steve. Especially now, when Ray finally has a friend to hang with. I understand how you feel, but I can't hate him. Sorry."

Libby and Cynthia exchanged a quick look before Libby spoke. "Robert wasn't just any cat, MJ. He is Shannon's familiar. Think of our coven, even if you weren't as close to Robert as the rest of us."

Her words didn't ease the anger burning in my gut. Now they were telling me how to feel? That wasn't going to happen! And Shannon's actions *had* been reckless. Ray could have been hurt or worse! "Well, I don't hate Steve the way the rest of you do. And I'm not going to twist myself in knots to bend to your wishes. So that's that."

At the tap on my window, I almost jumped out of my skin. Shannon stood next to my door, signaling for me to lower the window. But instead I got out, glaring at her.

"You caused that storm! And you never mentioned it when I saw you today! Ray could have drowned. All this time I've been keeping an eye on Steve, trying to cover your back while you're trying to kill my husband."

Shannon's mouth fell open, and she looked over at Cynthia who had gotten out of the vehicle. "It wasn't like that, MJ! I didn't mean to—"

I held my hand up, palm facing her. "It's always that way, Shannon! You didn't mean to cast a spell that made me a horn dog whenever I exercised. You didn't mean to have Devon fawning all over me making trouble with Ray. And now you didn't *mean* to conjure up a windstorm that almost drowned my husband!"

Libby stepped over. "She also got you healthy! She also wrote an article that made Old Man Cousins leave you his building! You aren't being *fair*, MJ!"

Scowling, I looked at each of them. Damn it! What she'd said was all true. I had lost a ton of weight, and the restaurant was all mine, thanks to Shannon. Shit! But I wasn't totally wrong in being miffed with Shannon. It was hard to eat my plate of crow, and my words were clipped when I glared at Shannon. "You can't ever do anything like that when Ray is around. You put his life in danger and I won't have it."

Shannon stepped over, but I couldn't return her hug, standing there stiff backed. "I'm so sorry, MJ. I promise this will never happen again. I'm working on this new power, to learn to control it."

The feelings and thoughts that flooded from Shannon into me backed up everything she was saying. "Okay." I watched her ease back, flashing me a shy smile. The next moment, she was herding us into her house to get prepared for Esbat at the well.

As I followed them, I thought of what Steve had said to me after Shannon left the coffee shop that morning. After Shannon was gone, he switched tables to join me. He mentioned Shannon meant well, but she was impulsive. Sometimes the things she did caused problems that she never intended. He'd tried to make a case that he'd shot the bobcat to prevent her from getting attacked by it. But, of course, he didn't know the whole truth about the magical bobcat.

What he'd said about Devon, though? That part I had to agree with him on. Devon was Shannon's blind spot, and that would lead her into trouble. You couldn't trust him. Everyone knew what Devon was like. I was through with helping her get close to Devon. As Steve said, it was for Shannon's own good.

THIRTEEN

Later that evening...

Libby

"Hey, Libby, I know you're worried about me suddenly feeling ill at Devon's office, but don't. I'm fine! Honestly." Shannon smiled as she handed me the glass of wine. Mary-Jane and Cynthia already had theirs in hand, sitting side by side on the sofa in Shannon's living room.

Before she could turn away, I grabbed her arm. "You shouldn't be so casual about this, Shannon. If it were just a stomach ache or nerves, why would your eyesight go wonky? That's the part that has me concerned."

She batted her eyes at me, grinning. "Maybe I need glasses. It's been years since I had my eyes checked." She chuckled.

"Whatever it was, I'm fine now. I really think it was a case of nerves because as soon as I got back to my truck, I felt fine."

I watched her walk across the room to stand next to Cynthia. "Could it have been a hot flash, Shannon? God only knows they happen at the weirdest times. Although I still don't understand how that could affect your eyesight."

Nerves didn't explain the sudden course change in how she'd been with Steve. Did any of this strange behavior and illness have something to do with that episode she had affecting the weather? Something was odd about her behavior.

Shannon threw her hands up. "Maybe! I don't know if it was a hot flash or nerves or drinking a gallon of coffee! I'm just glad I got out of there before I threw up. It could have been one of my tropical moments, who knows?"

Mary-Jane muttered, "I normally get my tropical moments at night. I've given up on nightgowns or PJ's, which is just as well, if you get my drift," she added with a wink.

I rolled my eyes. Trust MJ to bring the conversation round to her sex life. I shot a pointed look at Shannon. "If you get any more issues with your eyes, you need to see a doctor. This isn't something to take lightly."

Shannon tsked. "Duly noted. Now, are you ready for some exciting news?" She grinned, looking down at Cynthia."Do you want to share your news?" She smirked. "Unlike you, I haven't said a word to let everyone know what's going on with you."

Cynthia's eyes lit up, and a broad smile flashed on her face as she looked at Mary-Jane and me. "I'm going to have a daughter. I've been thinking about this for a while now, but I've finally decided."

Mary-Jane threw her arm around the young woman, but drew back after a moment. "Wait. You're not pregnant now." Her eyes became round, staring at Cynthia. "A turkey baster? You're not doing this the *fun* way? Why would you go for a donor in some clinic? It's not like you wouldn't have a ton of guys help you with this."

"Oh, for Pete's sake," I snapped at her. "Mary-Jane! This is a *big deal* for Cynthia! It doesn't matter how she chooses to do this." My chin rose. "In fact, it takes guts to have a child and raise it on your own." I'd know. After Hank was killed, I'd been in that same situation with three kids, left to raise them by myself.

"Yeah, yeah. You're right." Mary-Jane sidled closer to Cynthia. "Congratulations. But how can you be sure you'll have a daughter?"

Cynthia shrugged. "Of course, I can't be sure, but I'm willing to tip the scales in my favor. I'd like us to really do Beltane right! You know, the bonfire, decorations, chants, singing, and dancing! This is going to work out. I just know it!"

I rose to go over and give her a hug. Her excitement was contagious. "We'll do whatever we can to help you. Honorary aunts, that's us! Not to mention babysitters whenever you need a break."

Cynthia's eyes welled with tears as she looked at me and then Shannon and Mary-Jane. "I'm *counting* on it! I know this will be challenging but knowing you've got my back..." Her voice faded, and she shook her head, fighting a full-on gush of joyful sobs. "You know, I'm not sure I ever would have made this decision without being around you guys."

It was the first time I'd ever seen Cynthia get choked up and emotional. I watched Shannon rub Cynthia's back and murmur, "We're here for you. I know you never wanted to be a part of a coven, but I'm glad you're one of us."

Cynthia swiped a tear from her cheek as she nodded. "I am too. You know, I've never really had any close female friends. I always thought that was okay and I didn't need them. But being with you... It's weird. Even crying like this... I could never, ever show weakness around other people. But you three are different. I feel safe with you."

"That's the way you should feel, Cynthia." I squeezed her hand. "You can count on us to be there for you throughout your pregnancy and afterward. It'll be fun to hold a baby again, and I'm in no rush for my kids to start families. They're still way too young."

Shannon laughed. "Well, on that cheerful note, I think we need to get ready for Esbat, ladies! Now, we've got one more thing to set our intentions on—Cynthia's pregnancy, as well as Robert's safe return! Pitter-patter, let's get at her."

My gaze flitted to Mary-Jane, who had been quieter than normal. Of all of us, I would have thought that she'd be the most excited, planning baby showers and the preparation for Beltane. It was just a fleeting look, but annoyance smoldered in her eyes when she looked at Shannon. This thing with Ray and Shannon's windstorm had really gotten under her skin.

Ten minutes later, we headed out armed with candles, water, and the Well's favorite libation, a flask of Jack Daniels. I looked around at the forest surrounding Shannon's house when I stepped off her front porch. Dusk was falling, making the trees even darker and the shadowed undergrowth deeper. Despite the warmer temperatures, I shivered, pulling the sides of my cape tighter to my body. There was still no sign of Robert, and it had been over three weeks since he'd fled wounded into the forest.

At Mary-Jane's touch on my arm, I started. "Walk with me, Libby. I'd like to speak with you alone." She looked ahead of us where Shannon and Cynthia walked side by side, laughing at something one of them had said. "Sometimes, the two of them make me feel like an outsider. But you and I've always been friends, right?"

"Yeah, for sure! But you're not an outsider by any stretch, MJ!" I peered at her, trying to read her face. There was more to this than Shannon's new powers and what had happened to Ray. "Why would you think that?"

Again, her gaze fastened on the two friends walking ahead of us. "I like Shannon and Cynthia, but sometimes, it feels like high school, y'know. They're the cool girls, and we're just hangers on. If we don't see things the way they do, then we're the ones who are wrong."

She gave me a sideways look. "Like Steve. We grew up with the Murphy's. Shannon was only here in the summer, but we *knew* them."

"Yeah. So?" My hand rose, making her pause. "If this is about Steve shooting Robert, then I'm in total agreement with Shannon! Remember, I'm the one who can talk to that cat! Robert was trying to help Shannon. Steve had no business—"

"I get that! But Steve meant well. And technically it was Shannon rushing Steve and doing that thing with the weather which caused Devon to get shot! Yet she blames Steve for that too!" Again, she slipped a glance my way. "I just hope you can keep an open mind when it comes to him. He apologized to her. But she can't see past her silly crush on Devon Booker to be reasonable when it comes to Steve."

I shook my head and I couldn't help my voice getting louder with exasperation. "Where is this *coming* from MJ? When we learned Steve had shot the cat, we were all in agreement. What he did was unforgivable. That wasn't just a wild bobcat, that was Shannon's *familiar*!"

At the sharp snap of a twig behind us, I spun around, checking between the pines and cedars. A crow let out a loud caw before taking flight from a branch above us, scattering pinecones into the underbrush. The skin on my arms prickled as I stared into the woods.

Something was out there.

"Robert?" I stepped off the path but stopped at the edge of the trees. Not a sound, not even the rustling of leaves, from the old brittle dead growth of last year, could be heard.

"Libby? Is that him? Do you see Robert?"

I turned at Shannon's voice, seeing her wide eyes, the hope in her face evident. "No. Sorry. It must have been a raccoon or some animal nearby." Her shoulders slumped lower before she resumed walking next to Cynthia.

Her disappointment was mirrored in how I felt as well. I rejoined MJ on the path. As we continued, I kept one ear cocked for anything more from the woods while Mary-Jane, once more, grumbled.

"We agree to disagree, Libby. But does this mean you won't ever speak to Steve again? It's not that big of a town. When I talked to him today—"

"What? You talked to him?" I shook my head. "So it all makes sense to me now, MJ. He pleaded his case, and you bought into it, hook, line and sinker."

Her face fell. "So now you're pissed off at me?"

I sighed. "No one is telling you who you can and can't be friends with, MJ. But I wouldn't mention your conversation with Steve to Shannon, if I were you."

She nodded and when the path narrowed getting deeper into the forest and closer to the well, she stepped ahead of me. I couldn't shake the feeling that something was out there watching us. Casting one last look over my shoulder, I followed her into the glade where the well was.

No matter how many times I'd been at the well, it always filled me with wonder. The lush growth of grass in the surrounding clearing was early for this time of year, and especially in the forest where still some snow hid in shaded areas. The quiet of the glade, where even birds and chattering squirrels were hushed, added to the mystery of it.

We took our places, circling the stone structure, each of us aligned with each of the four directions like the well was some kind of compass. Vines bearing waxy green leaves wove around the upright supports of the small roof, while moss clung to the stone base.

I felt Mary-Jane's hand close over mine, and I reached for Cynthia's. Across from me at the north point was Shannon, tossing the hood of her cloak back before she joined hands with us. She cleared her throat and smiled as she began the familiar chant.

"We come to you tonight as four
Casting this circle evermore
To the north, the east, west and south
Only pure intents, no doubt.
Earth our mother
Air her breath
Water her lifeblood
fire pure energy
At this your sacred site

Homage for your light."

Shannon broke the bond, letting go of Mary-Jane's and Cynthia's hands to bend and lift the glass lantern holding the white candle. With her other hand, she held the lighter to ignite the flame. At her nod to her left, Mary-Jane held her fist over the mouth of the well, opening her fingers to let soil fall into the depths. Mary-Jane intoned as the dark earth fell from her fingers,

"We give thanks for the bounty this
soil provides.
Ever may we honor, let no man
divide.
We plead your blessings for Robert's
return.
Faith in your guidance, his
whereabouts we learn."

'Let no man divide'? The irony that it was Mary-Jane saying these words after what she'd said on the way to the well wasn't lost on me. When she looked over at me, it was my turn to speak. My hands lifted in the air to make a sweeping motion across the well's opening.

"Gaia, giver of life
Your bounty so fair
We honor your blessings
For this night in the fresh air"

My neck warmed and rose to color my cheeks. This was always the hardest part for me, to try to find words that were kind of mystical, which also rhymed. When I'd gone to school, science had been way easier than English. I turned to Cynthia, and a smile spread over my face. Her energy and excitement was contagious!

She looked at all of us as she held the small flask of Jack Daniels over the mouth of the well and let the contents drip out.

"The wonder of water so pure, giving
life.
To your depths, mingle with water
Hear my plea great Mother Earth
To carry and birth my own
daughter."

We had barely got the words, 'So mote it be' out when a booming voice burst from the well.

PAY HEED TO BE PURE OF
HEART.
YOUR INTENTION MUST
STRENGTHEN.
ONLY THEN WILL YOUR
REQUESTS ALIGN.

I jolted back, feeling my body stiffen. What the hell? The voice in the well had been curt... giving us shit? When I looked at the others, from their wide-eyed stares, they also were taken aback.

Shannon stepped forward, holding the lantern over the dark chasm of the well, looking into the depths. "We *are* pure of heart! And believe me, I have *every* intention of getting Robert back."

Cynthia's hands flew up covering her mouth. "Does this mean I won't get pregnant and have a daughter?" She looked at me and Mary-Jane. "Is it you two? My heart is pure, and this is something that I'm focused on in every ritual I do! One of us is causing this."

My gaze flitted to Mary-Jane. She'd been the one complaining earlier. And her anger with Shannon sure as hell wasn't helping. But as quickly as I thought that, my eyes once more locked with Cynthia and Shannon's. "That's not fair to assume it's me or MJ. The voice didn't single anyone out! This is something we ALL have to work on."

MJ's eyes were mere slits as she peered at Shannon. "Maybe if one of us wasn't so reckless in casting spells and affecting the weather, then we'd all be aligned in our intention. It's *you*, Shannon!"

ENOUGH BICKERING!
THE WHEEL IS TURNING,
BRINGING A NEW SEASON.
GATHER YOURSELVES AS ONE
FOR BELTANE.
NOW GO!

Shannon jerked back so fast she almost spilled the candle from the lantern.

Beside me, MJ muttered, "She started it with that windstorm. How come she's the one to get that power and not any of the rest of us? At least we'd take more care with it."

Cynthia stepped over to Mary-Jane. "This well is on Shannon's property. She was led to the well before you or Libby. It's not up to you what powers each of us have. If you're the reason stopping my intentions, so help me—"

"Stop this!" Shannon stepped in between Cynthia and MJ. "This is exactly what the well was getting at! We've got to stop any more bickering." For a few moments she was silent before continuing, "You know... I have a goal to get Robert back. Cynthia wants to have a daughter. But neither of you have ever said what it is *you* want."

Cynthia muttered, "MJ was pretty clear about that when she was afraid she'd lose the restaurant. And all of us focused to help her. Now that it's us wanting something, she's sniping about your powers being greater than hers."

I'd heard enough squabbling between Cynthia and MJ. It was like listening to my two kids! "We *all* want Robert to return. We *all* would like to see you have a daughter, Cynthia. For my part... I wish to hell I hadn't got that head nurse job! I hate making schedules and dealing with accountants. I'd rather deal with sick people. But what I'd really like to do is work with animals! Help the ones who are sick and can't tell us where it hurts. There! That's what I'd like, Shannon!"

But it was fairy dust. I needed the money from the hospital, especially the pay increase doing the head nurse job, although I hated it. I had three kids to raise and get into college. I had to follow the money to get through that.

Shannon's smile was grim looking at me with fire in her eyes. "That's honest at least. Now that we know, maybe we can actually DO something to make that happen, Libby." She turned to Mary-Jane and folded her arms like a schoolmarm. "Well? I'm waiting."

Mary-Jane's gaze bounced from Cynthia to me and then to Shannon. She opened her mouth to speak and then muttered. "You'll just laugh at me. So why bother? It can't happen." She turned and started to walk across the clearing.

Shannon yelled at her. "Stop! No one leaves until we have all been honest with one another. Mary-Jane? We promise not to laugh... that is unless you tell us your goal is to be some kind of exotic dancer. I can't promise we won't laugh at that."

Mary-Jane turned around and crossed her arms across her chest. "Why not? I'd be a damned good exotic dancer!" A smile twitched in the corners of her mouth. "Promise not to laugh?"

"Oh, for Pete's sake! Just tell us!" I marched over to her and shook her shoulders. "This is US, Mary-Jane. We help each other." If I could bare my soul about the colossal mistake I'd made in wanting that head nurse job, then she could also come clean.

I felt Cynthia and Shannon join me, staring at MJ, the three of us showing support.

Okay, I'll admit it—if she was so embarrassed about her secret goal, this had to be good.

She took a deep breath and blurted it out. "I want to work with the police finding lost kids and people. Or even lost pets. You know I can touch objects and know the history. So why can't I use that talent for something good? I want my life to mean more than just cooking a great meal."

Oh my good, goddess. This was the last thing I would have expected. Mary-Jane's face was twisted in a knot when she looked down at the ground.

Cynthia took a step closer to MJ. "You're serious. You actually think that you are somehow less than the rest of us. I *dream* of being able to cook like you." Cynthia tucked her thumb under MJ's chin, lifting it so that she could look into her eyes. "That's magic! Think of all the joy you bring to people, MJ."

MJ huffed, "I didn't go to college like the rest of you. Hell, aside from a year in cooking school, I've never even been outside Wesley. You guys are... well, sometimes I feel small compared to you."

"Not true at all, Mary-Jane!" I rested my hand on her shoulder. "You're smart and funny and not just a talented chef. When people come to your restaurant, it's not just for a wonderful meal. You always make them feel special." I thought of the times I'd been in there and seen her take a break from the kitchen and circulate around the dining room chatting with folks.

Shannon spoke, getting MJ's attention. "You said you want to help people find lost things. How about starting with Robert? Libby has tried to help me but maybe what we need is your touch. If anyone can do that, it's you."

Cynthia nodded. "Yeah. That's a great idea. You're better than I am in reading objects, MJ. I see only the present but you see what happened in the past as well." She let out a laugh. "It's so obvious! Why didn't we think of this sooner?"

Mary-Jane straightened, pulling her shoulders back as she took a deep breath. "I'll find your bobcat, Shannon. If it's the last thing I do, I'll find him."

Shannon stepped into MJ, giving her a big hug. "I know you will. I'm counting on it." When she pulled back she motioned for Cynthia and me to join her in a group hug. When we stood there under the crescent moon, all of us pressing together, Shannon's voice was light when she continued, "I'd say we made some progress tonight, ladies. It took getting shit from the voice in the well but it was worth it."

When we stepped back, Cynthia looked at MJ. "Don't listen to Steve, sweetie. I think he's trying to fill your head with bullshit. Remember who your true friends are. Your coven."

"What?" Shannon directed her question to MJ. "You spoke to Steve? When? Today, after I left you?"

My gut clenched tight. I should have known that this was going to come out. You can't keep secrets when one of the members is gifted like Cynthia. She'd picked that up when she'd hugged MJ. Was all our goodwill going to go up in smoke?

Mary-Jane nodded. "He sat with me for a few minutes. He explained what happened when Robert was shot—how he was trying to help you. He was also concerned about you getting close to Devon, Shannon. Steve may be a control freak but he's not really a bad guy, y'know."

Shannon's face became tight before she let out a long sigh. "Cynthia's right. Don't buy into his crap, MJ. But let's not let Steve Murphy ruin our night. We made a break-through and let's stay focused on what's important. Us. Our friendship."

I breathed a sigh of relief at hearing her words. At least the truth was fully out there and we were tighter than ever. As we walked back to Shannon's the feeling that something was out there in the woods watching us was still there though. If the knot in my gut was any indication, it definitely wasn't Robert out there. This was a heavily forested area so who knew what kind of animal it could be?

FOURTEEN

The next day...

Shannon

My phone beeped, almost vibrating right off the edge of the tree stump where I'd set it. My shoulders slumped before I raced over to grab it. I'd been outside for almost an hour, trying to get the leaves scattered in my yard to swirl up as Cynthia had suggested. This was damned hard to do! Yet I knew I could do it.

But maybe I needed to be consumed with rage or worry for it to happen?

Shit.

I picked up the cell phone and did a double-take. Devon? Swiping my finger across the screen, I opened the text message.

Are you feeling any better today? If you're up to it, you can meet me at the old Cousins' property and I will give you that interview. I'll be there at eleven at the main house.

The time on my phone showed it was a little after ten. He really didn't give me much time, but there was no way I'd miss meeting him there. My thumbs flew, typing a reply.

Much better today. See you there. Thanks.

I grabbed my jacket from the back of the lawn chair and hurried into the house to grab my camera. The day was already warm, and with the clear sky, I'd be able to get more great shots—this time with Devon in them. When I'd stopped yesterday to take pictures, I'd only gotten as far as the gate where a security guard was stationed. But I'd seen trucks and earth movers inside the chain link, busy making roads and digging what looked like a big foundation for a building.

Hmmm...I raised my arm and sniffed. A shower wouldn't hurt.

As I swept by the kitchen, heading upstairs to take a quick shower and change, Aunt Maeve drifted out of the room to follow me.

"Where's the fire? I thought you were going to practice your elemental work." Her voice trailed me as my feet pounded up the stairs.

"I did the best I could, Aunt Maeve, but no luck. I've got to rush now to meet Devon and get that interview. My editor's expecting my article by Thursday." I peeled off my sweatshirt as I crossed the bedroom.

"The work in gaining control of this skill is important too, Shannon! Promise me you'll get back to it when you come home."

"Of course." I headed into the bathroom, closing the door behind me, and ending that conversation with my aunt. If I'd even been able to lift one brittle leaf into the air, I might have been more encouraged. But it felt like the only thing I'd accomplished outside was getting fresh air and some sunshine. So not a total loss, I guess.

Thirty minutes later, I breezed by the security guard at the gate to what was now Devon's property and parked my truck next to the old Cousins' homestead. As I looked up at the two-story, sprawling home, I thought of meeting Estelle Cousin's ghost in Devon's office. It had been her wish that the house be used for some charity if it had to pass out of their family. Right now, it looked like it was being used as the site operation office.

I walked up the broad stairs to the wraparound verandah, framed by white spindles and a green topper. It wasn't hard to imagine children racing across it, playing tag or hide-and-seek in times past. The house was in serious need of fresh paint, but other than that, it looked pretty homey.

Devon stepped out the front door before I had a chance to get there. From the plaid flannel shirt and blue jeans, he could have easily passed for one of the workmen rather than the owner of what the temporary sign read as *Haven Energy*. His face was concerned yet unsmiling as he peered at me.

"You're looking better than yesterday. I thought we'd walk the job site as I explain to you what I'm planning here." He took two white hard hats from a hook on the column of the verandah and came down the stairs.

"Sounds good to me. I tried to get in yesterday after I left you, but security is pretty tight." I reached for the hard hat he extended. As soon as my eyes met his, a wave of nausea rolled up in my throat. I felt my mouth water as I stepped back, looking away. Sure, I was anxious that this interview go well, but not to the point where it could make me ill. Was it my nerves again? What the hell?

"You're sure you're up to this, Shannon?"

Another man, portly and wearing round glasses, stepped out of the building, wheezing slightly as he gripped the railing coming down the stairs. Before I could answer Devon's question, his head turned, and he introduced the guy standing next to him. "Saul, this is Shannon Burke, the news reporter doing the write-up."

He looked over at me and continued, "Shannon, this is Saul Jefferson, my old friend and partner in *Haven Energy*. He's the mastermind and chief engineer of this project."

I took a deep breath, willing my gut to settle before I shook his hand. "Pleased to meet you, Mr. Jefferson. You're also a friend of Devon's?"

"It's Saul, please. Yes. We roomed together at university. But Devon pursued business while I was the nerdy scientist."

All the while he talked, I kept breathing in slowly, letting it out to a count of four. This was ridiculous! Why the hell did it feel like I was going to upchuck? And just like the day before, when I was trying to get that interview from Devon!

Devon! Was there something about Devon that I was reacting to? I tried an experiment. Stepping over to Saul's side, and keeping him in between Devon and me, I gauged my gut. All the while my mouth was operating on rote. "Nerdy scientist! I'm sure that's not true. So, you specialized in energy research?"

My gut seeped back down from my throat, back where it belonged. It was still a bit queasy, but the urge to throw up had subsided. I pulled my phone from my purse and hit record, making a show of doing that in case there were any objections to it. But the scientist nodded when he saw it, continuing on with explaining his field of research. There was no way I would ever remember all that he said. I was too inwardly focused at the moment.

When Saul paused, Devon leaned forward, looking over at me. "Saul has made a breakthrough in capturing and the storage of renewable energy. Storage has always been the problem with renewables..."

Again, my stomach heaved, and it was only when I broke eye contact with Devon that I was able to hold my breakfast down. He continued talking while I held the phone high, trying to capture his words.

Shit! There was more to this than just being nervous. This *had* to be magic—magic being used to make me feel nauseous when I was around Devon! The only person who'd ever "spelled" me when it came to Devon was Mary-Jane! I'd been with her just before I met with Devon the day before. But the effects were still being felt today! I was going to throttle her!

It had to be MJ! But why?

It took every ounce of willpower to manage my next words, keeping my eyes averted from Devon even though my comment was directed at him. "Would you mind if Saul showed me the site and did the interview, Devon? You're busy, and I can call you later for further comments. I'd like to get the mastermind's take on the project."

I risked a peek over at him. The look on his face was confused before a hard glint showed in his eye.

"Fine. I thought I was doing you a favor, but if you want to interview Saul first, there's a ton of things that need my attention. I'll be available by phone after four today." He handed his hard hat to Saul and went back into the building.

For a moment, Saul looked like an owl blinking behind his eyeglasses, magnifying his blue orbs. But then he fell into step, leading the way to the construction area as he continued what was essentially a monologue.

His sciencey terminology was all Greek to me. I'd probably spend hours translating his jargon.

For my part, as soon as I finished getting enough material, I was going to pay a visit to my favorite chef in town. What kind of spell had MJ cooked up on me now?

***

It was two hours later by the time I tore myself away from Saul Jefferson. That man *loved* the sound of his own voice, especially when it came to wind turbines, solar collectors, and lithium ion! Despite all the techno-speak, I was able to pick up that he'd cracked the code in storing electrical power for way longer periods of time and disperse it for use at a fraction of the cost.

Who would have ever guessed that Devon's "nefarious" plan would benefit the region, if not the country! Hell, maybe even the entire world! Saul had really lit up when he talked about the implications of what they were doing—ending global warming, eliminating smog in cities. He went on and on; thank goodness I recorded it all. Talk about getting it totally wrong about Devon Booker!

As I drove into town, I wondered why Devon's reputation was so abysmal with most of the town's residents. Sure, he'd put up some housing developments that kind of changed the nature of the small mountain town, but that had also brought new people and money to the economy. Yet no one had *anything* nice to say about Devon. Hell, I'd hardly hit town before Steve was warning me about Devon.

Neither Mary-Jane nor Libby had a good word to say about Devon either. What had he ever done to either of them? Would Mary-Jane hate Devon so much that she'd cast this spell to make me nauseous whenever I was around him?

I shook my head. But she had also volunteered to read into Devon to see if there was a way for me to reconnect with him. Would she offer to do that only to totally blow any chance I had with Devon, by casting a spell? The more I thought about it, the less sense it made.

Still, I had to ask her. Mary-Jane wouldn't lie to me. Plus, she might have some explanation about what was going on. I parked my truck across from her restaurant, and as I was about to get out, Ray and Steve walked out of the front door. I pulled back, watching them stand there on the sidewalk talking and laughing. There was no way I was going anywhere near Steve, so I pulled out my phone to call MJ.

She answered right away. "Shannon! I was just going to call you. I convinced Ray to get Debbie in to work the kitchen so that I could help you find Robert."

"Huh?" It took me a moment to recall that she was going to put her psychometry skills to work. "Yeah! Great. Look, I'm just outside your restaurant. I was going to ask you something about Devon."

"What are you doing out there? Come in. I just have to put the finishing touches on this cheesecake, and then I'm free. We can talk while I do that." The clanging of a pot punctuated her sentence.

"I'm waiting for Steve Murphy to finish his conversation with Ray and return to his store. The less I see that guy, the better." My eyes narrowed as I looked across the street at his wide grin and his hand clapping Ray on the shoulder. How long was this going to take?

He must have sensed me looking at him because his head turned and our gazes met. Shit.

Mary-Jane spoke again, "Steve offered to go with me, Shannon. He was here when I asked Ray about leaving early. Steve said he wants to help you find the bobcat too."

Double shit! Steve broke away from Ray and ambled across the street to my truck. "I'll be in to see you in a minute, MJ" After clicking off the phone and slipping it in my purse, I got out.

"Shannon! I hear you're forming a search party for that bobcat. Count me in!" His hand rose to rest on my shoulder as he gazed into my eyes. "I'd like to help you."

I'd been ready to brush by him and tell him I wouldn't need HIS help, but instead I murmured, "Sure. The more hands, the better." I couldn't tear my eyes from his gaze even though on another level, I felt like kicking him in the knee.

"Is it just us, or will Cynthia and Libby be there too? You four are practically inseparable these days. I don't know how many times I drive by your place that I see their cars parked there." He squeezed my shoulder and made no move to remove it as he stared into my eyes.

It occurred to me that he was looking at me the way I wished Devon would look at me. But this was Steve, the guy who'd shot my bobcat! The last person I wanted to talk to let alone have him casually touch my shoulder was Steve! And why the sudden interest in my friends? Libby maybe, but Cynthia had broken it off with him?

But what came out of my mouth was, "No, Libby and Cynthia are both at work. How is it you're free to leave your store?"

"Jamie is covering the store today. It's not that busy right now. I'd rather spend time helping you. After all..." His voice trailed off, omitting the part he'd played in why Robert was missing.

I was saved from answering him when Mary-Jane yelled from across the street. "Hey! Shannon!" She hurried over to join us. "Great timing! I'll just get my car, and I'll meet you guys out there."

Steve turned toward her. "Are you sure you should be driving, MJ? I don't mind giving you a lift." Finally, his hand fell from my shoulder as he turned toward her.

She shook her head, scoffing. "I had one glass of wine with you and Ray! I'm fine to drive. I'm really eager to get out there. I've got a good feeling about this." She winked at me and rubbed her hands together.

Oh man. I wished she hadn't mentioned helping me find the bobcat in front of Steve. He was the very last person I wanted help from.

But what came out of my mouth was completely different: "Fine. I'll see you at my place." As soon as I got in my truck and drove off, I kicked myself for agreeing to let Steve help us. It was like how it had been in the coffee shop the day before. Why was I being decent to that jerk? My eyes narrowed as I tried to make sense of this. Nausea around Devon when all I wanted to do was reestablish our friendship... and being mealy mouthed around Steve when I really wanted nothing more to do with him.

My hands slapped the steering wheel. There was no logical explanation, which meant only one thing. It had to be some kind of weird spell that was affecting me with him too! And considering my history, specifically with MJ's involvement, it only made sense. But why would she do this to me? That's the part that didn't add up.

But what if it wasn't her? The only other people who could do this were Libby or Cynthia. I pressed the button on the steering wheel to call Libby. I didn't even bother exchanging pleasantries when she answered.

"Did you cast some kind of spell on me, Libby?"

"What? No! Of course not. Why would you even *think* I would?"

I sighed. Of course she wouldn't have done this. "I'm sorry, but I had to ask. There's something weird going on with how I'm acting, Libby, and for sure it's not some random hot flash... although I wish it were. It happened *again* today! I almost threw up when I met with Devon for the interview. And—"

"That's totally understandable." She let out a chuckle. "If I met with him, it would turn my stomach too."

There it was again! Her response was rote, almost like whenever Devon's name was mentioned, she'd have to say something negative about him. "*Why*, Libby? What did Devon ever do to you that makes you hate him so much?"

"Huh? What did he do?" A few beats of silence followed this before she stammered, "W-well, everyone knows what he's like, Shannon! You just moved back here. We've lived with him scooping up properties and turning things into... into these overpriced subdivisions or condos and—"

"That's no reason to hate him. He brought new life and money into Wesley. I would never choose to live in an overpriced mausoleum, but other people like them. There's no law against what he's done." From what I'd learned, he converted an old warehouse that was almost falling down into condos, as well as purchasing a tract of land near an abandoned logging road and creating a subdivision. So what?

"Aren't you forgetting how he tried to trick you into selling your aunt's property?" Her voice sounded like she was still in high school!

"He made me an offer which I refused. His *plumber* overestimated the cost of repairing my septic. Devon didn't do that. In fact, he's helped me on more than one occasion. I just don't get why everyone hates him!" No one complained about the money he'd brought with the new developments, getting wealthy people to retire in Wesley.

"Well, as far as I'm concerned, the less you have to do with Devon, the better. But it certainly wasn't me messing around with some spell, Shannon. I thought we'd all gotten closer after Esbat last night. Wasn't that what the Well wanted?"

"Yeah. Again, I'm sorry for accusing you of this. I just wish I could find out what's going on."

I glanced in the rearview mirror and saw Steve's burgundy truck behind me, and then farther back, MJ's Subaru. "If you can believe this, Steve Murphy is going to help MJ and me look for Robert. Mary-Jane mentioned that she was going to help me this afternoon, and Steve was all over it like white on rice."

"Oh. And you're okay with that? I thought you hated Steve. Why the sudden change of heart? I certainly don't want anything to do with him after what he did." Libby's voice was muffled, but I could hear her say, "I'll be right there, Doug. Give me a minute." When she spoke again, it was to end the call. "Look, I've got a meeting right now. I'll call you later, Shannon."

And the line went dead. I clicked the button, ending the call on my phone. That left only Cynthia. But seeing the familiar landmarks, the grove of birch trees, and then an outcropping of granite rock, I knew I wouldn't have time to talk to her before pulling into my drive.

The sharp whine of a police siren yanked my gaze to the mirror again. Flashing lights on the roof of a white car caught my eye. When Mary-Jane's car slowed and veered onto the shoulder behind the cop, my mouth fell open. Shit. The police had pulled her over? Why? We were all doing the speed limit.

I flipped my turn signal on and slowed down to enter my driveway. Steve's truck was right behind me. Great! Mary-Jane probably had a taillight out or something stupid, and I was stuck here waiting for her with Steve!

I got out of my vehicle and leaned up against the hood, watching for Mary-Jane to come barreling down the gravel drive.

Steve wandered over and shook his head. "I knew I should have insisted she drive with me. Maybe I should go back and see if she's okay."

"What are you talking about? It's probably a routine check. She'll be here in a minute." As I looked at him, his words outside the restaurant sounded in my head, him asking her if she was okay to drive.

"I'm not sure about that, Shannon. I think MJ had a few glasses even before I got there to speak to Ray. I've noticed that she's drinking a lot more than she used to. There was a time she'd never have a drink during the day and now..."

His eyes met mine again, and the sharp retort that was itching to leap from my tongue faded. Instead, I murmured, "But, Ray... he wouldn't have let MJ drive if she'd been drinking earlier. That can't be right, Steve."

He rocked back and forth from his toes to his heels, looking down at the ground. "When we were fishing on Sunday, he mentioned his concern about her drinking. He thinks it's because she's been hanging out with you and the others. I tried to tell him, but..."

The breath froze in my chest as I listened to him. Ray had said *that*? But MJ didn't drink that much! Sure, when she was here and staying the night, she'd tied a few on, but so had the rest of us! There was no way she'd ever be able to maintain her schedule of cooking six days a week in the restaurant if she had a drinking problem.

I pulled the phone from my purse and brushed my finger against the small screen to call her. There had to be a mistake in what he'd said. It rang for about half a dozen times before she answered.

"I can't talk right now, Shannon. I can't believe this, but a cop stopped me and I have to do a breathalyzer test! For *one* glass of frigging wine! I'll be there in a minute."

The line went dead. I looked at Steve and his head tipped to the side. "Maybe we should do this another day. I'd better touch base with Ray and let him know what's going on." He walked over to his truck and started it up.

As I watched him back out of my driveway, I blinked a few times. This was crazy. What the hell was going on? MJ didn't have a drinking problem, and she shouldn't have gotten pulled over. I'd seen MJ when she'd had more than a few Jack Daniels, her face flushed and cracking jokes like a madwoman. She'd been *sober* today.

Something seriously weird was going on with me, and now it looked like it was also happening to MJ. Again, I pulled my phone out to call Cynthia. Maybe she'd know what was happening.

FIFTEEN

Hi, Shannon! Can I call you later? You've caught me at a bad time. I'm waiting for a call back from the fertility clinic." Her voice was low and rushed. But considering the time, she was still at work trying to keep her coworkers from listening in.

"Sure. This won't take long, though. Mary-Jane's been pulled over for drunk driving." I paused and then dove right in. "There's something strange going on, Cynthia. I had that same nausea come over me today when I met with Devon. And then there's Steve! Why am I being so nice to that jerk?" The words gushed from my mouth like a faucet turning on. Even as I spoke, I knew I shouldn't be bugging her when she was trying to get her pregnancy appointment.

"Oh, my—" Her voice cut out for a second before she spoke again. "There's another call coming through. Gotta go!" The line went dead.

I held the phone out, scowling at it. It seemed like everyone was busy today. Just when I needed to talk to them! After slipping my phone back into my purse, I got back in the truck.

I had to find out about MJ. When I reached the main road, I saw the police car do a U-turn, heading back into town. Mary-Jane's Subaru was parked at the side of the road, but she wasn't in it. My gut fell lower into the seat as I continued driving. It could only mean one thing. She'd failed the breathalyzer and was in the police car headed back to the station.

I hit the button to call her again. As soon as she answered, I could hear her voice breaking.

"They think I'm drunk, Shannon! Honestly! I only had one drink. There's got to be something wrong with that damned breathalyzer thing they made me use!"

"I believe you! Something is going on... something weird, like some-kind-of-spell weird, y'know? I'm following you right now. Steve left to go talk to Ray. I'll be at the station with you, MJ. Try to keep calm, and we'll figure this out, okay?"

As I drove, I couldn't help but think of what MJ had said the night before, how she wanted to work with the police to help them solve crimes and find missing persons. Well, she would soon be at the police station, but not to help them. Poor MJ! Would she get charged with drunk driving? Fat chance of her being taken seriously when she offered to help them if she had that kind of record. This was TOTAL bullshit!

When I walked into the police station, I headed for the end of the large room, where a black officer stood behind a high counter. He looked over from the monitor that he'd been reading and asked, "Can I help you, ma'am?"

"I hope so. I'm here to see Mary-Jane Mathews. She arrived here just a few minutes ago?" Before he answered, his gaze drifted behind me and he muttered, "She's pretty popular."

At the touch on my shoulder, I turned and saw Steve Murphy standing next to me. "Ray is in with her. I'm afraid she's facing a charge of impaired driving, Shannon."

I looked back at the officer, whose eyebrows rose as he nodded. "It'll be about ten minutes till they release her. Have a seat."

I let Steve lead me over to the row of plastic chairs set out before a large plate-glass window in the waiting area. This was like a bad dream. It couldn't be happening.

"You might want to leave before Ray comes out. He's pretty upset about all this. He had a few choice words to say about you, Shannon." He lowered into the chair and sighed. "I wish she had come with me in my truck. And to think we were trying to help you find that bobcat."

My teeth ground together as I stared at him. The bobcat that YOU shot! But instead of blaring that at him, I murmured, "I know. But MJ wasn't drunk, Steve. I hope Ray gets a lawyer to fight this. There has to be something wrong with that machine."

He snorted. "Mary-Jane needs counseling more than a lawyer. I suggested that to Ray. It looks like your little get-togethers are going to be out of the question for her from now on." He smiled, but his eyes were hard when he asked, "Every Monday night I see their cars at your house, Shannon. What's up with that?"

There was something about the way he looked at me that set alarm bells blaring in my head. What was with him snooping around, checking who was at my house? What I did, and what my friends chose to do, was *none* of his business.

I was spared from commenting when I heard MJ's voice from across the room. She walked as if the weight of the world rested on her shoulders, while Ray, just two steps behind her, looked like he was ready to kill someone.

Standing up, I hurried over to her. "Mary-Jane. I can't believe this is happening. There's got to be some mistake—"

"There's a mistake all right!" Ray stepped in between MJ and me, his eyes narrow with anger, glaring at me. "And it started when she got involved with these Monday get-togethers. Too much partying and forgetting everything else."

I felt like he'd sucker-punched me in the gut. For a moment, I could only stare at him. "That's not true, Ray. Mary-Jane works really hard, and she definitely doesn't have a drinking problem!"

Before he could speak, MJ held up her hand, trying to silence both of us. "There has to be an error. In that machine! I had *one* glass of wine. Hell, I don't even like wine all that much." She fixed Ray with a hard stare. "And these Monday night get-togethers are not stopping, Ray. One freaking night with my friends, and you resent *that*?"

His lips clamped shut, and he shot me a dirty look before mumbling, "We'll talk about this at home, MJ. This is definitely not the place to air our differences. C'mon." He grabbed her arm, steering her toward the door.

But MJ wasn't having anything to do with being marched out on her husband's order. "No!" She twisted out of his grasp and took a step closer to me. "Shannon will give me a ride home, Ray. After I help her look for that bobcat, like I promised."

"Mary-Jane!" Ray's eyes popped out so far that it was a wonder they didn't jettison across the room.

Steve had been watching everything silently, but now he stepped forward. "Ray, I think you need to let her have some time. She'll be back later, and hopefully both of you will be calmer."

Ray sighed. "You really think so?" When Steve nodded sagely, he shrugged and said, "Okay bud, if you say so."

For the first time since I'd entered the police station I felt my head clear from the surreal situation. Frig! The whole day had been like this starting with being around Devon. I took Mary-Jane's hand and tugged her along with me to the door. "Let's go."

When Steve called after me, that he'd stop by to help us, I kept walking and didn't turn around. "Don't bother. Mary-Jane and I can handle this without your help! I'll drive MJ home later, Ray."

SIXTEEN

As soon as we were in my truck, Mary-Jane burst into tears. "This is a nightmare! I'm probably going to lose my driver's license. Ray is so pissed with me... and *you*! He's blaming all this on our coven meetings." She grabbed a tissue from her purse and dabbed at her eyes. "I'm not stopping though, no matter what he says. This is important to me."

I leaned closer and tucked a lock of her damp hair behind her ear. "I know you weren't drunk, MJ. We need to get a lawyer and fight this stupid charge. Ray is upset right now. He'll get over it once we get all this cleared up."

She twisted the tissue in her fingers, staring down at her lap. "He's supposed to be my *partner*. Someone who has my back when things are rough. But instead, he's acting like some kind of warden telling me what I can and can't do. And blaming me! When he *knows* I only had one freaking glass of wine!"

It was hard, but I kept my mouth shut. I totally agreed with everything she said. He should have taken her side, especially when he'd been with her and knew the truth, that she wasn't inebriated. Not. In. The. Least.

Her face was twisted in anguish when she looked over at me. "I thought he'd changed, Shannon. After he got that scare when I hurt myself running last winter, he was so kind to me. Even our sex life got recharged again. The weight loss helped. But for him to jump down my throat, assuming the worst is... well, it's like how things once were."

I rubbed her shoulder. "He's upset, MJ. He still loves you. This whole thing is upsetting." Poor MJ. She was a really good person who totally didn't deserve to be treated like this.

"Let's get out of here, Shannon. I can't stand looking at that police station. I'll help you look for Robert, but after that... I'm having a few drinks. More than a few. Ray thinks he's the boss when it comes to our marriage and the restaurant? Let's see how he makes out on his own." Her chin rose as she stared out the front window.

After starting the truck, I looked over at her. "You're welcome to spend the night at my place, MJ. Deal with Ray tomorrow if that's what you want. Personally, I don't think Steve is a good influence on Ray."

Her forehead furrowed. "Why? He's practically the only friend Ray has."

I took a deep breath as I steered the car out of the police parking lot. "Steve is a control freak, even a bit misogynistic. We all know that about him. That attitude isn't healthy for Ray to be exposed to. You and Ray are partners. He's not the boss and neither are you. But Steve..."

"You just don't like Steve, Shannon. He's not perfect, but he's not horrible either."

I held my hand out. "Hang on. I'm not finished. If you had heard Steve talking to Ray in the boat the other day, you might not have such a high opinion of him. He bragged about shooting Robert. Then he *bragged* about sleeping with me which was a total lie. There's something not right about Steve, y'know?"

She tsked. "That's a guy thing! Just talk. Whoever listens to that crap."

Well, there was nothing else to do but tell her my suspicions. The timing might not be perfect, not with her getting charged with a DUI and fighting with Ray but... "It's not just that, MJ. Something is weird about how I am around him. I mean, I can't stand him after what he did, yet I'm mealy mouthed around him, even nice to him. And Devon! The last two times I've been near him, I get nauseated to the point where I feel like I'm going to throw up."

She shrugged. "No surprise. It's Devon after all. He may be good-looking but he's a jerk."

Again, I had to hold my tongue at the rote response about Devon. These people sounded like a broken record where he was concerned. I reached out to squeeze her arm. "I thought it was you casting a spell on me. Making me nice to Steve but sick around Devon. But I know you didn't do it. Neither did Libby. I called her to confront her about it."

Mary-Jane snorted. "That only leaves one other person, Shannon. But why would Cynthia do that? It doesn't make sense. Unless she wants to take your place as the head of the coven."

I shook my head. "Cynthia didn't even want to be part of the coven. Not at first. Her big goal is to get pregnant and have a daughter. I can't see her casting some kind of spell like this. Plus, of all of us, she's got the most respect and knowledge about magic. No way would she trifle with this kind of thing."

Mary-Jane was silent for a few minutes—both of us trying to figure out what was going on. Finally, she looked over at me, "There's no way I should have gotten pulled over today, let alone charged with a DUI. Can whatever this is, be affecting me as well?"

I looked over at her. "Maybe. I don't know. But whatever is happening is damned strange. I think when we get back from looking for Robert, we should do a protection spell."

"It can't hurt." She brightened a bit before she added, "I'm looking forward to trying my gift in finding that bobcat. At least there might be one good thing about this horrible day."

SEVENTEEN

Later that day...

Libby

As soon as I turned the car off, the din of bangs and shouts filled my ears. What the hell? After the day I had at work, all I wanted was a hot bath, a cold drink, and quiet. Blissful quiet.

My shoulders slumped. Today was totally not the day to come home to drama. The meeting with HR still played in my head. Only a month into my probationary period for this new job and the feedback from Dr. Armstrong and the "bean counter" about my performance so far, was less than stellar. If things didn't change, there was a good chance I'd be let go.

I had to admit I was torn. The money was great, but administration had to be the most unrewarding job in the hospital. Going back on the floor as a registered nurse wasn't an option. They'd already hired someone to take my previous position. I *had* to make this work.

Emerging from the car, I frowned hearing the metallic clanging and my sons' shouts from the back of my house. The front door immediately followed this, opening with Dahlia sprinting out.

Her face was flushed with a big grin as she cried out, "Mom! You're not going to believe this! There're so many animals at the edge of the yard; it's like a zoo or something. Jack and Kevin are trying to shoo them away, even though I asked them not to. It's soooo cool."

Oh, for crying out loud! What I'd feared would happen, apparently WAS happening! So much for Miss Purdy Cat's assurance she'd keep them at bay. I was being swarmed by every animal in the forest.

The door in the house next to mine opened and Carol James stepped out. "What's going on, Libby?" Her knuckles were white, clutching the railing on her step, leaning over it to scowl at me. "Did you leave food out? Attracting wildlife? There's a whole passel of critters back there. I'm going to call the sheriff's office to get rid of them. Some friggin' skunk sprayed my patio furniture! It's ruined!"

I shoved past her as I strode up the walkway. "I *just* got home! Give me a break, Carol!" Turning to Dahlia—"Let's go inside. When did this start?"

Trailing beside me, she practically bubbled, "It was like this when we got home from school! There's a family of skunks, some raccoons, and rabbits... a whole *bunch* of rabbits. I took some carrots and lettuce out, but then Kevin made me go back inside."

When we stepped inside the house, I slipped my coat off, peering at my daughter. That cat had said that Dahlia was better at talking to animals than me, even if she didn't understand what the animals said to her. Part of this could be

Dahlia's doing, although she wouldn't even know it if she'd done anything.

I watched Dahlia carefully. "Ummm... honey, did you see any strays or animals on your way home today? Did you say hello to any of them?"

She tilted her head at me. "Nooo...and why would *that* matter, anyway?"

I wasn't going to tell her what I had learned—that animals *understood* her. Well, not yet, anyway. Come to think of it, how the hell do you tell your kid that she's a natural born animal whisperer?

"Did you see any rabbits or raccoons on your walk home today?"

At her questioning look, like I was speaking Greek, I added, "Is this happening to *anyone* else? That's what I was getting at." Although I knew it was just us! All because of setting Rascal the raccoon free so that he could gossip, spreading word about me. Although it wasn't gossip really when I actually could talk to animals. Crap.

"No! Come see! There's none in the neighbors' backyards, just *ours*." Dahlia tugged at my arm.

Massaging the tight knot of muscle at the back of my neck, I followed her to the kitchen. Through the glass patio door, I could see my sons clanging on pots with metal spoons as they walked the back part of the yard.

My eyes opened wider. In the forested greenbelt behind, a few raccoons chattered curses as they clung to the lower branches of a maple. At the side of the lot, a family of skunks circled my wild rosebush—no doubt the ones who'd sprayed Carol's furniture.

This was *insane*! To make matters worse, Miss Purdy Cat chose that moment to rub against my leg, purring as she looked up at me. *"I tried, but I've been a little busy with kittens."*

I yanked the door open and yelled to my sons. "Kevin! Jack! Come inside."

Kevin gaped at me, but his hand paused in clanging the side of the four-quart pot. "We can't, Mom! If we do, this yard's going to fill up with skunks and rabbits. I think I even heard a coyote at one point."

Jack weighed in: "Now I bet you wish you'd gotten me that twenty-two I asked for! What the hell is *with* these critters? Are they rabid or just stupid?"

"You can't stay out there all night, boys! Come in! *I'll* deal with this." I looked down at Dahlia. "Actually, we'll deal with this. I think we'll have better luck than your brothers at getting rid of these pests."

"They're not *pests*, Mom! They're probably hungry. It's been a long winter. Let me take something out for them." She started going over to the fridge, but I grabbed her arm.

"No! This is our *home*, not a sanctuary, Dahlia! How would you like it if the police showed up or even animal control to *shoot* them? They can't *stay* here, Dahlia. Feeding them will just encourage that."

When Kevin slipped by me, coming into the house, I asked, "You didn't see a bobcat out there, did you? A scraggly guy with one ear?"

"Noooo." He walked over to the counter to set the pot down. "This is bizarre, Mom. It's like we're Jurassic Park but without the dinosaurs. The animals have gone crazy. I agree with Jack."

"That's a first, bro!" Jack looked over at me. "I'm going to call Stan! I think he's got a shotgun. That'll take care of this, pronto."

"No! No! No!" I clutched the sides of my sweater together as I peered out at the yard. Three squirrels were now parked on top of my wooden picnic table, while four brown rabbits gnawed at the canes of my raspberry bushes. The raccoons had migrated to the main trunk of the maple making their descent. It was an open house at *my* place, apparently!

Jack was about to go back outside armed with his pot and spoon, but I blocked his way. "Let *me* handle this!"

He sneered, "What are you going to do that we haven't tried? I say we call Stan or even animal control."

Kevin stood at the window, gazing out. "Looks like Harold James is home. From the look in his eyes and the shotgun, this problem is gonna be solved pretty fast. It's rabbit stew tonight, folks."

I practically leaped through the door, racing over to the side of my yard to stop Harold. "Don't shoot them! I can explain!"

He turned his face to me, his eyes sparking under a unibrow. "What the hell's with these critters? I've lived here all my life and never have I seen animals act this strangely. I also *hunt*, Libby, so I know what I'm talking about!"

I looked over at Dahlia, who was squatted down next to the table trying to coax the rabbits out. "It's a science experiment, Harold. You've heard that animals are repelled by sonic hums, right?"

Oh shit! I was making this up as I went along, but Harold nodded sagely.

"Yeah. Steve Murphy carries them in the hardware store to get rid of squirrels in your attic. But that's to GET RID of them, Libby!"

I nodded fast, gasping a grin. "Yeah! See? The science project that Dahlia devised worked perfectly! She played around with vibrations to attract animals! Look at the result! Brilliant kid, right?"

"No. Carol's gonna have to turf the patio cushions." He fixed a glowering stare at Dahlia. "Tell her to turn it off, Libby. This isn't just a nuisance, it's unsanitary!"

"I will, don't worry!" I let out a long sigh, smiling at him like we were coconspirators. "I'll buy Carol new cushions. Just let us handle this. Dahlia will be traumatized if you shoot any of these critters."

He was silent for a few moments, gazing at Dahlia. "Do you think she'll lend me that gadget sometime? It would make deer hunting a lot easier."

I grimaced. "She's a pacifist, Harold. I wouldn't count on it."

"Then what *good* is it?" He rolled his eyes, disgusted, before he turned to go back into his house. "Make sure she turns it off, Libby! And never uses it again, not in this neighborhood."

Breathing a sigh of relief at one catastrophe averted, I looked over at Dahlia. She was cooing at the biggest rabbit and even had it sniffing her fingers. I glanced at the patio window where Miss Purdy sat between my two boys, gloating. That cat was getting sour milk tonight! She'd promised to take care of this!

"Dahlia?" I walked over and squatted down next to her. "You have a gift, being able to calm animals so quickly. I think on some level they sense that you're a good person who'd never harm them."

The rabbit turned its head, twitching its nose before whispering, *'She* promised *me food.'* It looked up at me. *"My mate is injured. Are you that woman? You can heal her, right? I heard about you."*

My gaze darted to Dahlia, but it was clear from the way she'd turned to the other smaller rabbit that she hadn't picked up on what the big rabbit had said, or that he was even conversing with me.

Turning back to the jack rabbit, I whispered, "I'll see what I can do. Hide under the maple and I'll be out later. But for now, you have to leave. It isn't safe here."

"Mom? Are you whispering to that rabbit? You like him too! Can we keep him?" She turned back to the rabbit, now stroking the fur between his ears with the tip of her finger.

"We can't keep *any* of these animals, Dahlia." I stood up and reached for her hand. Lord, help me be patient! "Letting them stay is a death sentence for every one of them. We have to convince them to leave."

She squinted as she pulled herself to her feet. "How are we gonna do that, Mom?"

"We will firmly, and politely ask them to leave. Most importantly, Dahlia, you must *believe* they will. Do you understand?" Still holding her hand in mine, I squeezed it.

"You've heard of horse whisperers? Well, we're going to try that trick but with these animals."

She brightened. "Like that guy, Caesar Milan with dogs! I love watching his You Tube vids."

I nodded. "Yeah, I guess. Now, you handle the squirrels and rabbits, and I'll look after the skunks and raccoons."

I left her, speaking in a calm voice as I headed to the little black-and-white stinkers. "You've gotta leave. Go back to the forest. It isn't safe here. Tell whoever is heading here, that I *command* it."

The smaller skunks crowded around the biggest one. It looked up at me. *"My paw. There's a thorn in it. They told me you'd fix it."* It lifted its left front foot, licking at the underside.

I bent over, extending my hand. "Don't bite me, okay? I'm going to have a look." I kept inching my hand closer, watching both ends of the skunk for any sign of trouble. Finally, I held its paw in my fingers. I could feel it, a stubble of something in the main pad of its foot. My fingers closed on the thorn and pinched it out.

The skunk yanked its foot back and then looked up at me. It was only a second, but I could hear it gasp a thanks before herding the rest of the brood toward the forest.

"Don't come back." They headed for the raccoons, cutting them off before vanishing in the underbrush.

I looked over at Dahlia walking behind the rabbits. Her hands shooed for them to leave, mirroring her words. The branches overhead swayed from the antics of the squirrels jumping from branch to branch going deeper into the forest.

Dahlia shook her head as she walked over to me. "It *worked*! I swear it was like they understood every word I said, Mom."

I pulled her close and kissed the top of her head. "They did, sweetie. Your words and your *intentions*. They knew you meant it."

When we reached the patio door, the cat arched its back, circling Dahlia's leg. "*Told ya, she's great with animals.*" Miss Purdy Cat looked up at me, blinking smugly.

Okay, maybe I wouldn't give her sour milk tonight. There was no sense making her any more miserable, considering she was feeding kittens.

The look in Jack and Kevin's eyes as they gawked at Dahlia and me made me smile. I held my fingertips close to my mouth and blew on them, gloating. "Sometimes the best man for the job, boys, is a WOMAN."

Turning to Dahlia, I said, "If our neighbor Harold ever asks you about your science project, tell him we broke it. Okay?"

Her eyebrows bunched as she looked up at me. "Okaaay?" She grabbed her cell phone from the table and headed out of the room. "That was seriously cool. I can't wait to tell my friends. Call me when dinner's ready?" With that she was gone.

"I've got this, Mom." Kevin opened the freezer door and took out a pizza. "I can hardly believe all that happened. What is up with these animals? Maybe we should put up a fence to keep them out."

I watched him turn the oven on and get the pizza ready. If he only knew. Beside him, Jack was busy rummaging around in the cabinets. When he turned, there was a highball glass with ice floating in amber liquid.

"You look like you could use a drink, Mom." He walked over to the table and pulled out a chair for me.

I didn't need to be asked twice. I practically fell into it and sighed. The burn of that first long sip of bourbon felt wonderfully soothing. "Thanks, Jack."

He handed me my phone from my purse. "Your phone went off when you were outside. I think it's a text from Shannon."

When I read it, my face tightened.

Call me. ASAP.

Crap. Now what?

EIGHTEEN

That evening...

Shannon

As soon as my phone buzzed, I knew it had to be Libby. I dropped the spoon next to the pot of spaghetti sauce, and raced to get it. But Mary-Jane was ahead of me, fishing it out of my coat pocket and handing it to me. Her shoulders slumped as she sat at the table, nursing the glass of Jack Daniels. It was awful seeing her so depressed at how the day had turned out—first charged with a DUI and no luck in our search for the bobcat.

As soon as I brushed the screen to answer, Libby's voice blared in my ear. "I got a helluva lot going on here at home, Shannon. This better be important!"

"Libby! Thank goodness you called back. I had to tell you about Mary-Jane. She's been charged with impaired driving, but I swear she was sober. We were on our way to—"

"Impaired! What the hell? Where is she? Surely, she's not in jail." I had to pull the phone away, her voice was so loud.

"No. No. No. She's here. Let me put you on speaker so she can talk too."

For the next fifteen minutes, we shared what had happened to MJ as well as my weird experiences with Devon and Steve. I wasn't ready for what she added to the mix: the wild animals showing up, and getting a terrible job evaluation at work.

"Shit! What the hell is going on, Libby? It's like we're cursed or something." I stood there, biting my lower lip. Cursed was pretty accurate. It had to be something like that for this much crap to happen all at once.

A hissing sound came over the speaker, and Mary-Jane's head tilted to the side. "What's that, Libby? Are you still there?"

"Sorry. I just started filling the tub for a long, hot soak. I had to come upstairs to talk in private so I thought, why not run a bath. The kids know nothing about my job situation."

Mary-Jane rolled her eyes. "Wish that were me relaxing in a bath, but I'll settle for another few of these." She lifted her glass of whiskey and took a sip. "If I'm going to get convicted of the crime, I might as well earn it."

I turned back to the phone. "It won't come to that, Libby. You'll get your job squared away. I know you don't love the head nurse job, but it's what you need, right?" Crap. Her financial problems made mine pale in significance. She had three kids depending on her!

"I *have* to keep it, Shannon. But what about this curse thing? The only one like us who could have done it, is Cynthia. But that doesn't add up. After Esbat, we were all so close to each other. But if it's not one of us..." Her voice faded, then she said, "We need to talk to her. I'd suggest a Zoom meeting, but I'm getting ready to have a bath."

Mary-Jane hovered over the phone and barked, "Keep your pants on, sister! I'm losing my driver's license, fighting with Ray, while Shannon's got some weird shit happening, and you're worried about your *bath?* Trust me. It'll still be there when we're through talking."

"Fine! I'll hang up and wait for you to set this up. I need another drink anyway," Libby sniped before the line went dead.

I looked over at Mary-Jane. "I'm not great at technology, but I'll give this a try. My daughter usually initiates the FaceTime calls." I flicked through my contacts and finally found the icon to set up a multi-call visual meeting. Cynthia was the first to accept, and the screen changed, showing her face. Rather than her normal smile, her mouth was a straight line, and her eyes were red-rimmed, like she'd been crying.

"I'm sorry. I meant to call you back today, Shannon." She dabbed at the corners of her eyes with a tissue. "It's just that..." She sucked in a deep breath and looked away.

"What's wrong? I've got MJ here with me, Cynthia. Libby is joining us soon, too. Tell us. Why're you crying?" I slumped down in the chair next to MJ, sharing the small screen.

Libby's face then flashed taking up half the screen. "I'm back." She held up a glass of amber liquid, with her bed and windows showing behind her. "Cynthia? What's wrong?"

We had to wait while Cynthia blew her nose before she spoke, "The fertility clinic. I have to wait for six months, and even then it's going to cost me waaaay more than I thought. It's not covered in my benefits." Her voice broke when she continued, "I thought this would be easy but it's soooo hard. Is this ever going to happen?"

I felt a chill on my shoulder, and the smell of patchouli oil drifted into my nostril. When I turned my head, Aunt Maeve's form wavered in the air. Another person, or rather spirit, taking part in this call even though I was the only one able to see her.

Mary-Jane's voice was soft when she spoke, "Do you *have* to use the clinic? What about that hot firefighter you were with on Saturday? There're tons of guys who'd gladly donate, Cynthia."

Libby weighed in before Cynthia got a chance. "That's not the same, MJ! She wants this child all on her own, no strings with guys demanding parental rights. Cynthia, if you need money, we'll all chip in to help you."

I nodded. "For sure! We've got your back. Whatever it—"

"I know! It's just that... I thought I'd be calling you with good news. Now..." Cynthia's voice trailed off.

Aunt Maeve floated over so that she was between MJ and me. "The curse, Shannon! It's coming down on Cynthia too. All four of you are under attack."

For a moment the consoling words of Libby and Mary-Jane drifted by as my mind digested my aunt's statement. We were under attack? But who would do that? Who COULD do that? And if they could, *why* would they?

I waited until Libby and MJ brought Cynthia up to speed with the awful things that had happened to them that day. Finally, when they were through and there was a break, I spoke. "Aunt Maeve has joined us, you guys. She thinks that we're being attacked. Every one of us has had a serious setback today. There's someone out there who's cast a shitty spell on us." I gulped. "Someone has it in for *all* of us."

For a few moments, this was followed by complete silence, each of them shocked but with their minds working overtime.

Mary-Jane was the first to speak, "Who? Who besides us practices magic? I've lived here all my life, and I've never known anyone who is even a Wicca, let alone a witch casting horrible spells?"

"But how would you know? None of us knew about Maeve! That she was a practicing witch! It's not like anyone wears a sign!" Libby shook her head from side to side.

Cynthia's eyebrows formed a tight bunch over her eyes. "Well, there was also my grandmother Ruth as well as Maeve."

"And who would be stupid enough to send bad wishes out against us? Don't they know it comes back to bite them threefold?"

Aunt Maeve once more fixed me with a hard look. "A reversal spell! You don't know who has done this to you. But you can find out!"

I held up my hand and turned to the phone's camera. "Hang on, you guys! Aunt Maeve has got an idea. Just give me a minute."

Turning back to Maeve, I asked, "What can we do? Whatever it takes, I'm willing to give it a try. But shouldn't we all be together for this reversal spell? Tomorrow—"

"What's stopping us from doing it now?" Cynthia leaned closer to her phone's camera so that I could see the flecks of gray in her blue eyes. "We're together right now! Not physically, but you get what I mean. Our intention! And didn't the well say that to us last night?"

Libby murmured, "Someone was following us last night, you guys. I could feel someone watching us the whole time we were together. It wasn't Robert; I know that for sure."

I jerked back at her words. "Why didn't you *tell* us? Look at what we've all gone through today, and it's only NOW that you feel the need to mention it?" This was ridiculous! Things had gone to hell in a handbasket and Libby... peaceful, placid Libby kept THAT piece of news to herself?

"Now, wait a damn minute! I wasn't sure! You don't need to bite my—"

"Stop bickering!" Aunt Maeve got right in my face, wagging her finger. "Now is the time to come together as a coven, not nitpick! Grow up, Shannon! This is serious!"

NINETEEN

My face warmed at Aunt Maeve's words. The others hadn't heard her, but her rebuke still rang in my ears. I turned to the screen again. "I'm sorry about what I said, Libby. How could you have known?"

"So how do we do this reversal spell? Does your aunt have any advice on that?" Mary-Jane looked at me, not the phone. Her face faded and wavered behind my aunt's amorphous body.

Cynthia broke in, "If we do a reversal spell like we did for MJ when we reversed Shannon's spell, that went wonky, or when we reversed MJ's spell on Shannon that turned her into a walking, talking phone-sex worker—"

"Ouch!" I said. "I wasn't *that* bad!"

The others all giggled. "Oh yeah?" MJ said, still laughing. "Ray wanted *me* to talk dirty like you did with Devon when you were under it!"

"Wait a minute. Let me finish, guys," Cynthia said. "What I'm saying is that we definitely can do a reversal spell. But that's not good enough. We have to add some extra spice to it."

We all stared at her. Cynthia closed her eyes and said, "We need to amp up the reversal spell. There's got to be a way that the effects of it are so obvious that it highlights who's behind this. That's what I mean. If we just reverse it, we'll never know who did this to us. But...if we add an extra element, something like, we make that person sneeze or get a constant case of hiccups. We don't want to harm them, just *reveal* who it is when we put an end to their spell."

Mary-Jane snorted, "Are you *kidding* me? That's it? That's all you want? No way. I want to make them pay! Hiccups and sneezing isn't embarrassing. That could happen to anyone with allergies or to someone who drinks too much pop."

"Make them strip! Make it so that they can't stand to wear clothes after noon tomorrow. Like when they'd be at work!"

I blinked a few times hearing THAT suggestion come from Libby and not MJ! But a smile curled my lips picturing it. Yeah! The weather had warmed with the advent of spring but it wasn't bathing suit weather... not by a long shot! And if it totally embarrassed whoever was doing this, it'd be perfect!

"Yes!" Cynthia sat back rubbing her hands together. "And you know what? I say we split up tomorrow and visit as many people as possible. We'll *uncover* the culprit!" She giggled at her pun, which started a chain reaction with the rest of us.

Mary-Jane sputtered, "I could set up a special night at the restaurant and install a stripper pole for her. That would serve the rotten witch! How dare she mess with us!"

Libby choked back a laugh. "What if the *she,* is a *he*?"

"No problem! He'll be the newest unofficial member of the Chippendales. We've got it covered!" Mary-Jane broke off, doubling over with laughter. "Please don't let it be old Ralph Riley. I don't think I could stand to see his bare beer belly."

Aunt Maeve once more got my attention. "Enough of your foolishness, ladies. Tell Cynthia and Libby to get the following items: a small mirror, a black candle, and reversing oil."

"Reversing oil?" I peered at my aunt with narrow eyes.

Before she could respond, Cynthia spoke, "I've got that. But if you don't have it, it's simple to make. Heat some vegetable or olive oil and add some sage, salt, lemon grass, and eucalyptus. It's not a perfect mix without the rue herb, but it'll do in a pinch."

Mary-Jane shook her head. "Everyone's a chef these days. Maybe I should start making these oils. I could probably sell them on Etsy."

"Yes, that will do for the reversing oil." Aunt Maeve nodded as she continued, "Basically, what everyone needs to do is after cleansing yourself with a sage smudge, is take the black candle and use a pin or nail to write in REVERSE, 'our enemy' on the side of the candle. Cut the top from the candle, flip it over and burn the bottom wick, placing it on the mirror."

I nodded, picturing this. "Reverse everything! The bottom of the candle, the name 'our enemy' written backward and the mirror reflecting back! Of course!"

She continued, "As you burn the candle, mindfully send the ill intentions into the wind dispersing it while focusing on your wishes—this crazy shedding of clothes—onto your enemy who cursed you. Don't forget the most important part; when you are finished, take all the items outside and bury them in the forest. But take care you don't bury them on your own property. You want to send this away, not keep it. Or you can put the items at any crossroad. Just get it away from you when you're done."

"Okay. Got it." I turned to the phone once more and relayed everything she'd told me. I glanced at the time and continued. "Can we all agree to do this in half an hour? That should give you time to get the stuff together and make your oil. Everyone in?"

Libby nodded. "Absolutely."

Cynthia leaned forward, grinning. "Count on it! I'll set the call up at eight, so we can do this together as a coven. Bitches don't know who they're messing with!" She clicked off, leaving Libby, who followed after a moment.

I smiled at Mary-Jane. "Guess our spaghetti dinner is gonna have to wait." I placed my hand on hers and squeezed. "This is gonna work, MJ. You will not lose your license, and I'm going to finally get my interview with Devon." And succeed in becoming friends again.

Shit. In all the commotion, I'd forgotten to call him. Oh well. By this time tomorrow I'd be sitting down with him—the hex spell demolished!

***

It was a little before eight when Mary-Jane, sitting across from me at the pentagram, smiled. "I'm glad we're doing this. Even if this is just a run of bad luck and not someone out to get us, it's better than sitting around feeling sorry for ourselves."

"I know what you mean. It's hard to believe that there's someone out there cursing us, but I think Aunt Maeve is right." I looked over to where she hovered near the window. "So! We've finished the cleansing smudge, and got everything together, so now it's just waiting for Cynthia's call."

When my cell phone rang, I grinned at MJ. "Here we go!" I brushed my finger across the screen and Cynthia and Libby's faces filled the space. "Ready?" Without waiting for them to reply, I continued, "MJ and I will start. If you duplicate our actions and then add your own words when we're finished, that should do it."

The scene on the screen changed as they both set the phones farther away, showing the pentagrams, candles, and mirrors that were set up at their houses.

I picked up the black candle and inscribed "ymeneruo" on the side of it with a pen. Next, I smeared the reversing oil over the candle's surface. Mary-Jane reached over to light the candle before I set it on the mirror.

As I spoke, my hand floated over the flame of the candle, pushing the tiny trail of smoke out into the room.

"Hex and spells that have us cursed
Rise into the air and thus disperse.
To the sender of ill wished upon us four
At noon on the morrow, we implore
Clothes on your body to heat and irritate
Revealing to us, the one doing us hate."

When I finished, I nodded to Mary-Jane. She gazed into the flickering flame as she started,

"Back to the party who cast this hex
Hot flashes, no matter the sex
Your harmful ill will be revealed
This spell reversal we do deal."

She repeated my gesture with the smoke tendril as she spoke. Finished, she looked over at the cell phone. "Libby?"

Libby cleared her throat and tightened the sides of her bathrobe against to her neck.

"By the light of the moon and stars
Return to the person this charm
Reveal yourself for all to see
Your body shed clothes with glee."

Mary-Jane and I exchanged a quick look. Not sure how much glee would be involved walking around nearly naked in sixty degree weather. But whatever. As long as it worked.

Cynthia inhaled as she raised her arms high above her head, letting them gracefully lower so that her hands cupped the candle on each side.

"Thrice will your hex return to your being
Transformed to your skin, for our seeing
Bare as your face, your chest find relief
Reverse and disperse, this our belief."

Mary-Jane and I finished the reversal spell, whispering,

"So mote it be."

Cynthia pulled her phone closer and winked. "That should do it, sisters! Now all we have to do is let the candles burn out, and then take this stuff away from our property. Since I'm in town in an apartment, I'm going to have to drive it to a vacant lot." She let out a true witchy-like cackle. "Tomorrow at high noon, our enemy will be revealed!"

Libby sighed. "I've got a date with a rabbit in my backyard to see what's wrong with his mate. So, I'll be burying this in the vacant woods in the greenbelt that borders the back of my yard when I'm done."

I looked over at Mary-Jane. "Don't get mad at me, but... the closest property to mine is Steve Murphy's. That's where I'm going to dispose of these spell items. It serves him right for what he did to Robert."

"I'm not going to argue with you, Shannon. After the day I had... I'm going to keep my powder dry for when I have to face Ray." She bent down close to the cell phone. "Blessed be, ladies! I'm starving. I'll talk to you tomorrow." With that, she walked away, heading for the kitchen.

I rubbed my hands together as I looked at the cell phone. "I can't wait to find out who this is. They're going to wish they'd never laid eyes on me, let alone hex me!"

TWENTY

The next morning...

Mary-Jane

Ray started in on me as soon as I walked into the house. "The least you could have done was answer my texts, MJ! That was not only inconsiderate, it was rude. You weren't here to explain to Chloe everything that happened and why you stayed the night at Shannon's."

Still nattering, he followed as I went up the stairs to change. When we came into the bedroom, I slammed the door. I'd had enough!

"First of all, you immediately sided with the police when you KNEW there was no way I was inebriated! Then you come down on me for hanging out with Libby and Shannon, like I'd joined some kind of outlaw biker gang!"

Seeing him jerk back and the roundness of his eyes, I pressed my case even further. "And furthermore, we're *partners*, Ray! You aren't my boss and I'm not yours! We're both trying to achieve the same things... to raise Chloe and to make a decent life for ourselves."

His breath came in a fast whoosh before he snapped back. "Well, you're setting one hell of an example for our daughter, MJ! Getting a DUI and then coming home the next morning, still reeking of booze. Steve told me I should give you some space, but... I can't tolerate your behavior anymore. Since Shannon moved here, you've become another *person*, Mary-Jane."

I jabbed his chest with my finger. "Maybe because I AM a different person, Ray! I've lost forty pounds. I'm as fit as I was when I was a teen, and... and..."

My words trailed off at what had come through when I'd touched his chest. Fear? Anguish? He really felt like our marriage was falling apart! And right after this, I saw things from his perspective. I'd lost a ton of weight, was looking after myself better, and then Devon Booker had hit on me in front of practically the entire town. It didn't matter that Devon had apologized for doing that. Ray was worried about the next guy who wouldn't back down and who I might be interested in. All of this hit in the space of a nanosecond.

Ray grabbed my finger, scowling at me. "And what, MJ? You're leaving? Is that what you were going to say?" He tossed my hand away before turning and stomping down the stairs.

I raced after him, standing at the railing and calling down, "I'm not leaving Ray! I love you, but you've got to give me some space... and trust!"

He paused at the bottom stair and looked up at me. "I *have* been giving you space. And look where it's ended up—the two of us arguing and drifting apart." He continued on, heading for the front door, muttering, "I gotta get out of here. I'm going into work."

At the thundering slam of the front door, I jerked back. For a few moments, I toyed with the idea of running after him to make him understand. But the only way that would happen was if I came clean about the coven and the psychometric abilities I now had. My jaw tightened at the thought of doing that. He probably wouldn't believe me, let alone understand it if I did.

Turning to go into the bedroom to change into fresh clothes, my head felt like it would burst open from all the thoughts whirling, plus my words coming back to haunt me. Ray was my partner, my husband. If I couldn't share with him everything that was going on in my life, then what kind of partnership was it? I should be able to share this. Maybe then he'd understand why I spent so much time at Shannon's house.

I paused after tugging my sweater over my head. But what about the well? I could share my newfound abilities with Ray but not the well. That secret wasn't mine to share without the others' permission. I don't know how I knew that, but I knew that I was right. And then there were my friends. There was no way I could tell Ray about Libby talking to animals or Shannon seeing spirits. Forget about her latest trick affecting the weather! And Cynthia had lived most of her life with special powers, devoted to witchcraft, with no one the wiser. It would be a betrayal to my sisters to let Ray in on any of this.

But if our reversal spell from last night worked, then maybe things would get better between Ray and me. After all, it hadn't been totally bad before... in fact, things had been *good.* It was that DUI that had started the real argument between us. If I could get that charge thrown out, then there'd be no need to tell Ray anything about what was going on with the witchcraft thing.

I glanced at the bedside clock. That reversal spell wasn't supposed to take effect until noon. There was plenty of time to pop into the restaurant to try to smooth things over with Ray. He would hit the roof again when I told him I had to take more time off from work. But with a little luck and copious amounts of magic, soon, whatever hex was screwing my life up, would end. There was nothing else to be done but see this through, with me scoping out the southwest quadrant of the town, while my friends checked the other sections.

After putting some lipstick on, I crossed my fingers that the person who'd hexed us would have a job in an office or some place public, and not be working from home. If that were the case, we might have to do the reversal spell again with new conditions; maybe make them scream like a banshee or something.

I looked up at the ceiling, muttering a prayer, "Please let it be someone easy to spot."

***

It was almost five o'clock when I walked into the coffee shop to join Libby, Shannon, and Cynthia. I had covered my section of town, popping into every store, office and even walking the streets, peering at houses, looking for a person prancing around in their birthday suit. But nada. Zilch. The closest I'd come to seeing anything strange was Old Man Wilson walking to his mailbox, wearing a pair of droopy boxers and a T-shirt under a gaping housecoat.

I grabbed a coffee and then took it to the last booth where my friends were huddled. Libby slid over to make room for me next to her. "Nothing, right?"

I shook my head. "My feet are killing me. I swear I walked fourteen miles but only encountered the usual oddballs. No streakers or naked gardeners, not even someone shedding his jacket."

"Well, I found 'em!" Shannon said, her eyes batting at the three of us.

All the air was sucked out of us and we stared at her. She rubbed her hair up and down like a preening kitty cat, with a grin on her face, watching our shocked expressions. She finished off with a shoulder shimmy. "I didn't want to say anything until all of us were here."

"WHO?" we all yelled in unison.

She put her hands palms down on the table. "I couldn't believe it. I wandered all over town with no luck, so I decided maybe if I wandered around some of the subdivisions? So I started out—"

"Who, Shannon!" I hissed at her. Whoever the hell it was, I was going to zap them with the mother of all hexes!

She batted her eyes at us. "So, I went down a greenbelt between the backyards of the homes on Brant Avenue and Harvest Avenue. You know, there's that laneway that divides the backyards..."

"Shannon!"

"It's Ida Red-Car!"

Cynthia's face knotted in confusion. "Who the hell is Ida Red-Car?"

Libby looked up at the ceiling and let out a sigh. "She's a woman Shannon had a run-in with over a parking space right after moving into town. She drives a red Ford Focus." She started shaking her head slowly from side to side. "Ida Watkins is her name. Shannon hexed her for it without even knowing she had any witching powers, and the woman's car caught on fire..."

"Ida Watkins? She's the one who hexed us? No way that oddball could pull it off!" Cynthia leaned over to Shannon. "How do you know it was her?"

"Because she was walking around her backyard in her birthday suit!" Shannon said. "I saw a couple of middle-school boys peeking through her fence. When they saw me, they took off. So naturally, *I* peeked, and there she was in all her glory!"

Libby let out a snort and looked at me. "Ida's not a witch, Shannon," she said while the two of us nodded in unison. "Is she, MJ?"

"Nope."

"What the hell do you mean?" Shannon said. "How the hell do you know?"

"Ida's our age, right?" I said. "Maybe a year or two older, even?" I looked over at Libby. "Is that right?"

Libby nodded. "Yeah, that's about right. After high school she went off to college in California, but came back to Wesley when she finished up her degree." She quirked a half smile. "Learned a lot of things out in LA, let me tell you."

"And brought her husband along too," I added. "That heir to an orange juice fortune or something?"

Shannon looked a little miffed. "But...what the hell are you guys talking about?"

"Oh!" Cynthia perked up. "I heard about her! That's right!" She looked over at Shannon. "No, it's not Ida Watkins. She's the town nudist." Cynthia glanced over at me and Libby. "We should have warned her about ol' Ida."

"Yeah, sorry, our bad," I said. "It's practically a rite of passage for boys in this town to peek through her fence, isn't it, Libby?"

Libby nodded. "Watchin' Ida Watkins? Yup. I know Kevin's been out there...and I'm pretty sure Jack went last summer."

"They told you?" Shannon's eyes grew wide. "Ewwww!"

Libby's jaw dropped in shock. "No! They didn't tell me! That'd be weird! One of the women I work with lives next door. She told me."

I reached over and patted Shannon's hand. "Ida's been like that for years and years. She's oblivious to it, all the Peeping Tom-ery—"

"Or else just doesn't give a hoot," Libby interrupted. She waved her arm around. "Pretty much any guy in this town who's in his twenties or younger knows about ol' Ida-the-Nudist.

Cynthia let out a bark of laughter. "Or thirties! Both my brothers growing up have been out there to her place to peek!"

The look on Shannon's face was priceless. Her mouth hung open as she looked at each of us in turn. "This is true? Ida's not the one, then?"

"No, she's not," we all replied in unison once again. I added, "She's just another one of the odd residents of Wesley, New York, that's all."

"Dammit!" Shannon rapped the table with her hand and blew out a huff. "I really thought I caught her red handed!"

"Nope!" I said. "Just bare-assed!" We all had a chuckle. I won't lie, it felt good to have a chuckle at Shannon's expense. Maybe just a little bitchy, I'll admit it; but it was fun.

We all were quiet for a moment or two until Cynthia took a deep breath, drumming the tabletop with her fingernails. "I don't understand this. I KNOW the spell worked, but we still don't know who the culprit is. It has to be someone who works from home. There're so many people who do that these days."

"Well, if they have any Zoom meetings or something online, we might hear some scuttlebutt about that. But it's kind of like finding a needle in a haystack." Shannon rolled her eyes. "So it's back to the drawing board?"

Libby leaned over, pushing me to the side with her shoulder. When I turned to say something about her hogging the bench, she muttered, "Is that Amy and Byron? I haven't seen Steve's kid since he was in the hospital with that concussion."

"Byron?" Cynthia's face lit up with a smile before she spun around, waving her hand to catch the nine-year-old's attention. Even Shannon turned to wave at the kid.

Much as it was nice to see Byron, it wasn't solving our problem of finding the slimeball who'd hexed us. I was still fighting with Ray and facing a DUI. But I forced a smile seeing Byron break away from his mother and sprint down the aisle of tables to us.

"Cynthia!" His arms went around her neck, hugging her as she scrambled from the booth. She squatted down on one knee planting kisses on the top of his head as she held him close.

"Byron! It's so great to see you, buddy. You've grown into quite the handsome little fellow." When she pulled back, I was surprised to see her eyes glistening with tears. But even though Byron's gaze flitted to Shannon, Cynthia wasn't letting go of her grip on his shoulders.

"Hey, Shannon. When are you going to visit my dad so we can play the video game you got me for Christmas?" The smile on his face, missing two front teeth, was adorable.

"Soon, Byron. I've missed seeing you. Aren't you supposed to be with your dad today?" Shannon reached over to muss up the kid's hair playfully.

I smiled up at Amy when she wandered down to fetch her kid. "Hi, Amy. I haven't seen you in a while." Not since the first night we'd hosted the school play at our restaurant, when she and Suzanne had been there.

Cynthia slipped back into her seat next to Shannon and smiled at Steve's ex. "Yeah, I thought this was Steve's day, or have you changed up the visitation schedule?"

Amy shook her head. "No. Steve asked me to pick the rug rat up at school. He's feeling under the weather today. We just stopped in to pick up some bear claws for breakfast tomorrow." She stood behind her son with her hands on his shoulders, murmuring a hello to Libby as well.

For a moment, the unreality of the situation hit me funny. Here was Steve's ex smiling and being friendly with Cynthia who had dated Steve for a few months and Shannon who had almost been an item with him. But everyone was friendly, and it was clear that Cynthia and Shannon adored his son.

"Well, buddy? We should get going. You've got some math homework, and Suzanne will be wondering what's keeping us."

Byron turned his head and gazed up at her. "Okay, but can I have one bear claw when I get home?" With the smattering of freckles across his nose and those adorable dimples, the lad was hard to resist.

"Okaaaay. Just one though. *After* you show me your homework." She lifted one hand to wave goodbye to us and with the other she maneuvered him around to leave the shop.

After they'd gone, Cynthia murmured as she gazed into her coffee. "I really miss seeing that kid. Actually a lot more than I ever miss Steve. We always had fun whenever he was there at Steve's."

Shannon nodded. "It's funny. After Bryon was injured and I cast that spell to help him get better, I kind of think of him as kind of a second son. He's such a good kid; it's clear he must take after Amy more than Steve." She chuckled and nudged Cynthia with her elbow.

"Well, that's all well and good, but we still don't know who the bugger hexing us is." Libby looked at Shannon. "What do we do now?"

I watched Shannon sigh before she answered. "We keep on with our spell. But maybe I'll add something even more ridiculous, like making whoever is doing this to bark like a dog, or scream obscenities. We might not see them if they're working from home, but we sure as hell will hear them. We have to find whoever is doing this to us and make them stop."

TWENTY ONE

Later that day...

Shannon

It was hard to stay upbeat on the drive back to my house after leaving my friends. I'd been so SURE when I'd left the house that day that we'd uncover the witch who was making trouble for us. The only thing we'd accomplished was aching feet from the miles each one of us had walked. The thought of a hot bath with Epsom salts and lavender sounded like heaven to me.

Seeing my mailbox flag raised, indicating that there were items in it, I parked the truck at the end of the driveway and got out to check it. When I lifted the metal door, I jerked back at what I saw in there.

My Grimoire? What the hell? My heart leaped into my throat as I grabbed the leather-bound text from the box, holding it close to my chest. My gaze darted to my house and the yard down the long gravel drive. Someone must have broken into my house to get the journal! But why leave it here for me in the mailbox? And why the Grimoire?

The muscles in my neck tightened, and a coldness sank into my chest at my next thought. This *had* to be connected to the spell and us trying to find the person who'd hexed us. I hurried back to my truck, but instead of starting it up, I flipped through the Grimoire to see if whoever had taken it had done anything to it.

The first section was all Alice Johnston's entries, and the second was filled with notes written by Aunt Maeve. My section was only about a dozen pages with the results of spells, feelings, phases of the moon, and my amateur sketches, but it was mine! Having someone else handle my Grimoire felt like I'd been violated. When I came to the last page that I'd written, my mouth snapped shut.

There in thick black marker were the following words:

> Enjoying your game of hide-and-seek? Nice try with the reversal spell. It was really cute even if it was like being attacked by a mosquito.
>
> But fun and games are over. It is time to join the big leagues, girlfriend! Join forces with me to know real power. Beltane marks new beginnings for me taking over your coven. Resist and I will destroy you.
>
> Sincerely Yours in Sorcery!

The playful tone made the threat even more ominous. I reread the entry, feeling my mouth go bone dry. Who the hell WAS this? Why were we being targeted by this person? Someone wanted to take over my coven... or else destroy me? What kind of bitchy witch was this?

I set the book aside and got back in my truck to park it. Whoever did this may have made a fatal mistake. Aunt Maeve might have seen the bitch break into my house to steal the book. Pray to the goddess, Mother Earth or whatever that my aunt had been there and not doing some ghostly stuff in the ether.

When I got to my usual parking spot in front of my verandah, I practically leaped from the truck, clinging to the book and my purse as I raced up the few stairs. "Aunt Maeve?" The door was still locked tight, and my fingers trembled as I slid the key in to unlock it. "Shit!"

Bursting through, I paused for a moment, my mind going a mile a minute! What if whoever had come into my house was still there? Should I arm myself? I grabbed the first thing I could find. My umbrella!

Starting at the kitchen and making my way back to the living room, I waved the tip of the umbrella before me like it was a sword, my gaze sweeping the rooms. The only sound in the house was the steady click of the cuckoo clock on the wall beside the staircase. I crept across the room to check the back patio door. Giving the handle a quick tug, I groaned when it slid open. Shit! I must have forgotten to lock it, and that's how the intruder got in.

I peeked outside at the small deck and lawn, but there were no footprints or any sign they'd left. I closed the door and flicked the lock, double-checking that it was secure. A little like closing the barn door after the horse had left, but whatever...

A hurried scan of the room made my eyes open wider when I saw my small makeshift altar in the corner of the room. The objects that I'd set there had been moved! The little seashell containing a handful of soil was now on the south side of the pentagram, while the white candle was on the north. And the east and west objects were also reversed. The small jar containing water was on the east and the feather on the west. Whoever had moved the objects had deliberately changed the placements.

My jaw clenched tight. Reversed. Just like the spell my friends and I had done the night before! This was a message to me, taunting me about the success of our spell. Whoever had come into my home had not only taken my Grimoire and written a nasty warning was also letting me know they could mess with my magic.

No freakin' way! I snatched the wooden tray where the objects were set and took it into the kitchen. The thought that some creep had touched my things was repulsive. I'd have to get fresh soil and water and replace the candle and feather. No way could I use these objects in my daily prayers and spells!

"Aunt Maeve? I need to talk to you!" I called as I returned to the living room and bounded up the stairs. It took me all of three minutes to check each room. But as I expected, nothing was touched. Nope. This little home invasion was all about magic, not theft or vandalism.

When I went down the stairs I saw the air near my altar kind of shimmer and bend. The diaphanous form of my aunt began to solidify. She turned from looking at where my altar had been to peering at me.

"Shannon? What'd you do with your altar?" Her wispy, white hair floated higher as she crossed the distance between us. "What's wrong?"

I sank down onto the stairs. "You don't know? So that means you weren't here this afternoon." Before she had a chance to answer, I blurted, "The spell didn't work, Aunt Maeve. Whoever hexed us came into the house and took my Grimoire. They left a warning in it. And they messed with my altar."

The touch of her hand on the side of my face was like feeling a cobweb brush your skin. "I'm sorry I wasn't here. After you left today, I needed to recharge my batteries, so I faded into the light." She shook her head. "I can't believe that anyone in Wesley is capable of this! To hex you was bad enough, but to come into your home? Who IS this person?"

"Whoever it is wants to take over the coven. And for that person to be powerful enough to resist the spell we cast, means that I'm not dealing with some wannabe witch. For Pete's sake, there were four of us casting it... *five,* if we count you!"

This was a scary situation that just got even scarier. Who would even know about us, let alone try to commandeer the coven?

"Let me read what they left in the Grimoire. There might be a clue." She clucked her lips and muttered as she hovered away from me, heading to the kitchen. "I should have reached out to other spirits today. I have to get better at this afterlife thing if I'm going to help you. Holy doodle. What a mess this is."

Feeling every one of my forty-plus years, I pulled myself to my feet, with the help of the stair rail. I should have known better than to think that we'd solved the mystery. Nothing was that easy, not when it came to magic. When I entered the kitchen, Aunt Maeve was seated at the table with the Grimoire open before her.

She looked up at me with round-eyed shock. "Beltane! Whoever wrote this expects to take over at Beltane? Why, that's only a week away! What I don't understand is *why* they're doing this? It goes against all the code of magic—do no harm, let live, blessed be, and all that! This isn't witchcraft; this is sorcery, *dark magic.*"

I paused in the midst of filling the kettle to make chamomile tea. "Sorcery?" It came out as a high-pitched squeak. On second thought, I grabbed the bottle of Jack Daniels. I definitely needed something to calm my nerves. Shit! Sorcery just sounded bad. "So it's not a witch?"

"It could very well be a witch, but one who practices black magic, not white magic. Or it could be a wizard, but I don't think there are any on this side of the Atlantic." Her lips turned down in a frown. "Or it could be voodoo... or—"

"What the hell? You're saying there's more than just us witches?"

"Of course, darling. Just like religions, there's many people who follow paths trying to understand or else control the unknown." She looked at me with her head tilted. "I thought you realized that."

"No! For God's sake, Maeve! Until last September I thought all of this stuff was just bullshit! Now you're saying that there's more?"

She nodded. "And my gut feeling is that you're dealing with a sorceress. The black arts." She shook her head. "It's the only thing that makes sense, Shannon. Whoever wrote this knows you're gaining in power. Instead of being happy for you, she wants to claim it for herself. That's evil and dark. You can't let her in your coven, let alone control it."

I gazed into the bourbon in the glass before swallowing half of it. "I know, but if they're more powerful than us, how can I stop them? Aside from giving up magic entirely, which I don't want to do. I know I've had some hiccups with magic, but I also feel empowered by it." I'd come a long way from being a homemaker in Philly, kowtowing to that cheating Ass-Hat. I totally liked the new me and to the growth happening with not just me, but with my friends.

Maeve rose, and in a flash, she was next to me. "You won't have to give up what you were born to be. There are some things I've learned since becoming a member of the afterlife set. We are all connected to one another, Shannon. Without getting into specifics—which technically I'm not supposed to do anyway—I've had conversations with our ancestors. It was no surprise to find that Alice Johnston is one of our line. She lived in Salem but ended up here in the Catskill Mountains. I was meant to buy this property, just as you were meant to live here and carry on with our heritage."

My head bobbed forward. "Alice Johnston who's in the well? She's our *ancestor*? How did it come to pass that she ended up as the voice in the well?" No wonder my offering of

Jack Daniels was so well received! We shared the same taste in our poison of choice.

Aunt Maeve's hand covered her mouth and she chuckled. "That's a story for another time, which *Alice* needs to tell you." Her eyebrows rose, and she sucked her lips in, trying to compose herself. "For now, we have to figure out who this witch, or sorcerer, is. Once we know that, we can stop her."

She floated over to the Grimoire and closed it. "I must go and visit with ones who will know." She turned and smiled softly at me. "Don't worry, Shannon. You're not alone. You're never alone fighting your battles." With that, her image faded until it was gone.

For a few moments, I stood at the counter, nursing my drink and thinking of what my aunt had said. I went over to the Grimoire and opened it to Alice Johnston's entries. It was still Greek to me with all the swirly flourishes in the handwriting, but now that I knew she was my ancestor, I'd have to make more of an effort to decipher it. That would have to wait for another day as well.

For now, I HAD to take a long, hot bath. My feet were sore and swollen. After my muscles stopped aching, I'd set up a Zoom call to let the others know what I'd come home to. As I walked up the stairs, my aunt's words echoed in my mind.

I wasn't alone in fighting this sorcerer. I had my friends and ancestors.

TWENTY TWO

The next day...

Libby

Morning, Libby!”

Hearing a deep voice call my name, I turned to see Len Miller put two fingers to his forehead and nod before resuming pushing the long broom down the hospital’s corridor.

“How are you, Len? Nice day today.” I continued going past the reception on my way to the stairwell and to the second floor where my office was. My new job wasn’t the most exciting one in the world, but it was a welcome break, from musing about Shannon’s call the night before. My gut coiled tight, knowing there was someone out there who not only knew about our coven but had their own designs on controlling it.

"Libby?"

I paused at the door to the stairwell and watched Len jog over to where I stood. "What's up, Len?"

The lanky man stuttered, his face contorting as he tried to get the words out, "Th-the postman dropped a piece of mail addressed to you. B-but I put it on your desk." He grinned like he'd just run the four-minute mile, before hurrying back to the area where he was sweeping.

"Thanks!" I pushed through and continued to my office. As I slipped my overcoat off to hang it up, I looked at the white envelope with my name scrawled across the front. After I'd settled in, booting my computer up and changing my voicemail message on the phone, I tossed the letter in with the other mail in my in-basket. I'd get to it in a little while.

Emails were the first to be dealt with before I could get to snail mail. The bean-counter, Al, popped his head through the doorway to remind me of a meeting in an hour's time with the head of the nurses' union and the comptroller. Argh. Give me patient care any old day over this. But I'd miss the extra money in my bank account at the end of every month, so I had to make this work.

It was close to lunchtime that I finally got around to opening the letter that Len had hand-delivered. When I opened it, my forehead pinched tight.

> Dear Libby,
>
> Do your bosses know that you spent the day yesterday gallivanting around town instead of working? I'm guessing not, especially if they knew WHAT you were hauling ass to find. Considering what you do for a living, I'd bet they wouldn't like it too much. All that sciencey stuff

versus magic and spells. It mixes as well as oil and water, don't you think?

I'd venture that your chances of keeping your fancy job as head nurse might be in jeopardy if they knew what you really are. But would losing that job you now have, be such a bad thing? Face it. With your newfound talents you'd much rather run your own veterinary clinic. That could be arranged. You'd be doing something you love, and you'd make triple the income.

I could make that happen, Libby. Unlike Shannon, I actually know what I'm doing when it comes to spells. You sense a catch though, don't you?

But it's no biggie. All I want in return is your support. Convince Shannon to work with me. I'm not her enemy or yours, or Mary-Jane's or even Cynthia's. There will be tons of benefits to all of us, when I run the coven. Money, satisfying careers and freedom. Did I mention that you'll be able to easily write a check to cover your kids' college education? That's after your mortgage is totally paid off, of course.

It's true that you can choose some misplaced loyalty to a woman who has always been self-absorbed, although it would be a shame if you did. Your new job could go tits up, your children in shock when they find out their mother dabbles in witchcraft. And then there's Stan. Not sure if he'd want to pursue a relationship if he knew you're a witch. He's an upstanding member of the community, after all.

But, that's not something I want to do, Libby. I'd rather celebrate Beltane with you than banish you to poverty and ridicule. Looking forward to the advent of spring celebration together!

Sincerely yours in Sorcery!

(Sorcery's where the real power's at)

I barely breathed as I reread the letter. What the hell? I picked up the envelope to examine it. No postage mark. Whoever had written this had come to the hospital and dropped it off personally. And must have used a glamor to look like a mailman to Len the custodian. The author of this letter has potent power, that's for sure.

I tossed the letter aside like it was toxic waste and sat back in my chair. Similar to what had been left for Shannon in the Grimoire, the tone was taunting, and darkly threatening. There was no way that I'd ever want to be involved with anyone who could do this. Shannon was not only my friend, she was a good person, unlike this *bitch.*

My fingers steepled over my chest as I considered everything in the letter. She'd threatened my career, although it probably wouldn't take an awful lot to make me fail the probationary period. I was doing a pretty good job of that all on my own. If not for the money, I really wouldn't care. But if

I lost it, another opening on the nursing staff might not happen for a long time, and then where would I be?

I snorted at how the carrot was extended—me running a vet clinic. It was something I'd considered after the kids were through college, when money wasn't tight. But from the sounds of it, money would never be a problem for me again. Using magic for financial gain? Wasn't that against the code?

If my kids found out that I was in a coven, practicing witchcraft, what would they think? It was hard enough for them to deal with the loss of their father without thinking that their mother had gone off the deep end in some cult or something. Or would they think it was cool? Not sure, I wanted to test that out. As for Stan... much as I cared about him, if he turned tail and ran when he found out, then maybe he wasn't the right guy for me. It would hurt, but...

I picked up the letter again and stared at it. I should tell Shannon and the others about this. They needed to know. But something held me back from reaching for the phone in my purse to call them. There were a lot of things in that letter that I needed time to process—things that would impact my life.

And the most compelling thing in the letter was my kids' welfare. Like always, they were my top priority. The longer I held the letter in my hand, the more convinced I was that I shouldn't be hasty in making my mind up. Not until I found out *who* this was, and what was their actual goal in using our coven. I could decide then if I should support them *joining*, not running, our coven. There was no rush in this. I had until Beltane, another week away.

The only thing I knew for sure was that I certainly wasn't impressed with their method of trying to influence me. It was sneaky and heavy-handed. If not for my kids, I'd tell them to pound sand. I lifted the letter to sniff it, for any telltale scent. Shit! If I had MJ's gift, I'd know who wrote this!

My mouth fell open. It wasn't Shannon I should confide in. It was MJ! I fished my phone out to call her.

TWENTY THREE

That same day...

Mary-Jane

Even the two-mile run did little to improve my outlook when I slumped back into the house. I kind of missed the days when exercising had gotten me fired up, and Ray and I would end up in bed. As crazy as that time was, at least we'd been close and not fighting like we were now. And that brought me around to Shannon.

She'd asked me to stop out to her place today to check out the note in her Grimoire. If we were ever going to find out who'd hexed us so that I could get things back on track with Ray, I needed to touch the page to get a reading on who had written it. That bitch wasn't as smart as she thought, writing that note. We'd find out who she was and then—look out!

I bent to unlace my sneakers and paused, hearing footsteps coming from the kitchen. When I looked up, Chloe stood in the entry, sullenly staring at me. Great. Was Ray's anger with me contagious? Slowly, I rose and took a step closer. "What's wrong, Chloe? Why aren't you still in school?"

"What's going on with you and Dad? You barely spoke to each other at all last night, and he slept in the spare room. Are you getting a divorce?" Even though her voice was steady, her eyes had filled with tears, which she swiped at with the heel of her hand.

Shit! I pulled her close, rubbing her back. "No, we're not getting a divorce. We're just having a difference of opinion. It happens sometimes, so there's no need for you to worry." But immediately after I got the words out, an image of her walking by a group of boys at school flashed in my head. The red-hot flash of embarrassment she'd felt as they taunted her, took my breath away.

"It's about the DUI, isn't it?" she whispered hoarsely.

Oh my God! That was what she had to endure at school. Being teased by a gang of thugs about my arrest and being charged. "Chloe, it's not the entire story. There was—"

"What was it, then?" She stepped back, throwing my hands off her. "I heard it in school, Mom. Joe Watkins's father is a cop. Joe overheard him tell his mother about you getting charged. He and a bunch of his Neanderthal buddies started teasing me about it, so I skipped class and came home." Her eyes were bleary and red-rimmed when she asked, "Is that why Dad's mad at you?"

"Chloe. I'm so sorry for what you had to go through. You don't know the entire story. I wasn't drunk when they pulled me over. Their machine is wrong. But yes, that's why your dad is angry."

"Shit, Mom! I just knew it." She spun around and raced up the stairs, her strawberry blonde hair swirling over her shoulders. And then a loud bang when she'd slammed her bedroom door shut, almost shook the house.

My fingers curled into fists as I stood there. If I could get my hands on the witch who'd cursed me, I'd throttle her! Not only was Ray angry as hell with me, but now my daughter was being humiliated by a bunch of assholes. And why was Gerry Watkins gossiping about me to his kids? Isn't there supposed to be some kind of privacy code with the cops?

I threw my sneakers against the wall and headed for the stairs to go up and talk to Chloe. When my phone chirped, I fished it from the fanny pack, and seeing Libby's face fill the screen, I rolled my eyes. "Not now."

I clicked it off and continued up the stairs. Whatever Libby had to say could wait. Right then, my daughter needed me.

After tapping on her bedroom door, I opened it. Chloe sat with her back resting against the headboard, her gaze intent on the small screen of her phone. "Can we talk? There are some things I need to tell you, Chloe."

"What? That this is all a big misunderstanding and that you never do anything wrong?" Her gaze flitted to me dismissively before fixing on her phone again.

"Oh, I do plenty wrong, believe me!" I nudged her legs to the side to make room for me to sit next to her. "But driving drunk is definitely not one of them. I'm going to fight this charge, Chloe. There was something wrong with the breathalyzer, which I'm going to prove. Actually I was going to call Edwin Smith, our lawyer, this afternoon. But, that's my issue, not yours."

She rolled her eyes. "Yeah, right. Tell that to that bunch of idiots having a good laugh about it, at my expense. I felt like everyone was staring at me, snickering about my crazy, drunk mom."

My gut twisted into a knot at her words. To see my little girl suffer because of me was hard... especially when I knew the truth—that I was innocent. I tried to keep my tone light. "Crazy, yes, but drunk... not by a long shot. I had one glass of wine. That's it. I swear."

Her mouth pulled to the side when she looked at me. "I believe you, Mom, but Dad doesn't. As for those guys in school, I can handle them. And if not, Jack sure as shit can. It's a good thing he wasn't with me or they'd be sorry. But it's Dad that has me worried. He's just... well, he's *devastated* by this. Is he going to leave you?"

I put my arm around her shoulder. "I don't think so, Chloe. He's angry right now. He also resents my friendship with Shannon. I think once this DUI is cleared up he'll be okay. But a lot has happened over the last year... stuff, that he's still coming to terms with."

"Your weight loss." Giving her head a small shake, she scoffed, "The ridiculous way Devon Booker treated you at the restaurant didn't help. What was up with that? Things have changed a lot since you started hanging with Shannon. Even Jack mentioned how his mom has changed since she moved here. Maybe Dad's right about her."

I took a deep breath as I watched her face. She was right about everything, but had no clue why things had changed. Was it fair to see her go through all this without knowing all that had happened? No, but the truth might make things even worse for her.

"You and your father are the most important people in my life, Chloe. Nothing will change that. But—"

"Of course, there's a 'but' coming," she huffed and returned to her phone.

I snatched it from her hands and held it to my chest. "BUT... I enjoy spending time with my friends too, Chloe." I decided to try a new track. "What if I told you I didn't want you seeing Jack again? Or Jasmine or Dahlia or Eve?"

She tried to snatch the phone back. "I get it, Mom! You need your friends and so do I. But Dad... he's kind of a loner, except for Steve Murphy, isn't he? He doesn't need people the same way we do."

It was hard not to smile at my daughter. She was growing up fast and showing a lot of insight into relationships. "That's Ray. I love him, but he's different from most people. We just have to give him time. He'll be okay." And I would make sure of that as soon as I found out who had hexed me.

My fingers grazed the curve of her cheek as I looked at her. Just that touch told me she'd be okay. She was a tough kid who could handle the teasing. It wouldn't be easy, but she'd get through it.

She turned to me. "Are you going into work today?"

"Nope. Debbie can handle things in the kitchen. And, I'd just as soon give your dad a little more time to cool off. Why don't you and I do something fun this afternoon? Or even just laze around eating ice cream and watching movies? We haven't spent enough time together lately."

She smiled. "I'm good with that. But I promised to meet Jack after school, so it'll just be one movie. He's building a fence around their backyard with his brother and I said I'd help. They had a bunch of wild animals wander into their yard the other day. Isn't that crazy?"

I stood up and then reached for her hand to help her to her feet. "Lots of crazy stuff has been happening lately, so I'm not surprised." But wild animals were the least of my concern right then.

When we went downstairs and started getting our pig-out feast ready, I remembered Libby's call. "Can you finish warming the chocolate syrup for the ice cream? I have to see what Libby wants. She called earlier."

Chloe nodded. "Sure. Take your time. I'll get everything set up. I'll see you in the family room."

I got my phone out and listened to the message she'd left me.

"That certain someone left a letter for me at work, MJ. You know, the same one who left a note in Shannon's Grimoire. That bitch wants me to work on Shannon to get her into the coven. Or else. She threatened my job, my children, and my relationship with Stan. I need you to touch the letter to see who this nasty bitch is."

Chloe passed by me, carrying a tray with ice cream, soda, and a bag of chips, heading for the family room. There was no way I was going to get into a long phone call with Libby, even though my fingers actually itched to get my hands on that letter—*that* and Shannon's Grimoire! I shot off a quick text to Libby.

Can I meet up with you when you're done with work? I'll give Chloe a lift to your house and hang around until you get home.

Next was my text to Shannon.

Sorry. Minor family emergency. I'll pop out after I finish 'reading' the letter that Libby got today. Apparently, our little witch wannabe has been pretty busy with the notes. See you around sixish.

I put my phone away and went to join my daughter in watching a movie. Too bad whoever was trying to manipulate us hadn't written a note to me. It would save me a couple of trips, and we'd know who our enemy was.

TWENTY FOUR

Mary-Jane

When the movie was over, I suggested to Chloe we pop by Libby's for a bit, and naturally she jumped at the chance.

I drove up to Libby's house, and her son Jack met us in the driveway. A lock of dark hair fell onto his forehead as he bent to set the bundle of fence boards down. When he wandered over to open Chloe's door, I looked across at the concern in his gray eyes staring at her. It was obvious he knew that she'd left the school in tears.

"You okay? Eve told me about Joe and those jerks." He'd hardly gotten the words out before she flew into his arms.

I got out of the car and tried to look at anything but their interchange, especially now that Chloe was tearing up again. But even so, I heard her reply.

"I'm fine. They're just stupid idiots with nothing better to do." She pulled back and continued, "Don't make it any more of a thing than it is, okay?"

"Oh, it's not over, Chloe. Not by a long shot. They'll wish they never said a word to you, when I'm through with them." He put his arm over her shoulder, walking up the drive to join me. "Hey, Mary-Jane. You want to help with the fence? We can use all the help we can get. Stan's got all the posts in, so it's just a matter of the stringers and boards."

My eyebrows arched hearing that Stan was there. Libby never gave many details about how her relationship with Stan was going, so it was nice to see they were still going strong. "Sure! I've got some time to kill till your mom gets home. Why not?"

"Here, Mom." Chloe handed me the four fence boards she'd plucked from the pile. "Too heavy?" Her brows pulled together as she searched my face. "Maybe just one more, then."

"Wait! I'm in my forties not twenties!" The boards were weighing my arms down. I looked over at Jack as I trudged along the side of the garage, heading for the backyard. "So, I heard you were invaded by animals. That must have been fun."

"It was actually kind of cool, although the neighbors sure didn't appreciate it. The skunks were the worst." He laughed and turned to Chloe. "Dahlia was in her glory. If she had her way, we'd be building a *hutch* for them instead of a fence to keep them out."

The whine of a table saw pierced the air as we rounded the garage. Stan had set up a workbench with sawhorses and a sheet of plywood and was busy cutting the end off one board. I added my stack to the pile of boards waiting and waved to Libby's other son, Kevin. They had about a quarter of the fence up, shutting off access from the forest behind Libby's yard.

Stan handed the fresh-cut board to Kevin and then turned to me. "Hi, MJ! Did you get roped into helping?" He stood with his hands on his hips, his green-plaid shirt swinging open above a white T-shirt. His eyes crinkled in the corners as he grinned at me.

I couldn't help but smile back at him. He was totally in his element, working with his hands and helping Libby's kids with this project. And from the easy way they were around him, it was clear they liked him too.

"Hi, Stan. I'm okay being a gofer, but that's the extent of my woodworking ability. It's a great day to be outside doing this! The fence will give Libby some privacy from her neighbors as well." I glanced over at Carol James's house, where she was ostensibly raking leaves but probably listening to every word being said. How Libby had managed to live next door to the town's busybody for so many years without killing her, I'd never know.

"Hi, Mary-Jane! Look what I've got!"

I turned just in time to see Dahlia bounce out the patio door behind me and wander across the deck, with two kittens in her arms. "Oh, my goodness! There's never a dull moment around here with you guys and animals." I took the orange cat from her and held it up, gazing into its small blue eyes. "This one's a keeper, I'll bet."

Stan guffawed. "Don't say that! Dahlia's been hounding Libby about keeping all of them. I swear, the kid's going to own a zoo some day." But even as he said it, he grinned at Dahlia and stroked the cat she held with his finger. "Where's Mrs. Purdy Cat? She's not going to like you absconding with her brood."

Dahlia winced. "A brood is for chickens, Stan. Cats have litters." She turned and called to the momma cat watching from the open doorway. "You don't mind, do you, Purdy? I'm still working on Mom, y'know."

"How's Ray? He must be holding down the fort at the restaurant." Stan looked over at me and smiled. "You're playing hooky today, MJ? I hardly ever see you when you're not at the restaurant."

I felt my stomach fall at the mention of Ray, but I managed to return Stan's smile. "He's fine. Yeah, someone has to do the heavy lifting. I took the afternoon off to spend it with Chloe, but I also need to see Libby and Shannon."

"Oh? Is everything okay?" He stepped closer to me and his voice became lower. "I know she's not too happy about the new job. I wish she had stayed with patient care. This is too stressful for her. I help as much as I can with the kids and doing odd jobs for her, but..." His eyebrows rose, and he looked at the ground.

I couldn't help myself from putting my hand on his arm. Sometimes I could give Carol James a run for her money when it came to being nosy. But I had to read him. As soon as my fingers touched the hair on his arm, I could feel how much he cared about Libby. He was even toying with the idea of asking her to marry him! Holy shit!

This was going to be hard to keep to myself! But I would. Although it probably wouldn't hurt to put in a few plugs for him with Libby. She'd be a fool to say no to a life with Stan. He wasn't only buff and stunning, but he was crazy about her!

I had to give my head a shake to remember what he'd said... oh yeah. Helping her with stuff around here. "I know she appreciates everything you do for her, Stan. I'm so glad that she finally agreed to go out with you. It was long overdue."

"Hey, you guys!"

At Libby's shout from the doorway, we turned to see her. It was such a change to not see her in nurse's clothes, wearing a pencil skirt and pink blouse, with a navy blazer topping it—office attire. Her heels clattered on the deck as she wandered over to give Stan a hug and a kiss.

"The fence is coming along well. Thanks for helping the boys with it." She looked over at me. "Come on inside, and I'll make us a cup of tea before I start dinner, MJ." When Dahlia stepped closer to her, she smiled. "Take those kittens back to the box, sweetie. I don't want you to get too attached to them."

I handed the orange ball of fluff back to Dahlia and followed Libby into the house. When we were inside, she murmured as she reached for the letter in her purse. "Whoever's leaving notes and letters has a lot of nerve. What happened to that spell we cast on her? Instead of revealing her, she's flaunting her power."

As soon as my fingers touched the letter, my forehead tightened. Instead of getting a flash of the person writing it, fluffy white clouds filled my mind. Clouds? I unfolded the sheet, and my fingertips grazed the black script. The words weren't important—Libby had already filled me in on what was there—it was the connection that I was seeking. The person writing the letter.

"Well? Who is it?" Libby leaned closer, her face clenched as she examined my eyes.

I shook my head. "I'm not getting anything... except for clouds. That's all I'm picking up from this letter." I closed my eyes, opening myself for any impression as I felt the smooth surface of the paper. But again, it was like being in an airplane, looking below at cottony white clouds. Why wasn't this working? Especially when I was focusing on the page so hard.

My eyes popped open. "There's a spell on this letter! It's...it's SPELLBOUND!" my voice was a shout. "That has to be it." I peered at Libby, the surprise showing in her face as clearly as what I was feeling. "This bitch sure covered her tracks! No wonder she's so brazen! She cast some kind of glamour on this letter after she wrote it."

Libby's shoulders fell. "So we still don't know who this is. And no doubt she's done the same thing with Shannon's Grimoire."

An icy feeling threaded through my gut as I looked at the letter again. Whoever this was had a lot of knowledge about spells and hexes. The only person I knew who had ever cast a glamour on anything to hide it was Cynthia, and that was the result of years of practice in the craft.

Holding the letter, a foggy sense came over me, like I was trying to read it through a haze. No... *clouds!* The bitch's magic was powerful! I took a deep breath and read the words in the letter to see if perhaps that might help to get a sense of who could have written it. Libby was right about the taunting tone and the threat.

Libby snatched the letter from my hand, slipping it back into her purse before she spoke. "If this witch is powerful enough to cast a spell on this, while *our own* spell never even slowed her down, why does she want to control our coven? She doesn't need us, obviously. And this person is dark. Why would she want to be involved with us? We do white magic, and we're still learning that."

Without the letter in my hand, everything in the room seemed sharper, more distinct. Shit! That had to be some potent spell on that letter! Immediately the answer to Libby's question popped into my head.

"The Well. That has to be it. It's what gives Shannon, you, and me our power. Whoever this is wants to join with us to use the well."

Libby shook her head. "And they want it by Beltane. If this bitch is powerful enough to do what she's already done, will we be able to stop her? Plus, she's threatening to do some awful things if we don't go along with her plan."

"I don't know, Libby. We've got a week to figure this out. I've got to go see Shannon now, although I'm not optimistic that I'll get a reading from her Grimoire."

TWENTY FIVE

Two days later... (Saturday)

Shannon

"Hey! I never heard back from you about finishing the interview, Shannon."

I jerked back from placing the last bag of groceries in my truck, almost bumping my head on the roof. Shit! With all that had happened with the spells on my Grimoire and Libby's letter, that interview with Devon about his project had fallen between the cracks.

When I turned to face him, my stomach did a flip. His blue eyes were hooded while the shadow of his beard growth appeared even darker against the white denim shirt. A lock of lustrous blonde hair had fallen over his forehead from the gentle spring breeze. Damn! He still looked as good as he ever had, but thankfully I was now able to keep that thought to myself rather than blurt it out because of MJ's hex.

I did a check on my stomach and was relieved that I felt fine being around him. At least we'd been successful in one thing—removing the spell that the nasty wannabe coven member had cast on me.

"I'm really sorry about that, Devon. I've just been... well, I've had a few things I had to deal with. I was going to call you on Monday to see if we could get together so I can finish the article."

His lips pressed together as he shook his head. "That's not going to work for me. I'm tied up all day Monday, but I've got a couple hours now. I'd like to get this over. It'd be good to end the rumors and speculations about what I'm doing with the Cousins' estate." His eyes narrowed as he peered at me, reminding me of the part I'd played in those rumors.

My cheeks warmed at that thought, but embarrassment was way better than throwing up, like the last time I'd seen him. "Sure, that works for me, but weren't you going into the grocery store—"

"That can wait." He glanced up at the sky and took a deep breath. "It's such a nice day, why don't we just walk... maybe go to the park? I'll answer your questions, and you can record it on your phone. How does that sound?"

It was hard to believe that he was being this civil with me. Could it be possible that he had forgiven me for all the trouble I'd caused in his life? Whatever. I'd take it. "A walk to the park sounds great. I'll even buy you an ice cream cone for giving me this scoop." I smiled up at him.

"Cute play on words; you oughta be a writer." He pressed the button on his fob, locking his Beemer. "You'd better make it a double scoop." A hint of a smile brushed his lips, and he started walking across the parking lot.

I locked my truck and hurried to catch up with him. Before I started, I took my phone out and hit record. "So, your energy project... when do you think it will be complete?"

"Phase one will be ready by September. I'm not going to get into all the details, as I'm sure my engineer, Saul, filled you in on that. I'm more concerned with talking about how *Harvest Energy* is going to help the town's economy and create jobs."

He looked over at me. "Before I get into all that, what's going on with you, Shannon? Frankly, I was a little concerned when I didn't hear from you. If I hadn't run into you today, I was going to call. I really thought this interview was important to you. Didn't you have a deadline at the newspaper?"

I focused on the street, looking both ways as we crossed it, buying time to come up with a plausible answer. I certainly couldn't tell him about some witch hexing me and that I was trying to figure out who that bitch was! I was already on thin ice with Devon when it involved my sanity.

"The interview *is* important. But I had some things with Mary-Jane and Libby to take care of. Nothing catastrophic but kind of involved, y'know."

"Oh." He continued. "Did you ever see that bobcat again? That was such a freaky thing that day. So crazy how Steve Murphy tried to kill it and the gun going off, hitting me."

My stomach fell at the thought of Robert, but also because I knew the truth of what had happened—my calling down that bolt of lightning to stop Steve. Thank the goddess that Devon wasn't hurt worse than he was.

"No sign of the cat at all, and I've looked, believe me." We left the sidewalk and stepped into the village green, where there were kids tossing Frisbees and a few couples walking dogs along the pathways rimming the big fountain.

Devon paused and put his hand on my arm, stopping me. "Speak of the devil, and there he is. I didn't know he was seeing Cynthia again."

My head turned to where he was peering. My eyes popped wider, seeing Cynthia sitting on a bench between Steve and Byron, the three of them eating ice-cream cones. Although it was apparent that Cynthia was paying more attention to the young boy, with her arm looped over his shoulder, leaning in and sharing a laugh. But why? Even though she missed seeing Byron, she wouldn't enjoy having to suffer through a visit with Steve to do that? Not from what I knew...

"I didn't know they were so chummy either, Devon. She never mentioned anything to me about reconnecting with Steve." But as soon as the words were out of my mouth, I wondered what else Cynthia hadn't told me.

Mary-Jane hadn't been able to read Libby's letter or the entry in my Grimoire to find who was behind it. Both threats had been charmed to hide the identity of the writer. The only one I knew who could cast a glamour like that was Cynthia.

I watched her chatting with Byron, noting the easy way she had with the kid, and shook my head. No. It couldn't be Cynthia. She was already a member of the coven, tapping into the well's power the same as the rest of us.

Devon huffed. "Personally, I don't see the big attraction to Steve. I asked Cynthia out at one time, but she ended up dating him for a few months. There's no accounting for taste, I guess."

As I looked up at him, I wondered about that myself. Steve was drop-dead gorgeous, but his personality? He was way too controlling and sexist—especially after overhearing him on the lake with Ray. Devon and I had our differences, but at least he'd always treated me with respect. When he wasn't questioning my sanity, that is.

So why had Cynthia turned Devon down flat when he'd asked her out? Actually, I really didn't know why Devon was still single, or if he'd ever been married. Despite the mutual attraction, we'd never really even gone out on a date, let alone talk at any length.

"Have you ever been married, Devon? I know it's none of my business, and you don't have to answer me. I'm just curious."

He steered us onto another pathway, away from where Cynthia and Steve were. His mouth pulled to the side in a smirk when he looked down at me. "Is this going to be in your article?"

I looked away, rolling my eyes. "No. Okay, it's none of my business. Got it." I'd probably be better off sticking to what I needed for the article. I was pushing things... as usual.

He sighed. "I'm *teasing*, Shannon. And yes, I was married a long time ago, but it didn't last long." He made a small shrug. "We both realized we made a mistake and ended it pretty quickly."

My gaze flew to his face. "I'm sorry to hear that." Double shit. Even without Mary-Jane's spell making me say outrageous things, I managed to put my foot in it anyway.

His lips pulled back in a grim smile as he looked at me. "It was a long time ago. We should get back to the subject at hand—*Harvest Energy*."

I nodded and held the cell phone up. "Tell me everything about it that you want in the article. I may not understand all the technical stuff, but I can see that it's going to be good for the town."

We continued on the walkway as he continued on, telling me all about the energy project. It was a good thing I was recording his words, as I have to admit, I was more interested in watching the way his eyes lit up and listening to the excitement in his voice. A warm feeling infused my chest as he became lost in the marvels of renewable energy and sustainability. Could this be the start of us resuming our friendship?

By the time he finished, we ended up outside Mountain Flavors, the ice cream shop on the main street. He paused in front of the wide plate-glass window, and his eyebrows arched.

"You owe me a cone. And after talking nonstop for the last twenty minutes, I could use one." He stepped to the door and held it for me.

"I'm good. Thanks for the interview." I took a couple of steps away before spinning on my heel, laughing. "I'm teasing! Of course I'm buying you a cone!" I was about to enter the shop when I heard a high-pitched voice calling my name.

I looked down the street and saw Byron break away from Cynthia and Steve, running toward me. My gut tightened, even though it was nice to see Byron's freckled face and the wide grin as he approached. Cynthia's hand rose and she waved, walking arm in arm with Steve. What the hell?

Beside me, Devon murmured, "Great. And I was having a decent day before this."

My arms went around Byron as he almost bowled me over when he got to me. "Hey, buddy! Nice to see you!" But my gaze was drawn to Cynthia. She smiled at me as if it was as natural for her to be walking beside Steve as breathing. And Steve looked kind of... Oh my God. *Smug?*

Byron's eager voice caught my attention. "I'm playing softball at four this afternoon. Do you want to come and watch me? I tried out for shortstop, and they're letting me play that spot. Say you'll come, Shannon!"

I grinned at him. "Gee whiz, I wish I could, Byron. But, I've got some things I have to take care of this afternoon. Maybe your next game though? I'd like that."

By this time, Cynthia and Steve were right behind Byron. Steve murmured, "Byron, Shannon's busy." His eyes were flinty when he looked over at Devon. "Booker. Surprised to see you here. I thought you'd be out at that abomination you're building on the Cousins' Estate. Trucks are coming and going all the time, kicking up dust right next to my land."

Devon glanced down at Byron before he answered. "It's a great day for an ice cream cone, so I thought I'd take a break. Even those trucks you're talking about stop on the weekend. But you'll read all about that in the paper next week." He nodded to Cynthia. "Nice to see you, Cynthia."

I wasn't even aware that my fingers were digging into poor little Byron's shoulders until he shrugged and stepped closer to his father. I smiled an apology at the little guy before my eyes skewered Cynthia's, silently questioning. The tension between Steve and Devon wasn't bad enough that I also had to wonder what the hell my sister witch was doing?

My mouth was dry as dust while my glance bounced between Steve and Cynthia. "We were just going in for a cone. It was nice seeing you both but..." I stepped closer to the ice cream shop's door and shot a pointed look at Cynthia. "I'll call you later?"

Although there was a smile on her lips, it didn't quite make it to her eyes when she nodded. "Sure. I should be around after Byron's game."

Steve's gaze flew to her. "But you promised to have dinner with me. I asked Mary-Jane to save us a seat at the restaurant." He looked over at me. "It's a new performance from the school's theater group. They're doing *Into the Woods*. I'm surprised you aren't going. It sounds like something you'd enjoy."

As I watched him, I wondered what he was up to. He HAD to know that if he was trying to make me jealous, there was no way he was even coming close. What did he mean about the play? I'd have to look it up when I got home. But before I could answer, Devon spoke.

"Well have fun with that." Devon smiled at me. "Shall we? I'm dying for some mint chocolate."

I gave Byron one last muss of his hair before saying goodbye to Steve and Cynthia. As I went inside, my mind was a maelstrom, wondering about the strange encounter. Cynthia had been so quiet, totally unlike herself, while Steve was all *puffed up*. The only normal one was Byron.

After we'd placed our orders, I looked up at Devon. "Have you ever heard of that play, *Into the Woods*? What's it about? I'm kind of out of things when it comes to books and plays."

He scoffed. "I'm not much better, but I know that one. It's kind of a mash-up of traditional fairy tales with *Red Riding Hood, Cinderella* and magic witch stuff. Meryl Streep was in the movie. I only caught half of it as I'm not a big fan of musicals."

I nodded numbly and then took the cone that the young teenage server handed to me. Magic witch stuff. What the ever loving hell was up with Steve saying I'd enjoy it? He had no idea what my taste in entertainment was. And the irony that an actual witch was clinging to his arm, focused on his every word, wasn't lost on me.

TWENTY SIX

That same day...

Mary-Jane

Four more lasagna and two veal, MJ."

I grabbed the order form that Sylvie set on the shelf and set it at the end of the line. I'd expected it to be busy, but this was *crazy*! Ever since we'd started dinner theater and live entertainment, the restaurant was busy on Saturdays, but this was over the top.

Debbie set four plates of veal scaloppini on the stainless-steel warmer and signaled to Kevin to take them out. She turned to me and grinned. "Aren't you glad I insisted we make an extra tray of pasta? At this rate, we're going to burn through the first three like wildfire."

Ray popped his head in the swinging kitchen door. "We're at capacity, ladies. Only forty minutes till show time. How are you doing in here?"

The fact that he directed the question to Debbie rather than me didn't go unnoticed. He was still miffed with me, despite Steve's best efforts. Steve might be in Shannon's and Libby's bad books after what he did to the bobcat, but he was still a good friend to me. He texted me after he and Ray had gone to the local watering hole for a few drinks to let me know Ray was softening. It was thanks to Steve's pleading my case to Ray that we were even on speaking terms.

Debbie chirped back at Ray, "We're good! Just make sure you don't serve all the Canadian Club rye tonight. I'm going to need a drink or two to unwind when this place clears out." When he disappeared out the door, she turned to me. "Thank God you were well enough to work tonight. I've missed you in the kitchen the last few days."

"Yeah. I've kind of missed it myself. But I'm feeling way better today." It was a white lie that Ray had told Debbie to cover the fact that I was MIA—a result of Ray and me arguing. Getting caught up in the hectic pace of the kitchen was a welcome break from all the ruminations about the mystery witch.

I was beginning to agree with Libby on that badass bitch. She was more powerful than any of us, easily sloughing off our curse on her. Even though there was no way any of us wanted her in our coven, I had to admit I was curious about who it was. You'd think that living in a small town, where everyone knew everyone else's business, I'd have some hint as to who it could be, but nada.

We had just finished getting the plates ready for the next order when I heard my cell phone ringing. I rushed over to the table at the end of the kitchen where my purse was. When I saw Shannon's face on the small screen, I toyed with the idea of letting the call go to voicemail. But Debbie had things well in hand, so I answered.

"Hi, Shannon. I can't talk for very long. It's a zoo in here tonight. You're missing an excellent performance." The fact that Chloe and Jack had scored brilliant spots in the cast added to my excitement.

"Did you know that Cynthia is seeing Steve Murphy?"

Without so much as a hello, she'd launched right into the reason for her call. As annoying as her self-absorption could sometimes be, her question about Steve and Cynthia made my mouth drop open. As far as I knew, Cynthia had nothing good to say about Steve, but now she was *dating* him?

"No. That's news to me." As I spoke, I walked to the other side of the kitchen to peek out the door's window overlooking the dining room. I scanned the tables at the window, where I had saved a spot for Steve. When I saw Cynthia in a glittery dress, leaning over the table toward him, I did a double-take.

"Oh my God! She's here with him tonight! What's she doing with Steve?" I had to bob to the side when someone blocked my view, but I saw his hand reach across the table to cover hers. They sure were hitting it off!

"That's what I want to know! I saw her and Steve together today with Byron. She... She acted kind of odd, MJ. You know how she's normally chatty and a bit snarky... Today, she acted kind of *docile*. I don't think she said two words to me!"

I had to step back when Kevin approached the door, coming through to pick up his order. "That *is* strange. I know she really likes his son... maybe she was trying to be nice so she could visit Byron."

"That doesn't explain why she's having dinner with him!" There was a pause before Shannon spoke again. "Is Libby there tonight?"

"Yeah. She and Stan have a table close to the stage. Jack's in the play, you know." Of course, Libby wouldn't miss this for the world! I only wished I could get out there to see Chloe when she was on the small stage performing.

"Ask her to stop by Cynthia's table. I'd like to get her take on what's going on with Cynthia."

I grit my teeth. As usual, *my* gift, reading people, didn't register on Shannon's radar. "I'll ask her, but I'm going to make it a point to stop by their table. I'll put my hand on her shoulder, and then we'll know what's going on! Y'know... that magic thing I do... READING people!"

"Oh shit! I'm sorry, MJ! Of course! Do that. Then when you know, call me back. I'm just working on that article for the newspaper. I'm so behind that I'll be lucky if the editor doesn't fire me. Otherwise, I'd be there to see all this for myself. Chloe's in that play too, right?"

The tightness in my chest dissolved at her mention of Chloe. "Yeah. She's Cinderella. Jack's the big, bad wolf." I smiled before adding. "I'd better go. I'll call you once I scope this Cynthia thing out."

It was a half hour later that the main courses had been dished out and I heard the musical score for *Into the Woods*. I slipped my white cook's jacket off and looked over at Debbie. She was busy slicing cheesecake and setting them on plates for the servers to pick up.

"I'm going out to visit with customers and catch some of my daughter's performance. You good here?"

Her ebony face broke into a wide grin. "Go! I got this covered, MJ. If you don't get out there, your daughter will be disappointed." To emphasize the point, her hand rose, shooing me away.

The first performers were just making an entrance when I stepped out into the dimly lit room. I threaded through the tables, pausing at a few to mouth a greeting. Finally, I arrived at Libby's table and leaned down to whisper in her ear. "Check out Cynthia with Steve. The midway table at the window." When she bobbed forward, my fingers dug into her shoulder. "Not like that! Be discreet for Pete's sake."

I noticed her gaze scanning across the room, and her eyes became round as she locked in on Cynthia and Steve. Her head swiveled to me and she hissed, "What the hell? What's she doing with *him*?"

"I have no idea. I thought she was interested in Eric the fireman."

Stan must have heard the last, because he shot me a puzzled look. I leaned in closer to Libby's ear. "I'm going over to check it out, but if you see her go to the ladies' room, follow her. Shannon said she was acting weird earlier today."

Libby's eyebrows arched as the same thought I was having darted through her head. Cynthia was capable of putting a glamour on the letter and Shannon's Grimoire. And her showing up with Steve after the way she'd cast so much shade on him earlier was weird. What was going on with her?

I eased away, trying to slip by people who were trying to watch the play. Thankfully, Chloe wouldn't appear on stage for another ten minutes, so I wasn't missing her performance. When I got to Cynthia's table, she looked up at me.

For a moment she looked confused, but then she smiled. "MJ! Dinner was fabulous, as usual." Her gaze darted to Steve when he leaned closer. "I'm glad Steve talked me into coming tonight."

"Thanks." My hand rested on her back, and I looked over at Steve when he spoke. But his words fell on deaf ears as I tried to sense what was going on with Cynthia. I blinked quickly as the image of clouds filled my mind. It was exactly the same picture and sense of nothingness as when I'd tried to read the letter left for Libby and the note in Shannon's Grimoire.

My gut tightened as I looked into Cynthia's eyes. She was purposely blocking me! Of all of us, she would be the only one capable of doing that. But why? She had to be hiding something, and there was only one thing that could be. She had written those notes threatening Shannon and Libby.

At the touch on the small of my back, I turned to see Ray there. Once more his eyebrows were bunched in a knot, darkening his narrow eyes. His voice was smooth, but there was no mistaking that angry look.

"Mary-Jane, you're interrupting Steve and Cynthia's—"

"It's fine, Ray. We haven't missed much. Would you get us another bottle of wine?" Steve interrupted, flashing a confident smile at me. When Ray huffed off, Steve continued, "He's coming around, MJ. Just be patient with him. In the meantime, maybe you should join him at the bar, so the two of you can watch your daughter together."

I nodded numbly. Just when things were thawing between Ray and me, I'd pushed things by trying to figure out what was up with Cynthia. It was like I took one step forward and two back. Thankfully, I had Steve in my corner, trying to smooth the troubled waters with my husband.

Cynthia squeezed my arm. "Steve's right, MJ. I'll talk to you later. Just go and be with Ray right now." Her gaze drifted back to Steve, dismissing me.

As I walked away, my mind whirled in a maelstrom—fear that Cynthia was behind all this coven-snatching crap and disappointment that my marriage depended on Steve Murphy acting as my advocate. Ray was supposed to be my mate, someone who'd have my back no matter what. Instead, he had been so damn quick to condemn me for that DUI charge. He HAD to know I was innocent.

And Cynthia. Even though I'd been skeptical about her joining the coven, she had won me over countless times. But now... it looked like that had been a setup for her ultimate goal. She wanted ALL the power that the well and coven could offer.

My world had certainly tipped off its axis.

TWENTY SEVEN

The next day... Sunday

Shannon

I hit send and let out a long sigh. Finally, the article on Devon's *Harvest Energy* project was complete, and the copy was on its way to Wayne Silver, my editor. It had taken me into the wee hours of the morning to finish it, but it was done! This would keep the wolf from my door for another while and hopefully open another door for Devon and I to get closer.

Snapping the laptop shut, I got up from the kitchen table to make some lunch. I had barely finished cutting my sandwich when the smell of lavender and patchouli oil drifted into my nostrils. The air at the other side of the room shimmered and sparkled for a few moments, and my Aunt Maeve's form materialized.

It had been a few days since she'd popped in to visit. I bit back the sharp reprimand that threatened to leap from my lips. Here I was being threatened by some nasty witch-bitch with designs on stealing my coven, and my aunt had been MIA.

"I know that look, Shannon. Before you say anything, I've been busy too." Aunt Maeve's hazy blue eyes sparked as she drifted closer to where I stood. "My path isn't easy either. This afterlife stuff is hard to get a handle on. But I've learned a few tricks that might help you."

"Oh, yeah?" I brushed by her to have a seat at the table and eat my lunch. "So you know who's leaving threatening notes and trying to take my coven over? That'd be helpful. How about stopping them cold and maybe throwing them in the well? I could get behind that."

She clucked her tongue, drifting closer to gaze out the window. "Whoever the crafty bitch is, throwing her in the well isn't the answer. They must never be allowed anywhere near it."

"But what if they've already been to the well? In fact, the person who I suspect is behind all this visited that well as a young girl." I bit into my sandwich and scowled at her. It was a good thing Libby and Mary-Jane were coming out soon so that we could compare notes in person and figure out how to destroy Cynthia's plan.

Aunt Maeve's hand flew to her neck and she gasped. "*Cynthia?* You don't honestly suspect Cynthia of trying to hijack the coven and the well?" Aunt Maeve's gaze fell as she continued, "I just spoke to her grandmother Ruth! We were bragging to Lillian and Emma about you girls—how well you were doing in mastering witchcraft."

As nice as it was to hear she was proud of me, her humble-bragging was totally missing the mark. "I know you and Ruth were best buddies but Cynthia... well, she's been acting really weird the past few days. And then there's the glamour on the note in the Grimoire and the letter to Libby. Cynthia is the only one of us to ever use a glamour. She's hid her hot tub from her landlord for years."

Aunt Maeve sank down into the chair at the end of the table. "No. I can't believe it's Cynthia. To tell the truth, it surprised me to see her join up with you three; she's always been more of a loner. And she was doing remarkably well on her own in the craft." She shook her head slowly. "No, her being willing to be a part of your coven was a surprise; the idea of wanting to lead it just doesn't make sense to me. Why would she want to control everything? She should know better! That kind of selfish ambition would rain down all kinds of terrible things on her."

As I looked at the shock in Maeve's eyes, I knew she had a blind spot when it came to Cynthia—probably because of her close friendship with Cynthia's grandmother. I softened my tone when I spoke. "I don't understand why she would do this either, Aunt Maeve, but all signs are pointing to her. Even that thing she told us about not being able to get a fertility appointment for months and months... as well as the expense. She might have been trying to throw us off her tracks."

Aunt Maeve rolled her eyes. "She certainly doesn't need to use a clinic to get pregnant. There's more 'natural' ways of accomplishing that."

The sandwich in my stomach felt like a ball of lead as I pictured Cynthia walking arm in arm with Steve Murphy. I scoffed. "It looks like that's the route she's opting for. She's back with Steve. At first I thought she was with him so she could see his son Byron, but now I'm not so sure. If Steve can father a kid as great as Byron, maybe she thinks he's a suitable candidate for the daughter she wants to have."

Aunt Maeve's eyes widened as she blurted, "Beltane! It's the celebration of new life. That's why she put that as a deadline. She wants to *really* get into the spirit of the festival, if you know what I mean."

Eeew. My nose crinkled up at the nasty picture flooding my head. "Well, she was the one who made such a production of planning Beltane. Little did I know what she had in mind. If she plans on asking Steve to our celebration so he can be the Green Man, she's got another think coming."

Maeve floated over the room to me. "Green Man? Oh, dear Shannon, I don't think that's a good idea. You're not planning to invite one, are you?"

I shook my head. "Nope... but with Cynthia's attempts to take over the coven, I wouldn't put it past *her* to extend an invitation on her own."

"That's a terrible idea, Shannon. The energy that's brought up in a Beltane celebration... the fertility, the fecundity... It's not"—her mouth pursed as she looked up for a genteel way of expressing herself — "proper," she finally added with a sharp nod.

I'm sorry, but I couldn't help but giggle at Maeve's awkwardness. "You're worried about some moonlight orgy or something!" I burst out laughing. "Well, they don't call it 'the horny forties' for nothing!"

"SHANNON!" Watching a ghost gasp and blush is a sight to see.

I reached out and tried to pat her shoulder, and, of course, my hand went right through her. "Don't fret, Maeve. There's not going to be any funny business like that going on, believe me. Cynthia's out. I can't allow her anywhere near that well or in our coven again."

"I never would have thought this of Cynthia. Even Steve Murphy surprised me when he tried to kill Robert. He used to be such a sweet and gentle boy when he was younger. It's true his big brother always overshadowed him, but he tried, y'know." She shook her head and sighed.

"Yeah. Like he tried to kill Robert." My eyes narrowed, thinking of my familiar, the bobcat. We'd just started to get along well together when Steve had barged in and shot him. How Cynthia could have anything to do with Steve after that was beyond me. It was hard to say who I was angrier with—Cynthia or Steve.

"So what are you going to do, Shannon? If it *is* Cynthia, then you're up against a powerful enemy. But, you can't condemn her without proof."

That was the rub. Much as Libby and Mary-Jane agreed with me that it had to be Cynthia, we had no actual proof. We wouldn't have that until Beltane. By then it might be too late. But one thing I knew. There was no way that I would allow the person who sent those messages anywhere near the well. Even if it meant breaking up the coven and giving up on magic, that was a small price to pay. Anyone who threatened us like this was not the sort of person who could be given access to the well's power.

And I'm pretty sure that person is Cynthia. Damn it.

My voice sounded more confident than I felt when I looked over at Aunt Maeve. "We carry on with Beltane. Except, it will be here in my yard rather than going to the well. At least we will know for sure who our enemy is. I only hope that whatever power the well has given us, will help us defeat this witch."

At the sound of a car outside, I peeked out the window. "Libby and MJ are here, Aunt Maeve. I hope you stick around to hear what they have to say about all this."

Behind me she murmured, "Holy doodle. This is a mess. I'm staying, don't worry. I'll confer with Ruth about all this later. If it is Cynthia, she's going to be heartbroken."

I turned and grabbed my hoodie from the back of the chair. "Okay. I'm going out to help them bring in the stuff we need to decorate for Beltane." I grimaced. "This is pretty sad, you know. I was really looking forward to my first one. It may be my last one."

As I walked toward the door, she called to me, "Don't say that, Shannon. I always taught you to be positive. We need good intentions right now."

I took a deep breath as I stepped outside. Aunt Maeve was right. All of us had come too far to accept defeat so easily. Cynthia might be powerful, but had she ever influenced the weather? Could she talk to animals like Libby? Okay, she could read things like MJ and even move objects with a thought, but she was outnumbered. Plus, I owned the well.

Mary-Jane carried a tray of food in her hands as she stepped up onto the verandah. "I've been at this since early this morning. I've got enough food for a dozen people, I think. But with Ray hardly talking to me, at least it kept me busy."

There were dark cusps under her eyes and her face was pale. This argument with Ray and the DUI charge she was up against were really weighing her down. "Let me take that, MJ. I cleared out the bottom shelf of the fridge for this. I'm glad you could do this."

As we walked into the house, Libby commented, "I brought ribbons, flowers and grapevines to decorate, but since we're missing a Maypole, maybe we can string them around your birch tree. I read that lots of people do that. The important thing is making everything festive, rather than what it really is... a showdown at the OK Corral."

Mary-Jane held the door for Libby and me to enter. "I know how you feel, Libby, but we have to go through the motions to draw Cynthia out. I still can't hardly believe that she'd do this. But the way she's acting around Steve... who knows?"

As I shoved the tray of food into the fridge, Libby mused, "What if it isn't Cynthia? Just because she's reunited with Steve doesn't mean she's turned against us. If she's chosen to use him as the sperm donor, she might be feeling a bit of shame when she's around us. She knows how we feel about him."

"Libby has a point, Shannon." Aunt Maeve was right in my face when I closed the fridge door. "I have a hard time thinking that Cynthia is behind this. And for all you know, her seeing Steve might be because of a spell that's been cast on her. She dated Steve but broke it off from him."

Mary-Jane, of course, hadn't heard what Aunt Maeve had said when she answered Libby. "You know, Cynthia has always been really self-assured. She doesn't hesitate to call bullshit if it's being dished out. The Cynthia in the restaurant last night wasn't the Cynthia we all know and love. Add to the fact that when I touched her to get a reading on what's going on, it was clouds that blocked me. The same thing I picked up when I held the note in your Grimoire and the letter to Libby."

I stared at Libby and MJ. "Aunt Maeve just said almost the same thing, MJ. Instead of thinking that Cynthia cast the glamour spell on the letter and my Grimoire, what if she's had a spell cast on her? This witch-bitch wannabe coven leader might have spelled Cynthia."

Libby scooped her cell phone from the front pocket of her hoodie. "Instead of sitting here speculating, we need to get her out here. If she's a victim like us, she needs our help, not our suspicions."

Mary-Jane shrugged. "At the very least, she can help us with the decorating." When Libby and I shot a dirty look at MJ, her cheeks flared and she stammered, "H-hey! I'm kidding! Of course she needs to be here so we can get to the bottom of this. Help her if she's a victim or stop her if she's the villain."

Libby shushed us with a flutter of her hand before she spoke into the phone. "Hi, Cynthia. How are you doing?"

For the next few minutes, Mary-Jane and I watched Libby maneuver the conversation and finally get Cynthia to agree to come to the house to help decorate.

When Libby clicked the phone off, her eyebrows arched. "She said she'll try to be here in half an hour. I heard Steve in the background. He must have spent the night. I hope she can ditch him, now that he's served his purpose."

"Ha!" I rolled my eyes. "If he shows up here, I'll charge him with trespassing. He wouldn't dare come onto my property."

But as soon as the words were out of my mouth, another thought popped into my head. He'd been at my house to help find Robert the day MJ got the DUI charge. That pompous ass probably thought that things were better between us. Well, this time I wouldn't be all mealymouthed like the last time. He was in for a surprise if he showed up with Cynthia.

TWENTY EIGHT

Later that day...

Shannon

I peered up at Libby, watching her stretch from the ladder's top rung, to tie a pink ribbon around the trunk of the birch tree. She'd already managed to get streams of blue, purple, and yellow ribbons up, and this was the last one. The four ribbons fluttered in the light afternoon breeze.

Mary-Jane stood below, holding the stepladder steady. She looked up the length of the trunk, musing, "I don't think this is the first time this tree's been used as a Maypole, Shannon." Still keeping the ladder steady, she waved her arm at the tree. "There're no branches for the first ten feet, and it's pretty damn straight. A naturally grown Maypole, huh?"

I nodded. "Well, why don't you touch it, then? See if there's a history to this tree?" She had a point. While it wasn't in the center of the yard, it stood apart from any other trees, leaving plenty of room for the four of us to prance around it, braiding the ribbons on it in our Beltane celebration.

MJ turned and looked at me for a moment, then sighed. "How about I wait until Libby gets down, okay, boss?"

"That'll be fine," I replied, watching Libby pick her way down the ladder. "You afraid of heights, hon?" I called to her. The ladder shifted a little. "MJ! Hold it steady!" I dropped the bundle of branches and sprung over to help.

"Relax, Shannon," Libby murmured. "I'm fine."

When she got to the ground, we stepped back to admire our work. Like banners, the wide ribbons undulated in the breeze, wavy streams of color in the air. With the sun casting diamonds across the surface of the lake and the warm breeze, it was hard to imagine that there was some nasty bitch out there plotting against us.

While I gathered up the branches I had dropped and tossed them into the firepit I glanced at MJ. "Any word from Cynthia, MJ?"

"I didn't talk to her last, Shannon. You did. She hasn't contacted you since?"

I turned around. "No, nothing. That's why I'm asking you. How about you, Libby?"

Libby rolled her eyes and sighed. "Shannon, I've just spent the last twenty minutes ten feet up in the air. My cell phone is in my purse. How the hell would I know?"

Sheesh! What the hell was up with these two? From the time we started setting the place up, they've been all sigh-ey, just this side of full blown huffy. As if I didn't have enough to deal with. "Well, you guys want to check?" I replied, gesturing to their purses on the picnic table nearby.

MJ's eyes narrowed for a moment before she tossed me a quick salute. "Yes, boss."

Now, wait a damn minute. "What's your problem?" I said. "Don't you want to know what's up with Cynthia too?"

"Yeah, I sure do! But"—she jabbed a finger at me—"you've been a goddamned drill sergeant since we got here! 'MJ do this! Libby do that!' and it's a real pain in the ass!"

"Are you kidding me? If you had your way, we'd still be in the house gabbing and yakking!"

Libby held up her hand. "Take it easy, Shannon. You've been pretty pushy lately; that's all MJ's trying to tell you."

"Pushy is putting it mildly," MJ sniffed, chin tilted up.

"PUSHY? You gotta be kidding me!" Someone had to get things moving, and as usual, that was me.

"See?" Mary-Jane's face tightened when she turned to Libby.

"There's no need to yell, Shannon," Libby said. "We can hear you just fine."

MJ just stood there, shaking her head. "Here we go again."

"What the hell's that supposed to mean?"

"Look—since you found the well and got us involved, you've been running the show, more and more. To the point that there's some witch out there right now so fed up with you that she's zapping us with spells and shit." She folded her arms. "What the hell's happened to you, Shannon? You used to be fun, lighthearted, and great to be around. But lately..."

"Lately, what?"

"You're a pain in the ass, that's what."

My jaw dropped so far it could have bounced off my kneecap. "Whaaaat? You're kidding me." I looked over at Libby. She sure as hell wasn't jumping in to back me up. She stood there quietly... and then slowly nodded. Nodded? What the hell? "So you're on her side too, Libby."

As I waited for her to reply, that dark sense of futility which, by now, had become a familiar friend, descended on me.

"Well... kinda," Libby finally answered. "MJ's got a point, Shannon. When you first came home to Wesley, you were kinda beat up, for sure. But you had a plan to fix up Maeve's property and start over. But then... with the well and everything? You're coming on pretty strong, y'know?" Her voice was gentle and soothing in tone, belying the knife she just thrust in my gut.

"Yeah, what the hell's going on with you?" MJ asked. "We're your best friends, and you're treating us like we're inept busboys!" She shook her head. "You're acting like your back's up against a wall and lashing out at everybody!"

I took a deep breath. "THAT'S BECAUSE IT IS!" It came out like a howling wind, scattering loose leaves across the yard.

"Whoaa..." MJ's eye spanned wide, looking around. "Hey, Shannon..."

"Don't '*Hey, Shannon*' me!" I stormed over to both of them. "Everything... *everything* in my life I ever counted on has always, *always* crumbled." I should be crying over that, but I was just... just *mad,* dammit!

"Look at me!" I thumped my chest. "Forty-three goddamned years old! I did everything right, despite—" My breath hitched so hard in my chest, I couldn't speak.

Libby stepped over to me. "Hey... despite what?" she asked, rubbing my arm.

I lurched away from them both. "Despite the fact that my own *mother* didn't give a shit about me!" I looked at them both. "We first met when we were twelve, right?" They both nodded, all of us remembering coming all together at that Wesley Town Summer Celeb For Kids that Maeve made me go to. "I was up 'visiting' my Aunt Maeve, right? Well, the fact of the matter is that my mother wanted to go on some freaking camping trip with some of her drinking buddies and sloughed me off to Maeve. And after that summer, every damn year until I left for college, she had some kind of reason to dump me on Auntie Maeve."

Damn, the waterworks started, and I rubbed my arm across my face, wiping away the beginning tears and snot before they got out of hand. "The only, *only* thing that saved me was you two guys."

I shook my fist at the both of them. "In the last year, my goddamn husband leaves me for a younger woman; I'm barely hanging on to a relationship with my *children*, walking on eggshells with every text, email, and phone call." Collapsing forward with my hands on my knees, I looked up at them. "Are ya seeing a pattern here, ladies?"

They stayed silent, just staring at me. Fuck it. Yeah, *fuck it.* I straightened and swept my arm at Maeve's house. "Now, for some stupid reason, I've been given this gift of magic...so I try doing spells, that leave MJ's marriage on the rocks, Robert's shot and vanished, and Devon thinks I'm a nutcase!" I bent at the waist again. "Is it coming through to you guys yet?" I said, staring at them in the face. "Y'see what's happening here? Huh?"

MJ just shook her head while Libby said in a low voice, "No... what *is* your point, honey?"

Shit! I straightened up, spread my arms out to the side. "I'M A DAMN FAAAILLLURE!" One at a time, I stabbed the air with my fingers. "I was a failure as a daughter! A failure as a wife! A borderline failure as a mother! And the world's worst witch!"

Without warning, a furrow shot down the lawn between us, like some invisible lightning bolt had hit it. There was no boom or crash or zap; it just ran down the lawn like a zipper. MJ and Libby jumped back, staring at it, then at me, when a wisp of steam wafted from it.

"Dial it down, Shannon," MJ said quietly. "Please..." Her eyes were enormous.

I took a couple of deep breaths, trying to calm down. Well, at least the truth of the matter was out there now. Shit, to tell the truth, I didn't even realize that was how I really felt until the words flew out of my mouth. But they were the truth; that was for sure.

What a screwup I am.

Libby spoke up. "Your life's not like that, surely. Ass-Hat leaving you was all on him, not you, Shannon."

I scoffed. "Bullshit. He traded me in, Libs. He decided he could do better." I took a deep breath, but if I was being as honest as I could, the hell with it; I was gonna tell her the truth. "Look, I'm really sorry Hank died,. But you're going through life with 'the poor widow' label while I'm the woman with 'the failed marriage' sign around my neck, okay? I'm used goods on the market."

"Now, wait a second!" MJ chirped. "That's not fair!"

"Fair?" I said, spinning toward her. "Y'know what's not fair? You and Ray drive each other absolutely crazy! You both have been sniping and nattering at each other ever since we were kids! Ray's a royal pain in the ass sometimes, Mary-Jane, but so the hell are you! But still..."

I wiped my eyes again. "Still...in my marriage I fought harder to 'keep the peace' than for anything else and look at me now! You two guys fight it out, and you're coming up to your goddamn *twentieth* wedding anniversary!" I took a deep breath. "Yeah, you with your stupid one year of college could write a goddamn self-help-book on how to make a marriage work!"

I was exhausted. My legs went weak, and I just sank to the ground. "Now I got Alice in the well, Maeve's ghost, some other witch gunning not just for me but *all* of us, and I still owe a fortune in land taxes. Not to mention what the hell I'm going to do with Devon Booker. I'm so hot for him." I looked up at them.

"I'm not bossy, guys. I'm just trying to keep from losing my freaking mind."

And yes, I started to cry. Bawling like a three-year-old, to be honest. Those hiccupping, crouping sobs too, not the lovely waterworks in the movies. Not. At. All.

Fuck it.

"You're such a jerk," MJ said, flying over to be next to me.

"You're so wrong, Shannon," Libby said, joining her from the other side.

MJ cradled my head. "You're starting over from zero, Shan," she said. "But you're doing pretty damn good, y'know. Your kids touch base with you every week. Devon's as hot for you as you are—still don't get his Jell-O kink, by the way—and your magic..." She cupped my chin and pointed my face at that plowed-up rut in my yard. "Strong with you, the Force is, young Jedi!"

Libby leaned her head on my shoulder. "From the day we met at that fair, MJ and I, *you have blown away both of us*. For years and years, we've always looked up to you, Shannon baby. You were the first to go to college! The first to have kids! The first witch we've ever known! I *love* talking with animals! It's so cool! And without you in my life, I'd just be another nurse with varicose veins!"

"And I'd be the dumpy, frumpy lady with a restaurant, instead of the next Sherlock Holmes!" MJ added. "Screwup? You're such a jerk." Rubbing my back, she added, "Oh, and yeah, that birch tree you just 'happened' to pick out as our Maypole? The memories of coven celebrations it's witnessed, oh wow." She hugged me again. "Ya jerk."

The three of us; me and my super best friends I could ever have held one another in a silent, quiet circle of love.

As the ground continued to steam.

***

Until we heard the car pull up in my driveway and not one, but two doors slammed. Cynthia was here.

And she wasn't alone.

TWENTY NINE

We all got to our feet as Cynthia and *Steve*, came around to the side of the house. He had his arm around her waist.

"Ah! There you are!" he called jovially. "Sorry we're late, but dear Cynthia was just,"—his eyes glinted with mirth—"so... *insatiable* this afternoon!" He looked down at her and squeezed her into his side. "You're such a minx!"

She was looking up at him, smiling.

But there was something odd about Cynthia's smile. It was the sort of smile you see on those princesses at Disney World; they're happy to be there because they're actresses and they're *supposed* to smile. A fake plastic smile? Not exactly—more like a "it comes with the job" kind of smile. With about as much joy and happiness behind it as you have changing a tampon. More "eewww" than "ooooh," that's for sure.

There was no jealousy on my part, let me tell you. Despite coming close to hopping in bed with him on more than one occasion, the idea of doing the horizontal rumba with Little Stevie Murphy was now about as appealing as a root canal. And seeing that disturbing expression on Cynthia's face was unnerving.

MJ nudged me and whispered, "Looks like Cynthia's trying to seal the pregnancy deal." Her eyebrows bobbed up and down. "You got to give Steve credit; he makes wonderful babies, judging by how Byron turned out as a kid."

The three of us stood there as he approached with a shit-eating grin plastered on his face. Before I could say a word, Mary-Jane said, "Sorry, Steve, this is a girl's-only thing today. Thanks for giving Cynthia a lift, but I'm afraid you'll have to leave."

He paused and hooked his thumbs in the pockets of his jeans, squinting a little as his gaze drifted past Mary-Jane to the lake and our Beltane decorations. "Well, y'see, that's the thing, MJ. Maybe it's time you gals were more inclusive. That's the buzzword these days. It's all about being inclusive."

Oh, for shit's sake! My teeth clenched as I strode over to him. But as soon as his gaze locked with mine, my mouth opened, and the diatribe I wanted to hit him with melted. What came out was the same milquetoast that I'd mouthed in the coffee shop. "Please, Steve? We don't mean to be rude, but Mary-Jane is right. This is just for us—"

"Get the hell out of here, Steve!" Libby bellowed, coming to my aid when she stepped over to my side. "They tried to be nice, but believe me, I'm not. You came in your truck, right?" When he nodded, she said, "Then get back in your truck, and get off this property, or we'll call the police and have you charged with trespassing."

Steve smiled at Libby like she'd paid him a compliment instead of the threat she's just yelled. "No. I don't think that's going to happen. Frankly, you surprise me, Libby. I really thought you'd be my biggest ally."

"Ally? In what?"

"You don't realize? C'mon, you're just playing dumb now."

"What the hell are you talking about?"

He let out a sigh. "Oh, Libby, I gave you too much credit. I mean these other bimbos are ditzy; I'll grant you that. But you?" He chuckled. "I imagined you'd put two and two together, like that!" He added with a snap of his fingers. When she continued to stare at him blankly, he said, "I *did,* after all, send you that memo, by courier even."

Like a cobra, he held Libby's gaze as she stood still, staring at him.

"What memo?" I asked.

With a careless wave in my direction, he said to Libby, "I know all about your worries about your problems at work and your kids' well-being. So why so nasty when I'm offering you freedom from your problems?"

"You...*you* wrote that letter?" she replied.

Steve nodded, a prim smile on his mouth.

What the hell? My eyes felt like they would pop right out of my head as his words sank in. "You? You wrote the letter to Libby? *You're* the witch?" The last word came out kind of as a high-pitched squeak.

"The correct term is warlock, you fool."

Mary-Jane spun to face him. "What? That can't be! What the hell is going on?" She practically leapt with her hand outstretched to touch him. Releasing his grip on Cynthia, he sidestepped out of the way, letting out a chortle as her arms windmilled, caught off-balance with her toes caught in the furrow in the grass.

Cynthia gave her head a few quick shakes, like someone who had just woken up, and darted to MJ's side, steadying her. "It's no use trying to read him, MJ. He's more powerful than any of us. I'm sorry. I wanted to tell you but—"

"Enough! This is *my* tale to tell, Cynthia." Steve flicked his fingers at Cynthia and MJ. Immediately, they both bounced back, letting out yelps of pain and surprise when they landed.

I started to go over to them, but Steve said, "Nuh-uh, Shannon." He made an odd gesture with his hand, and my feet were glued to the lawn.

Holy shit. Try as I might, I couldn't pick up either of my feet. He'd done all this—freezing me in place, dropping Cynthia and MJ to the ground with a flick of his fingers! The look on MJ's face mirrored the same shock that froze me to the spot. If he could do that to them, what else could he do?

Still holding his hand in that strange gesture, anchoring me in place. In the calmest of voices, he continued. "This is a takeover, Shannon. I tried doing it friendly with you, but that didn't work out, sadly. So it's a hostile one. But I'm taking over from you."

Why did he want to control our coven if he was already so powerful? Oh damn. It wasn't just taking over the coven; he wanted control of the well. Of course.

Libby rushed over to help Cynthia and MJ, snarling at Steve, "You got another think coming if you think I want anything to do with you, jerk face! I could be homeless and I'd still hate you. You're nothing but a—"

"Whatever." Steve brushed past me, taking a step to get a better view of the yard. "I see you decorated for Beltane. That's good, but the celebration will not take place here." He turned and stepped close to me. "We all know where it needs to be done, don't we, Shannon?"

Before I turned to face him, Cynthia shouted, "Don't look at him, Shannon! That's how he's controlling things, with his eyes." Just in the nick of time, I stopped, and my gaze swept over to where my three friends stood.

It was odd, but peering at Libby, MJ, and Cynthia emboldened me. Steve might be powerful, but there were four of us. "You will never, ever be part of us, Steve. And hell will freeze over before I allow you *anywhere* near that well."

There was a cool touch on my cheek, and my aunt's voice whispered close to my ear. "Stay strong, Shannon. White magic is more powerful than his. Each of you, but together, can prevail. Just as the well has always commanded, support each other in your coven."

"You will OBEY me!" Steve roared. An icy pressure enveloped my face like a freezing mask. It pushed my head around, facing Steve. I couldn't even shut my eyes. I kept them averted as he drew close to me. "Look at meeee..." he hissed, now pulling at my chin with his hand.

Instead, I crossed my eyes, probably looking like a lunatic version of Homer Simpson. But hey, it worked. He could control my body, but not my mouth. "Why are you doing this? You know I will never bring you to the well. And you can't get to it without me." The words were garbled as I fought for control of my jaw, caught in his viselike power. It hurt like hell, but I couldn't give in. No way was I falling under some kind of spell so that my real intent and words got trapped in my head.

Mary-Jane's shock was clear in her soft voice: "I trusted you, Steve. I *defended* you! All the while it was you behind me getting arrested! You're behind the problems between Ray and me! How could you? Why are you doing this? I feel like I don't even *know* you."

"Oh, sweet Mary-Jane. You don't know me." He let out a wild laugh. "But you will."

THIRTY

Steve let me go and turned to where the others were grouped on the ground. When MJ started to get up, he snarled, "No." Flicking his fingers again, my friends plopped onto their behinds, looking up at him.

His voice took on a sickeningly sweet tone, like a TV preacher asking for donations. "I was always Seth's kid brother—the one everyone tolerated because they adored Seth."

"Seth was everything you weren't!" Libby spat out. "Part-time job after school, straight A's—"

"I know! Believe me! Everybody loved Seth!"

"And you were always a sniveling, little brat acting like the world owed you something!"

Shit, I forgot about that. How many bonfires or softball games over the years had I been at when Seth's car would pull up, and everyone breathed a sigh of relief that Stevie wasn't with him? How the hell did I have memories of him being such a great kid? He was a... a *punk,* as they would say in Philly.

His back was to me as he faced down Libby. The memories flooded in. The genuine memories. Little Stevie Murphy getting caught Peeping Tom'ing through the bathroom window at Libby's house at a slumber party. It outraged Libby that night. She would have killed him back then if it wasn't for the fact that Seth was his brother.

The little perv.

I had completely forgotten about all that! Seeing the look of disgust on MJ's face, her memories of this guy must have come back all at once as well.

"Holy shit!" MJ yelled at him. "I just remembered! You took those kids' candy that Halloween!" She was shaking her head in wonder. "And not just that! You were getting caught up in all sorts of stuff as a kid! How the hell did I forget all about that?" she asked aloud.

"He glamoured all of us, hon," Cynthia said. "The whole damn town!"

"That's right, bitch. The whole damn town loooves Stevie Murphy now, don't they? They remember me getting kittens out of trees, shoveling old people's walkways in the winter, buying other kids ice cream in the summer..." He laughed. "That Stevie Murphy grew up to be one hell of a good man, eh?"

He pointed at Cynthia. "You couldn't *wait* to hop into the sack with me, could you, Cynthia? All I had to do was crook my finger at you and you came running like the bitch in heat you are." He looked over his shoulder at me. "She's just the warm-up for the magnificent prize; *you*, Shannon. You'll have to change the sheets in the morning when I'm finished with you, babe."

Oh God. I wanted to throw up. Doing it with Stevie Murphy? Shit, I'd join a convent first!

"In fact," he said, turning back toward me, "I think I'll just have a bit of a sample squeeze right now."

I watched over his shoulder as MJ, Libby, and Cynthia all got to their feet. There were too many of us. He wasn't strong enough to keep all of us at bay! To keep his attention as the others spread out behind him, I thrust out my chest. "Just try to touch 'em, you bastard. Just try."

Libby edged away from MJ and Cynthia, her eyes focused on the forest at the side of the yard. I had no idea what she was up to until she turned suddenly to face Steve. Her arm shot out, pointing at him. "This is for Robert!"

An arc of light flashed from her fingertips, and Steve stumbled to the side. But he quickly caught himself. Like a striking viper, he reached out and clutched at Mary Jane. "You want to touch me, you bitch? Want to read me? Here I am!" he grunted. He wrapped a hand around her throat and spun around, facing all of us. "You're going to watch each of your stupid friends suffer," he growled into her ear.

My gaze darted to Cynthia, and our eyes met. I screamed inside my head, *Move away from him! He can't fight all of us at once!* Relief inched into my chest, seeing her pull back from Steve and Mary-Jane. Thank the goddess she'd picked up on my thought. Steve's power over Cynthia was dead. As well as over me. I could move with no problem now as we formed an arc around him and MJ.

Steve's face roiled with rage as he glared at Libby. "That's the best you can do? Send out a puff of energy that you think will stop me?" His hand lifted from MJ's stomach, and a rippling wave of gray energy shot across the yard at Libby.

All the while, MJ caught in his viselike grip, struggled to breathe, her face turning a darker shade. My own steaming anger was reaching the boiling point. Time slowed, the seconds drawn out like stretched taffy. Libby grunted when the wave of dark energy pounded her, jettisoning her into the air to land ten feet away.

Cynthia's chin dropped. A stray branch on the lawn spun through the air, striking Steve behind his knees. His grip on MJ loosened, and she fell to the side at the exact moment Steve's legs gave out.

Power burst from every cell in my body, sparking down my legs, through my feet, into the earth. A loud crack rented the air, and the ground under Steve opened up. What had been a furrow in the grass was now a crevice in the earth, twenty feet long. His hands grasped at nothing as he tumbled in, screaming in terror.

I gasped. My body tingled painfully as I tried to catch my breath and stay on my feet. Holy shit, I did it again!

From the trench, Steve's voice bellowed with rage. A numbing wonder gripped me as a thought came through my consciousness: *Well, I didn't kill him, did I?*

The three of us gathered at the edge of the trench and gazed down at the crack in the earth that was easily fifteen feet deep. Below me, Steve clung to a tree root, his feet dangling a few feet above a mud-covered, jagged rock. Streaks of brown soil creased his forehead, while his eyes were white rimmed, staring up at me.

"How? How d'you do that? Help me, Shannon!" His other hand reached up to grab the tree root but missed, leaving him clinging with one white-knuckled hand.

I squatted down, about to extend an arm, but then something barreled into me. Once again, I was knocked on my ass. Son of a bitch!

THIRTY ONE

"You can't look into his eyes, Shannon! Stop it!" Cynthia stared down at me and then reached to help me up. "How do you think he could control me yesterday? It's dark magic, and it's powerful."

By this time, Libby was at MJ's side, examining her neck. "You're going to be okay, MJ. You're badly bruised, but that's all." She took her hands. "Can you stand?"

The four of us, no. Correction *five*—Aunt Maeve floated next to me—stared down at Steve, carefully avoiding looking into his eyes. His feet flailed in the air, trying to get a toehold in the sheer sides, but kept slipping against the muddy walls.

Holy shit. Holy freaking shit. I made an *earthquake!*

Mary-Jane gasped out gravelly words as she held her hand to her throat. "You rotten bastard! You tried to kill me. And Libby. You were a strange, bratty kid, and you grew up to be a goddamn psycho!

***

Mary-Jane

As I watched Cynthia, the spiking hurt in my throat eased. She squatted down on her haunches, looking at each of us in turn. "I hated seeing any of you while I was under Steve's spell. I couldn't warn you, but that doesn't mean I wasn't desperately searching for his weakness." Her eyes narrowed as she nonchalantly dropped a handful of loose dirt down onto Steve's head. At his sputtering curses, she smiled.

"It's not fun being victimized, is it, Stevie? You're hanging by a thread and unable to use your magic. You're trapped in the bowels of Mother Earth—the mother who came to Shannon's aid. Your dark powers can't function down there."

"You crazy bitch! When I get out of here, I'll make you pay! *Your* bowels will be strewn from the treetops for the crows to eat. All of you!"

Libby picked up the stick that had caught Steve behind his knees. She jabbed at his ivory knuckles a few times. "Shut up, Steve. Real witches are talking now."

Smirking, Cynthia continued, "Stevie's not only a flash in the pan sexually, he's like that with magic." Her hands rose, fluttering her fingers. "He puts on a big, impressive show with all his power, but he can't sustain it. And he's got a one-track mind, only able to tackle one thing at a time."

She looked at Shannon. "You picked up on that. He didn't stand a chance once we came at him from different directions."

"Duh!" I replied. "We're women! Multitasking's in our genes!" I croaked a giggle. Almost manically, but still—it was kinda funny.

Shannon replied, "To tell the truth, it wasn't me. Aunt Maeve helped me with that little insight about all of us taking him on at once."

The last penny dropped in my head. "That's why he wants the well. He needs the boost, to sustain his power." But something else niggled in the back of my mind. "But why is he after more power? He's got a pleasant home, a good business, and a great kid. What else does he want?"

Shannon weighed in. "It's greed. People like him will never have enough. Plus, there's that overblown ego. It wasn't enough to ask to work with us. He had to control us, be the boss, the *man*."

Cynthia brushed the dust from her fingertips and sat back onto the grass. "Oh, it's even worse than that, Shannon. In his warped little mind, he thought he'd have his personal harem of witches. There's me wanting a baby. Then, creating problems between Ray and MJ, she was supposed to turn to Stevie. He thought he could win Libby over, and, of course, he's always crushed *majorly* on you." She nodded. "Yeah, his *ego* is ginormous. But,"—she held up her thumb with her index finger spread just a little bit, and with a cackle... yeah, a cackle, she added, "not his *dick*!"

But my mind was still reeling from what he'd planned for me. He was no friend to Ray. It was thanks to Steve that Ray and I were arguing. There was no doubt in my mind that he was behind that bogus DUI charge.

Cynthia started up again. "Y'know? When I dated him a couple of years ago, he wasn't like this. Sure, he's always been sexist as hell, but he wasn't totally warped by dark magic. I would have known. I think his descent into the dark side is something more recent."

"But he admitted to following my aunt and your grandmother when they were doing Esbat. He's been into witchcraft for a long time." Shannon looked off to the side silently for a few moments. "Aunt Maeve thinks it was when he moved into that house. Do you guys remember Alan Thornton? He was the old guy who lived there before Steve. She said he was a nasty recluse."

From the bowels of the earth, Steve yelled, "You bitches don't know what you're talking about! Get me out of here!"

Ignoring Steve's outburst, I looked over at Shannon. She'd hit a nerve when she'd mentioned old Thornton's name. "He was a creepy guy. The odd time I'd see him in a store or on the street. I always gave him a wide berth. I thought he might be some kind of sexual predator."

But as soon as the words were out, I realized that the bad vibes I had picked up were black arts. That had to be it. And Steve had bought his house when the old reprobate died.

Libby looked to the side, thinking before she commented, "When Steve moved into that cabin and started remodeling it, Amy left him. We always thought it was because she'd come out of the closet, meeting and falling in love with Suzanne. But maybe moving to that house did it?"

Old Man Thornton practicing dark arts in that ramshackle cabin? If Steve was curious about magic and witchcraft trailing Shannon's aunt, then maybe he'd been drawn to the place. At the very least, he'd be close to that glade in the forest where he knew Maeve went. Drawn to the Witching Well, even though he'd never been invited to visit it. These fleeting thoughts were interrupted when Steve yelled once more.

"Hey! Let me up, or I'm going to tell everyone about you bitches. I'll ruin each one of you if you don't get me out of this pit!"

I edged closer to the rim of the hole and peeked over, keeping my gaze on his shoulders and avoiding his eyes. He waved his free hand, clutching a cell phone, while a maniacal sneer flashed on his lips. My chest tightened as I watched him. He might be trapped, but he was still fighting.

"It's all here... on my phone. My email to Ray, and Stan, and Devon. Even that stupid fireman you're so hot for, Cynthia. They're all going to know what kind of women you are—that you four are witches! I followed you the last time you went into the forest. Hell! I've got evidence. Photos and recordings of you in your witchy robes. Too bad they don't burn witches anymore, but you'll still be ruined. Let me out, or I'm sending the email."

My gaze flew to Libby and Shannon, all of us dumbstruck with Steve's latest threat. Even Cynthia's eyebrows were pinched together.

If Ray found out I was out here casting spells and hexes, dabbling in magic, he'd be shocked before he totally blew a gasket. He'd be angrier than he already was. If he knew the truth of our weekly meetings, he might even leave me!

And then there was Chloe. If she thought the teasing about her mother getting a DUI charge was awful, wait till everyone found out I was a witch. Her life would be in shambles.

Steve chortled. "Okay. You've had your fun. Now let me up, or I'm hitting the button to send it with the photos." Even though he tried to sound like he was holding all the cards and not just that root from the tree, there was a hint of fear in his voice as well.

Libby was the first to speak. "I don't know about you three, but there's no way I'm going to be blackmailed by this loser. My kids might be shocked at first, but they love me. And if Stan leaves, well, his loss." Her mouth was set in a firm line, her eyes flinty when she peered at each one of us.

Cynthia rolled her eyes. "Most of the town hates me now. Well, at least the women do—not like I give a shit. I say, bring it on." She shrugged before holding her hand up to give Libby a high-five.

Shannon was the next to put her hand up, fist bumping Libby and Cynthia. "Devon already thinks I'm nuts. This would just confirm it. But, y'know? Who the hell really cares? I've got you three and my aunt on my side. My kids... well, I'm like Libby. They'll survive this. Although Thomas is going to freak." She laughed. "That'll be a sight to see when he does! I'm thinking of Will Ferrell in that *Bewitched* movie!"

That left me. Each of them turned to me, watching. My heart hammered fast in my chest before I took a deep breath. Really, what choice did I have? Word would get out, and the chips would fall where they fell.

Screw it. All for one and one for all and all that jazz.

"Do your worst, Steve. You're still an asshole!" I joined my hand with theirs, my sisters in the coven.

"I'LL KILL YOU ALL!" His voice was a roar. "I'll drink the blood of your children as you watch! OBEY MEE!"

The absolute *evil* that spewed out of him was frightening. I backed up a couple of steps, along with Cynthia and Shannon.

But Libby stood her ground. She put her hands on her hips and leaned over. "Yeah, tough guy. Dime a dozen in the ER on a Saturday night, you creep. Now, shut the hell up."

"You'll die first! I'll..." He kept up his rant and started cursing a blue streak. The air was filled with the most vile, evil diatribe I had ever heard. I like horror movies, but this was real life. Steve was scaring the hell out of me.

But not Libby. She just waited him out. And as soon as he stopped to catch his breath, she said, "My turn." She pointed at him and said:

"As long as you are in that pit
Your lips will now be completely
zipped!"

And silence descended.

"So there!" Libby said, brushing her hands and turning to us. "Yeah, yeah, my rhyming sucks, but it worked, okay?"

The three of us stared at her in stunned silence.

Note to self. Don't screw with a nurse. The force is strong in them.

It was at that moment that a spine-tingling howl filled the surrounding air. I jerked straight up, and my fingers clutched the grass. What the hell? As awful as nails creaking over a blackboard, the sound made the hair on the back of my neck spike.

And was sooo wonderfully familiar!

"Robert!" Libby jumped to her feet. She raced across the lawn to the forest, calling over her shoulder, "Oh wow! Robert! He's back!"

THIRTY TWO

Shannon

My heart stopped at the high-pitched yowl. I knew that screech! Could it be? For a moment I barely dared to breathe, but when Libby clambered past me, I was right behind her, both of us flying to the wooded edge of my land.

When the mottled, one-eared beast stepped out from behind a giant oak, tears filled my eyes. "Robert. Oh my stars and moons, my wonderful cat. You're back!" I stopped, collapsing to my knees when we locked eyes.

He kept his gaze on me as Libby sank down on her knees to hug him. His ear twitched while his eyes blinked slowly, the golden orbs rimmed in white practically glowing as he stared at me.

Libby pulled back and her head turned to face me, tears streaming down her cheeks. "He's alive, Shannon! Praise the goddess, he's returned."

I buried my tears in his fur, hugging the bobcat like I wouldn't let go. Ever. I felt his rumbling purr beneath my fingers, smelled the scent of the forest in his fur. "Robert. I missed you so much!"

I've had pets before. In Philly we had a couple of dogs and one cat for a time. Our last dog, Major, was *my* dog in that he latched onto me; everyone else in the house was the supporting cast in his eyes. When I would leave the house, he would sit by the front door, waiting for my return. Even if it was to just dash out for a gallon of milk, when I came back it was like he had yearned for me for years. Covering me with love and licks when I returned like a sailor from an ocean voyage. When he grew too old and his time was done, I cried for months and months; I never got another pet after Major; the pain of letting go was well, brutal for me. Him leaving my life hurt in that single special part in our heart that only a loyal pet could access.

Until Robert. I'll never stop loving and honoring Major. But this mangy bobcat, with his chewed off ear and crappy superior attitude, had moved into my heart, stretched out on the most comfortable furniture, and had become an important piece of the puzzle that is my life.

Just thinking about him, even as I held him in my arms, made me cry even more.

Stupid bobcat.

"I missed you oh so much, Robert!" I sobbed into his fur. "You stupid cat! Don't you ever do that again to me!" How can you love someone so much you want to kill them? I don't have a clue, but that's pretty much how I felt.

Libby laughed. "He missed you too! Can't you feel it? It's coming off him in waves!"

MJ and Cynthia crowded in, all of us stroking the big cat's fur and cooing at him. He let out another yowl and shook us free. My mouth dropped open as he crouched lower, stalking slowly away from us to the edge of the crevice where Steve was. His ear flattened against his head, and loud snarls followed.

Libby stood up, extending her hand to help me up. "C'mon. It looks like Robert has some unfinished business with Steve. We'd better get over there before your bobcat kills him."

As I followed Robert, I was still in a state of shock, swiping tears and snot from my face with the cuff of my sweatshirt. But seeing Robert's stumpy tail twitch sharply and the fur on his spine spike, I picked up my pace. Even if Steve deserved to face the cat he'd tried to murder. The last thing I needed was Robert falling into that hole.

I kneeled on one side of the cat, while Libby was on the other, both of us gripping Robert's fur. It wasn't hard to get a handful with the way it was puffed out around his neck and along his back. "Easy, Robert. He isn't worth risking your neck to take a piece out of him."

The bobcat let out another screech before his lips drew back, exposing long, sharp teeth. He looked over at Libby, continuing his caterwauling.

He was doing it again. He was saying something to Libby that he wanted passed on.

As I waited, my gaze fell to Steve. He had managed to get himself down to the bottom of the pit. He was covered in mud from his face to his feet; he must have slid down the wall. I squinted, trying to get a better look at the dark stain in the crotch of his jeans. Had he pissed himself? From the white face and eyes that looked like they'd pop any second, it sure looked like it.

I probably would, too, if I had an enraged bobcat snarling at me the way Robert was.

I looked up at Libby. "What's he saying?"

"I'm not getting all of it," she said. "I *think* he's swearing like a sailor, but I don't understand the language." Robert stopped his snarls, shot Libby a look, and gave a couple of screeches before turning his attention back to the pit.

"Oh! Well, that makes sense!"

"What did he just say?" I asked.

Libby snorted. "He said he's using his native tongue for Steve. Humans don't need to hear such"—she laughed lightly— "imprecations. That's the word he gave me, and I don't even know what it means!"

Steve stood silently, taking the bobcat abuse. But what the hell could he do? He couldn't even reply because of Libby's spell cast on him.

Finally, Robert went silent. He stood up and edged to the rim of the shaft. Raising one leg like a German shepherd, he relieved himself over Steve. The guy couldn't say a word, but the sputtering and wheezing as he jumped out of the way only to land face-first on the bottom was priceless. Looked good on him.

Like a mincing little prince, Robert lowered his leg and pranced away from the edge to sit down, looking up at us. I didn't need to read his mind. His expression was plain as day: *"Well, what do you think of THAT?"*

"Good job, Robert," I said. "Damn fine job."

MJ peered over the edge, keeping an eye on Steve. She gave voice to a thought that had crossed my mind earlier: "What are we going to do about this asshole? Is there a spell we can do that will neutralize him, erase all this and his magic from his memory? We can't just leave him in there." She tilted her head. "Right? I mean, or can we?"

Cynthia stepped up beside her. "Why not? I think he looks good in that pit. Maybe we can build a trapdoor over the hole and let him suffer. It's a suitable spot for rats like him." Again, Cynthia tossed in a few pebbles, letting them fall on Steve's head.

Aunt Maeve once more materialized above the crevice. She stared into my eyes. *"What you put out into the world will come back to you with the power of three, Shannon. You must show mercy to your enemies, but you also have to stop him. His magic is twisted and dark."*

Little did I know it would be Robert who would have the solution about what to do about Steve. Libby reached over and tapped my arm. "Robert knows all about Steve. Your familiar has battled many times against dark magic. That's how he lost his ear."

"What?" I looked over at him. "What do you mean?"

He let out a few grunts and bobcat sort of meows.

"He's got some stuff to tell us," Libby said. "I'll translate, as usual."

You won't believe this, but bobcats can clear their throats. Robert made a sort of *ahem* sound and began...

As Robert stared at me and began, Libby spoke at the same time. But in my mind I heard, really heard, Robert's voice. *"I have been the familiar to the keeper of the waters for as long as I can recall."* He looked up at me, holding my eyes in his gaze. *"You are the latest of a long line of water keepers."* He turned his head in the well's direction. *"In the past it was a bubbling spring, looked after by generations of the shamans of the Esopus people."*

"Do you mean Native Americans?"

He dipped his head slowly. *"Yes. After the white man expelled them from the land, I slept, I think. I have no recollection of the time that passed until Alice Johnston arrived."*

"That was 1901 or so," I said.

Robert gave his head a shake. *"Your time is meaningless to my kind. For me, the era of Alice Johnston was but a moment ago."* He tilted his head at me. *"But dear Alice was not the only one of her kind. Her mate, was also magical. Like that beast in that pit, he quickly became enamored of magic, and wished to control it for his own selfish ends."*

Beast. A wild animal just referred to Steve Murphy as a beast. "You sure got that right," I said.

"Damn right," Cynthia added.

We quieted our chatter as soon as Robert resumed his tale.

"Alice banished her mate. But mark me"—he cocked his head at us— *"they lived apart, no longer mates. He wished her to die, but could not bring himself to do her harm. Nor her him. Just as light needs the darkness to keep at bay, as the Earth itself needs dark clouds above to restore itself, Alice and her mate went about their own lives, as the moon*

spins over the Earth, or the Earth dances around the sun itself...keeping the balance of the universe."

"Alice built the well over the spring, but glamoured it so that none but those invited could behold it or partake of its gifts."

Robert stopped suddenly and jerked to his feet, looking past me.

"Hello, my dearest Maeve! 'Tis good to see you!"

I spun around to see Maeve's spirit hover.

"It's been a time, no?" she said. She was in a much, much younger form now. A young woman, younger than even Cynthia—a lithe lass of bygone times. She wafted over to Robert, and I watched her crouch down and hold him. "I've always wanted a familiar, but you never revealed yourself to me. Even so, I knew you were there."

He nodded. *"Always watching, always protecting, yes."*

Maeve's spirit turned to me and back to Robert. "Why did you reveal yourself to her then?"

He barked a laugh. Yeah, bobcats can laugh. It's a weird sound—a high-pitched grunt. I didn't need to see Libby's mirthful look to know he was laughing.

At me. I had the realization that he's laughed at me before.

He kept his eyes on me as he spoke to Maeve's spirit. *"Two reasons, actually. First and foremost... she* really *needs assistance. You took to the white arts with an elegance I haven't seen in ages. Far more than Shannon."*

Maeve gave a little smirk. "Why, thank you, Robert!"

"Thanks a lot, Robert! Like I don't feel enough like an idiot?"

"But... there's something about Shannon." His eyes focused on me. *"She started off as awkward as a newborn fawn."* He slowly blinked and looked over at MJ, Cynthia, and Libby. *"And brought her coven together much, much too soon. They're all so immature."*

Libby blanched. "Hey! That's not fair! We're doing the best we can, y'know! How about *you* try waking up in the morning thinking you're in hell only to realize it's just another damn hot flash!" When Robert shot her a look, along with another series of grunts and hisses, her face lightened. She tilted her head at him. "Well, in that case, okay, I guess. It still stung though."

"What'd he say?" I asked.

With a huff, Libby said, "He said despite our shortcomings, our progress is amazing. He's never seen a coven come together and reach the truth about itself together as well as we have." Robert grunt-hissed at her some more, and she continued, "And he's very proud of us."

Robert continued, and Libby went back to her role as UN translator.

"At the same time as needing me so acutely, Shannon is true hearted, and has powers unmatched, in my experience." He pointed with his chin at the gouge in the earth. *"I've heard of such power, but I've never witnessed it."* He looked up at me. *"I am the familiar to a legendary witch, Maeve. Legendary."*

So, yeah, I smirked at Maeve. "Legendary." I shimmied my shoulders. "I sure like the sound of that!"

Maeve nodded to me. "Yes, I think he's right." She turned back to Robert. "We've only just met, yet now I must bid you fare-thee-well."

Robert snuggled into her, distracted from his tale, and purred and mewled as Maeve stroked his fur. "You'll be as good to Shannon, as you were to me, won't you?" she cooed at him.

"Of course. She's coming along nicely," Libby translated. "I assume Maeve's making an appearance, Shannon? I can't see her, but I feel a glow of energy from Robert."

"Yeah. She's here, finally able to talk to him."

Robert dropped his head, showing respect for my aunt. *"A remarkable bloodline,"* he said in a gentle purr. *"But her time has passed."* He lifted his head. *"Now, you have work to do. Just as Alice Johnston's mate remained in the area, he passed his powers on as well. That beast over there"*—he pointed to the pit where Steve was—*"is a twisted one. Alice's mate passed his knowledge onto a man named Thornton, who then built that home over beside this lake. But Thornton became darker and darker over time. And that beast... he* relishes *the darkness. His power has become too strong and must be diminished."*

He then proceeded to make a series of yowls and grunts. Libby was silent, taking it all in until he grew quiet again. I asked her, "What else did Robert say?"

"Robert and Old Man Thornton got into a huge fight many years ago. That's how Robert lost the chunk from his ear—the bastard set a bear trap that almost worked! When the old guy died, that was the end of it. But Steve bought the old shack, and the dark energy surfaced again. It was always there, ready to flare up, when the right person showed up. Steve with his interest in witchcraft *was* that person."

My gaze dropped to the side as I thought about what she'd said. Well, actually, what Robert had said through her. I stroked Robert's neck, directing my question at him. "Steve rebuilt that house. He told me everything was brand new except for the original stone fireplace."

Robert's head turned, and he blinked slowly, looking into my eyes—the only way he'd ever been able to say yes when I'd tried talking to him.

"The fireplace?" My mouth fell open, picturing the large fieldstone structure. Oh my good goddess! "Whatever evil energy the old man brewed up is *there*? But how? I don't understand how that's possible."

Cynthia scoffed. "Yet you have no problem believing that the well is a repository of power? It's white magic, but magic nonetheless. So why wouldn't that old geezer's juju be lingering on in that fireplace, just ready for some warlock to tap into?"

"If that's the case, we need to destroy that fireplace and end that dark magic."

"Hang on, you guys!" Libby said when Robert started growling again.

"It's not the entire fireplace. You will find a black stone of shungite in it. Either the keystone of the mantle, or in the center of the fireplace's hearth floor. Get that shungite away and break it. Failing that, throw it into the lake—water shall keep its power at bay." He gestured with his snout to Steve's pit. *"He'll no longer be a threat if you succeed."*

"Okay, got it." Libby leaned over the edge of the split in the earth. "But what about him? His power source would be gone, but he's still hanging around. Literally. He still has some power, and he'll always be after ours. We need to put a strong restraining spell on him or erase his memory of everything he's done."

Maeve hovered behind Robert, shaking her head. I noticed the look of alarm in her eyes as she stared at Libby. *"This is where it gets really tricky, Shannon,"* sounded in my head.

I rolled my eyes. "What happened before was no cakewalk, Aunt Maeve! MJ was almost strangled to death; Libby was hurled about ten feet into the air, and Cynthia... well, you know what he did to her."

"You talking to Maeve?" MJ croaked quietly. When I nodded, she said, "Steve was no cakewalk for you either, Shannon! He had to have put some kind of spell or mind control on you so that you'd be nice to him. Remember in the coffee shop when you really wanted to slam him?"

My eyes closed as I thought of how I'd been with Devon after spending time with Steve. I'd been sick to my stomach whenever I was around Devon. Steve had done that as well. He'd worked on each of us.

"What are you gonna do about Steve?" Cynthia pulled me back to the burning question.

I pushed myself up and stood there, peering down at Steve. There was another consideration. Steve's son, Byron. As angry as I was with Steve, I had to consider my decision carefully. "Libby is right. We need to destroy the fireplace in Steve's house. But I'm not leaving him alone here to try any tricks. I'm staying to keep an eye on him."

When the other three stood up, Mary-Jane peered over at me. "You're going to be okay here alone with that monster?"

My smile was tight as I rubbed Robert's mangled ear. "I'm not alone. I've got my familiar again. And Aunt Maeve. You go, find and tear that obsidian stone apart. Destroy it. I need time to think about what we're going to do about Steve."

THIRTY THREE

Libby

Breaking into Steve's house was the easiest part. Cynthia managed that with just a snap of her thumb and forefinger, making the deadbolt slide back and the door pop open.

Mary-Jane shifted the sledgehammer to her other hand, mumbling, "Wouldn't it be easier to destroy the fireplace with magic? I mean, you're good at getting objects to move, Cynthia, and Shannon can create an earthquake, so why are we slogging it out with all these tools?"

As I followed Cynthia into the entryway, I wondered that myself as I toted the pail with hammers, chisels, and safety goggles. It would also be faster so that Shannon wouldn't be left alone with that maniac.

Cynthia turned and shook her head at MJ. "If that fireplace is the seat of dark magic, there's no way I'm using my own magic to tamper with it. If I lost, it would have dire consequences for me, for sure, but also for the rest of us. No, ladies, we have to do this the conventional way. Even then, the force in that spot is going to resist us with every ounce of power it can muster."

A chill went down my spine as I followed Cynthia into the kitchen. I couldn't help but notice how modern and well appointed the work in the spacious room was. But the fact that Steve had been drawn to this spot and did all these renovations was because of the dark energy present made it feel obscene rather than homey.

The atmosphere was oppressive in its silence, weighing on me.

"Before we start this, should we do something to protect ourselves?" I directed the question at Cynthia, but it was MJ who answered me.

"I have it covered. I grabbed Shannon's bundle of sage and sweetgrass. We'll burn it and do a cleansing before we start swinging hammers." She set the sledgehammer down and pulled the dried bundle of herbs from the back pocket of her jeans.

"Good thinking, MJ." Cynthia took the bundle from MJ and lit it, sending a spiral of blue smoke from the orange tips.

In no time, she performed a blessing ceremony on me and MJ, who took the smoldering bundle and did her. I'll be honest, I didn't feel any different body-wise, but I felt a stronger sense of purpose to the task at hand.

When she was finished, MJ said, "Let's leave this burning as we work. I got a feeling we're going to need all the help we can get on this job." She grabbed a saucer from the cupboard. She looked at the rest of us before nodding to the living room and fireplace. "You guys ready to do this?"

"Can I say 'no'?" I asked. "I mean, when I was about to have my first baby, the nurse asked if I was ready. I told her no...so...?" I made a stupid toothy grin.

"So did I," MJ said. Tilting her head at me, she added, "And what did the nurse reply?"

I dropped my head. "Same thing I say to patients today... 'Too late!'"

"Let's go, guys," Cynthia said. "Duty calls."

"Still don't wanna...," I said, trailing them.

When I stepped into the living room, I ignored everything, my gaze focusing on the fireplace that dominated the longest wall. You could tell at a glance that it was older than the rest of the house. The stones were mottled and flaked with age, and the mortar joints were corroded with gaps. A rough-hewn log embedded above the arched opening of the hearth served as the mantle.

My eyes were drawn to the arched opening. At the center of the arch was a smooth black stone, practically gemlike in appearance, reflective as glass. It glinted at us, almost in defiance.

Cynthia murmured as she stepped forward to clear the items from the mantle. "Even with the protection cleansing, my stomach is feeling this. It's all I can do to keep from throwing up."

As soon as the words were out of her mouth, I felt my stomach roll. "Oh yeah, we found the damn thing, didn't we?"

"Damn thing's the right word, fershure," MJ said. She held the sledgehammer out like it was a baseball bat. Her first swing clanged against the black keystone and bounced back so hard it swung her around. "Ow!" She dropped the hammer and blew on her fingers. "That hurt me more than that rock!" She winced as she flexed her hand.

She was right. Despite being hit with a sledgehammer, there wasn't a mark on the damn thing. Oh boy.

"Hang on!" Cynthia strode out of the room to the kitchen. I could hear her slamming cupboard doors. She returned with a box of table salt. "This will lessen its power."

She rubbed a handful of salt on the rock's surface. It could have been my imagination, but I could have sworn I heard a hiss and crackle as she massaged the surface. Whatever. It felt like it was working. Even the air felt clearer when she was done.

She stepped away and grabbed a pair of safety glasses. When she was armed with a hammer in one hand and a chisel in the other, she spoke. "We need to attack the weakest part. We'll break the bonds to free this rock by going at the mortar joints holding it. Once it's free, we'll pulverize it, and if that's not possible, we'll throw it into the deepest part of the lake." She looked at me. "Help me, Libby. Mary-Jane's hurt her hand."

It was tedious work, chipping away at the mortar, but between the two of us we made fast headway, tapping and scraping the chisels into the surface. Cynthia kept whispering a chant under her breath as she hammered at the old cement.

"What are you saying?" I asked.

She paused. "Sorry. It's kind of a prayer I say when I'm scared."

"Well? You want to share it with the rest of the class, Cynthia?"

"Yeah, good idea. Sorry. I'm still getting the hang of playing witchcraft with others, I guess." She took a breath and said, "Divine Mother, dear God, power of goodness, help us."

MJ and I repeated the plea. And together, the three of us said it over and over while we worked: "Divine Mother, dear God, power of goodness, help us."

I actually think it worked, if for no other reason than my fear had lessened. Over and over, as we worked at it, all three of us chanted that mantra in unison.

At one point I missed the chisel and barked the side of my hand with the hammer. "OW!" I said, dropping my tools and rubbing my boo-boo. Damn, it hurt!

"MJ, take over! We can't stop!" Cynthia said. "Libby, grab something from the freezer and ice that right away!"

"I *am* a nurse, you know!" I countered, even though the thought hadn't occurred to me. "Thanks though." MJ was already banging away in my place as I grabbed a bag of frozen peas from Steve's freezer.

"You got it!"

No sooner were the words out of MJ's mouth than the rock tumbled out and fell onto the stone hearth with a resounding bang. My mouth fell open, seeing it shatter into four large chunks. An iron sledgehammer hadn't caused even a chip in that hard stone, yet hitting the floor had broken it?

"Eeeeewwww!" MJ cried out, jumping away from the void in the wall. Like from a hose, dried maggots and dead bugs poured out of the hollow, covering the stone's remnants like sand. A putrid stench filled the room. MJ flew to the patio door at the side and flung it open.

"Shit!" she said. "No wonder I felt sick to my stomach during all of this!"

It did not bother Cynthia in the slightest. She grabbed the sledgehammer and shoved at the four heavy stone pieces separating them from the disgusting mess. When she had them off to the side, she said, "shungite is usually a good stone for protection, but that old bastard even twisted it for his own purposes. Let's get this outside. I can't stand being in this house a minute longer."

I totally agreed. The arch of stone now looked like a six-year-old's gaping smile with a tooth missing.

Mary-Jane walked over to us with a canvas shopping bag. At my questioning look, she shrugged. "I found it in his kitchen drawer. I don't think any of us should handle that rock anymore than we have to. My gut is telling me that would be a bad thing for us."

Cynthia grabbed a poker and nudged the largest piece while Mary-Jane held the open end of the bag next to the hearth. "You aren't just a pretty face, MJ. You've read this one exactly right. This shit's got some bad juju on it."

When all chunks were inside the bag. Cynthia looked over at me. "Let's take this out to the lake side of the property. There's a flat granite stone where the dock starts. We'll set the pieces on it and destroy this evil."

Now things got strange. When we got the shards into the bag, I lifted it up. No problem, right? But the moment I stepped off the raised hearthstones, it was as if someone yanked the bag from my grasp! It fell to the living room floor with a thud.

"What the hell?" I said.

"Sorry, Libby," Cynthia said. Both of you gals have hurt your hands. I should…" She bent over and grabbed the handles of the bag. "Oof! This weighs a ton!" She pulled at the bag, yanking it about three feet from the fireplace. "What the hell? It's getting heavier?"

She tugged and pulled. But that bag wasn't going anywhere.

"Let us help, Cynth," MJ said. "Power of three and all that?"

"Fingers crossed," I replied.

The three of us pulled the bag. I don't know why, but the canvas didn't tear in the slightest. But as we got farther and farther away from the hearth, it got heavier and heavier. By the time we got to the front door, we were exhausted.

"Let's take a break," MJ said, "then we give it the ol' heave-ho." She giggled. "Heave-ho! I think some of Shannon's spell is still on me! From all the exertions, I'm feelin' kinda randy!"

"You ain't the only one, kiddo," I said. "At first I thought it was a hot flash, but to tell the truth, if Hank came through that door right now, you'd really see something."

"Well then, three's a crowd, girls," Cynthia chimed in. She peered at the fireplace. "I wonder if this is Steve and Old Man Thornton's demon at work?"

By this point, we were all sitting on our butts two feet away from the front door. I shrugged. "I don't know. Since me and Hank started getting...y'know..." I felt a blush rise on my neck.

"Getting laid!" MJ said. "It's okay, Libby—no virgins here!" She giggled. "Shannon's back at her place!"

I spluttered. She was kind of right, though.

"Yeah," Cynthia said. "Poor Shannon. The last time she was in the sack with a guy, I think it was her ex before he walked out on her!" She shook her head in wonder. That's more than a year now, isn't it? No way. I can't remember the last time I went that long without doing some guy!"

"Yeah, more than a year for poor Shannon," MJ said. "No wonder she's so cranky!" We all burst into laughter.

I couldn't believe what came out of my mouth. "Well, I'll gift her my vibrator collection to get her through this dry spell!" My hand flew to my mouth. Did I just say that? Me?

"Ewwww! Libby! Used vibrators? Eeeeew!"

Cynthia stuck her hand out between the three of us. "Let's make a pact, just us three. Let's get Shannon laid, the sooner the better!"

"Deal!" MJ put her hand on top of Cynthia's, and I put my hand over hers. We pumped our hands three times. "One! Two! Three! Sex!" we cried out and broke our little circle.

Cynthia got to her feet. "Let's finish this damn job guys!"

The work was just as murderous, those last few feet. It was like pulling a car that had no wheels. We groaned and snarled as we yanked and pulled, but we managed to get that damn bag of freaking rocks over the threshold and outside.

The second the bag crossed the threshold, it became normal again. "Whoa!" I said, as I tumbled onto my ass from the release of weight. All three of us wound up on the ground for a second.

Cynthia got to her feet first and lifted the bag with no problem. "And that's that," she said, swinging it gently.

"Let me go in and get the rest of our stuff," MJ said.

"Not alone," I replied. We went back in together, closed the back door and gathered up our tools and whatnot. We were back outside in a jiff.

Cynthia was waiting for us at the dock. Just as we reached her, Mary-Jane's phone, that had been in her backpack with Cynthia, started chirping. There was a clatter of tools falling to the ground as she cursed, "Shit! That's Ray's ringtone!"

My heart leapt in my throat. Shit was right! After breaking into Steve's house, destroying his fireplace, we still had things to get done. He must have gotten the email Steve had sent! "Don't answer it! Let it go to voicemail. We got to keep our focus and finish this, MJ!"

"Ummm, that's the third time it's gone off, hon," Cynthia said.

"Uh-oh." She grabbed her phone. "He sent some texts. Oh shit..." Her mouth fell open. "He's on his way here!" She squeezed her eyes shut, correcting herself. "Well, not here, here, but to Shannon's, where he thinks I am. Oh shit!"

"What's wrong?"

He's gonna find Steve in that hole, and if he finds out about this"—she brushed at the bruises on her neck— "he'll kill Steve."

"Forget smashing these rocks." Cynthia looked as shocked as I was. "Toss them into the lake. Let's hope that the water will drown out any vestige of power they still have. Hurry! We got to get there before Ray!"

THIRTY FOUR

Mary-Jane

When we turned down Shannon's driveway, my gut sank. Uh-oh—the white van with the restaurant's logo on the side was parked next to Libby's car. Ray had gotten here before us.

"Damn it!" Cynthia wheeled the truck in next to Libby's car and braked so hard, I was thrown forward, barely catching myself from banging into the dashboard.

The three of us scrambled out of the car and flew around to the side of the house.

Ray was standing toe to toe with Shannon. Well, not really. Robert was on one side of the hole in the ground. Thank goodness too. Despite Shannon impassively staring at Ray, he was yelling his head off.

"What the hell did you do to Steve? Why is he stuck in this hole in the ground?" He looked down into the chasm. "You okay, buddy? Say something!"

We must have gotten there right after him. Hearing us, he turned to face me. "Mary-Jane! What the hell is going on with you? Why is Steve in the hole?" He held up his cell phone. "And what the hell is this all about? Is this some kind of joke you guys are playing? Have you been drinking again? What the hell is going on around here?"

Behind him, Robert tilted his head to the side and looked at us, then back up at Ray. I swear to God, I was positive he was thinking, *Who is this nutcase?* I took a deep breath and asked, "What did Steve say in his email to you?"

"That you and your friends think you're some kind of witches; you attacked him and have him trapped at Shannon's house! That you're doing some kind of crazy drugs or something, thinking you have magic powers!" He looked down at Steve. "What the hell is this, man? Answer me!" He shot a look back at me. "What did you women do to this poor guy? Steve Murphy is my friend!"

Cynthia let a huff from behind me. "There's no way we're going to be able to get this cat back in the bag, hon," she murmured.

"Yeah." I looked over at my husband. "Well, honey, it's kinda a long story..."

Never looking away from the ice in Ray's scowl, I walked over to stand next to Shannon. The only thing separating Ray and me was the trench in the yard.

"How?" Ray's gaze drifted from me to Shannon and then to Libby, before he looked down in the pit where Steve was. "Don't worry, Steve, I'm going to get you out of there in a minute. I just..." He shook his head and once more locked eyes with me. "Start talking, MJ! Tell me what happened. I'm waiting." He folded his arms and stood up straighter, like some high-school principal about to dole out detentions.

My fingers curled into a fist as I peered at my husband. Again with the tone. That same tone he'd used berating me for the DUI that Steve had somehow caused. If he hadn't used that belittling tone, I might have felt some empathy for him being dragged into something beyond logic and reason. But no—again, he was treating me like the junior partner.

Once more.

I spat my words at him. "It's true. I'm a witch, Ray. But so is your new BFF, Steve! He attacked me. He would have strangled me if not for my friends. They saved me."

Libby's voice brought my attention to the surface again. "Ray. I know this is a lot to take in, but Mary-Jane is telling you the truth. Steve isn't who you think he is. We were defending ourselves. He tried to kill MJ."

"Do you realize how crazy you sound, Libby?" Ray's mouth fell open as he gaped at her. "How did this pit happen? I feel like I just stepped into the set of some Stephen King movie. And my wife's a witch?" He looked up at the sky. "Oh Lord, give me strength." He dropped his gaze and marched around the pit to get into my face. "The only people I see hurt here is Steve, MJ. He can't even talk, and he's fallen into that damn hole in the ground."

He looked over at Shannon. "What's with the hole? You putting in a swimming pool or something?" His eyes got flinty. "You. This is all because of you, isn't it? You've even got that mangy bobcat that Steve tried to kill. You're behind all this crazy shit!"

It did not surprise me to hear the cat let out a piercing yowl before he hissed. Ray jerked back, staring at the bobcat.

Libby said, "No you *can't,* Robert. That man is Mary-Jane's mate, and she'd be upset. He's just angry and confused for now." Robert replied with a low-pitched grunt and sat back down at Shannon's feet. "Shannon will be fine, don't worry."

Ray's jaw dropped. "Are you trying to talk to that animal, Libby?"

"Nope. I *am* talking to this bobcat. And his name is Robert. Show some respect."

Cynthia let out a light laugh. "Well, this cat's fully and *completely* out of the bag now!"

Ray's mouth moved, but no words came out. His jaw went up and down as he looked at each of us wide eyed.

"Baby, this is a lot to take in, I know..."

"A LOT TO TAKE IN? YOU'RE OUTTA YOUR MIND!" He ran around to our side of the pit and reached for me, grabbing me by the arm. "We're leaving! I'm gonna take you home to dry out, and then I'm taking you to the mental ward over in Margaritaville. You need professional help, Mary-Jane!"

"Let go of me!" I wrenched my arm free and backed up.

And then...well...

With a shout, Ray lunged at me. But he only got a half a step before he was blown off his feet and landed on his ass. "What the—!" he grunted.

I looked to the other side of Libby where Cynthia smiled, blowing on her fingertips. When Ray tried to get on his feet, she flicked her hand in his direction, and he flopped back onto the grass. "Not yet, big boy," she said. "Calm down a little, okay?"

His face went white. "A talking bobcat, Cynthia's doing Jedi shit..." He looked up at me. "What the hell's happening, Mary-Jane?"

I went over to him and squatted down. "Baby...I'm a witch." I put my hand on his chest.

I almost burst into tears at what flooded into me. Ray was genuinely frightened that I was crazy. He didn't know what to do to make me better, and it scared the hell out of him. He gave a fleeting thought to Chloe, but then his heart went out to me wondering how he could help me and make this all better." I misted up. "You love me, right?" He nodded silently. "So just catch your breath, and listen to me, okay?"

His own eyes were tearing up. Not because he got knocked on his ass, but because he was dead certain I was losing my mind. Which, of course, made me let out a little sniffle too.

Good grief, this man loved me. "It's going to be okay, hon," I said. "Weird as shit, yeah. But it's going to be okay,

okay? Can you just trust me enough to hear me out?" He nodded, and I stood and helped him to his feet.

"How... what the hell knocked me on my ass?" he asked.

"Sorry for the hard landing, Ray, but I just thought you needed a little demo to cut through the bullshit." Cynthia brushed her hands against each other. "That, my friend, was magic! Now it seems to me like you have a choice. You either accept that your wife is a witch with magical powers and trust that she's telling you the truth, or you believe that jerk in the pit that she's doing drugs."

"*You* did this?" he said to Cynthia, pointing at the pit.

Shannon spoke up. "Cynthia knocked you down, but it was me. I made the earth open up to swallow Steve because he was trying to strangle your wife!"

"What?"

I stepped into him, holding him around the waist. "A lot of stuff was going on, but yeah, Steve grabbed me by the throat, hon." I lifted my neck to show him the finger marks that were still there.

"What?" He stared at me dumbly—that expression was becoming familiar now. But as gentle as a feather, he touched the side of my neck. "Mary-Jane...?"

The absolute, white-hot, murderous rage that erupted from him staggered me. I had no idea a human being could be so *dark*. He didn't want to beat on Steve—he wanted to kill him! Slowly! So he could scream in agony, gasping his last breaths! Visions of broken bones, blood, and screams filled my head. Holy shit. "Honey! I'm okay! I'm okay! And we took care of that son of a bitch!" I said. I grasped his shirt, giving him a shake. "I'm okay! We're okay! I love you!" Ray was panting now.

I had an idea. "Baby, hold me? Just hold me for a minute, please?"

His arms encircled me like pythons. He crushed me to his chest. Looking up, I watched his face as he looked at the edge of the pit. His breathing evened out from the ragged, enraged gasps back to normal as I squeezed him back.

This has been a real bitch of a day, you know that? I got choked out, almost broke my freaking hand taking a sledgehammer to a demon stone, and now I was in the mother of all bear hugs.

I really, really needed a bubble bath.

And a drink.

As he held me, Ray looked over toward the girls. "So what is it? You guys like the Avengers or something? You each got superpowers?"

Shannon grinned. "I really like that idea!" Smiling, she said, "Not exactly. But each of us has developed supernatural gifts, yeah." She pointed to each of us. "Libby can *really* talk to animals, Ray. Cynthia's got some wicked telekinesis abilities and other stuff. And... when I get really upset..." She gestured at the split in the earth.

"What about you, hon?" he asked me.

I grinned. "I can read minds."

"Bullshit!"

"Oh, yeah?"

"Yeah! That's crazy!"

I stuck my tongue out at him. His rage was gone, but his blood was running hot. "Think of something sexy." I paused. Then I snatched at the back of his neck and pulled his head down so I could whisper, "Oh you bad, baaad boy! Spankings, huh? That's *hot*!"

"Ohmygod."

I let go of his neck. "I'm glad to know *that*!"

He threw up his hands. "OKAY! I BELIEVE! OKAY?"

He stepped to the side of the pit and stared down at Steve. "So what do you got to say for yourself, you son of a bitch?" When there was no response, he yelled, "Answer me, you bastard!"

"He can't," I said. When Ray looked over at me, I pointed to Libby. "She put a spell on him to shut him up."

"You guys do spells too?"

I nodded. "Kinda. That's what's made stuff so crazy these last few months, babe."

"We're trying to figure out just what we can do, and how to do it," Shannon added. "We're really new to all this."

"This all started when you moved up here, didn't it, Shan?"

She nodded. "I came into realizing that there's magic, and I shared it with my two best friends in the world." She looked over at Cynthia. "Cynthia joined us because she's been practicing the white arts on her own and got wind of what we'd been doing." Her face softened. "She's the baby sister I never had."

"Oh Shannon..." Cynthia said. She went over and put her arm around her waist. "Shannon..." She turned to Ray. "Let me introduce you to the witches' coven of Wesley, New York!"

With a sick laugh—a chuckle bordering on the maniacal, to tell the truth—Ray took a deep bow. "How do you do, Witches Of Wesley!"

He straightened up and went back to the edge of the pit. "And this bastard's been giving you a hard time?" He put his fists on his waist.

"Yeah. Pretty much," Shannon said.

Ray horked a huge goober that only guys can do and launched it down the pit.

"Let's get that bastard up here."

THIRTY FIVE

Shannon

"Ray," I said. "I want you to control yourself, okay?"

He looked over at me. "I hear ya." He pointed at Steve. "Why isn't that candy-ass saying anything?"

Libby raised her hand like she was in class. "Like we said, I kinda put that spell on him? He's unable to speak until I remove it." She looked over at me. "What are we going to do about him?"

Well, that was the million-dollar question, wasn't it?

"Maybe put a spell on him to remove his memory of magic?" Cynthia said.

"Can you do that?"

She shrugged. "I've never done one, but I'm happy to try. I mean, if I fry his brain, so what?" She stepped to the edge of the pit. "Bastard was happy to put a spell on me and get me in the sack!" She kicked a clod of rocks and dirt from the edge down on him. "A goddamn supernatural roofie!" She leaned over the edge. "And you didn't need to, asshole! We had great times together, didn't we? You needle dick!" She turned and faced us. "It wasn't *exactly* like a date rape. I mean, we had a thing a few years back, right? And I was pretty attracted to him, but it was his damn spell that kept me from being able to talk to you guys, y'know?"

"Yeah," MJ added, "I hear you. Making Devon Booker swoon all over me sure as hell made my life complicated. I say let's give it a try, brain fry or not."

Ray nodded. "Yeah, Devon's all right, but when he kept hitting on you, it really got under my skin."

"Wait a second," I said. "You think Devon Booker's a good guy?"

Ray looked at me. "Sure! He's doing a lot for the town with his developments. He brings in new residents, and that factory he's putting up... yeah, he's a solid citizen, for sure." He looked at me curiously. "And he's a pretty nice guy. Don't you think so, Shan?"

"Yeah, Shannon," Libby said. "Devon Booker's a good guy."

"Devon's yummy. I wouldn't kick him out of bed," Cynthia said. She shrugged.

I stared at all of them. "You guys used to slag him all the time!"

"Who, us?" Libby said. "Whatever are you—" She went still. "Shit! You're right!" She looked around. "We used to hate that guy! How the hell..." She stopped, and we all looked at the pit. She chewed her lower lip and shook her head slowly. "Steve, you're such a goddamn bastard." She turned to me. "Yes, I'm for erasing his memory as well."

But the idea of messing around with someone's memory just gave me the chills. I mean, I screwed things up with love spells, and when I wanted MJ to get fit, that sure went sideways. I just didn't think it was a good idea.

Robert let out a long series of spine-tingling yowls before stepping over to the edge of the pit and hissing. It was clear he felt the same way as Libby, but I had to be sure.

"Robert wants to finish him, but he'll support you in whatever decision you make, Shannon." Libby stared across the pit at MJ. "He tried to choke you, MJ. Surely, you want to see him go to jail."

Ray barked a reply, "He needs to be punished for hurting MJ! All this time we trusted him, and he lied, pretending to be my friend."

Mary-Jane patted Ray's arm and stepped forward, peering down at Steve. "You practiced dark magic with the goal of getting rich and being more powerful. When we do magic—white magic with good intentions—sometimes it boomerangs and we pay the price."

Her eyes were narrowed when she looked over at the rest of us. "Why doesn't it work like that for him? He hurt all of us with his magic, yet he gets a free pass from the universe? That doesn't sound right to me."

As she spoke, I heard Aunt Maeve's voice in my head: *"Mary-Jane is right on this, Shannon. You're taking too much on yourself in deciding his fate. If you truly trust in the power of magic, you need to step back and allow retribution to play out for Steve as the universe wills it."*

My eyes closed as I let out a long sigh. Aunt Maeve and MJ had raised good points.

Also, if I stopped trying to manage this by casting the memory spell or even pressing charges to have him thrown in jail, there might be a way that his son wouldn't be deprived of his father. That was actually a bigger concern than Steve's well-being.

I looked at each of my friends. "We believe in magic, so we must trust in it as well. His punishment will be doled out by an order of three, but it won't be by our hands."

Mary-Jane was the first to answer. "Are you sure, Shannon? We just let him walk and trust in fate or karma or something?"

"Yeah, I mean, none of us are familiar with memory spells, right? What if we do it wrong? Will we be able to undo it?"

She shrugged. "Beats me."

"And that's my point. Messing with someone's memories is a big deal. They're such an important part of what makes us who we are." I gestured at Steve. "And he's got a long track record with magic, going back years and years. How could we tease it out to figure out which ones to remove or keep?" I shook my head. "No. Instead of taking the chance of making things worse, I'll trust the universe." I crossed my arms and looked over at each of my four coven sisters. "Look—it's been pretty strict with us, right?"

A series of nods and yeahs were their replies. "So, I think that what we do, is we trust in the universe to balance out Steve's punishment? Now that we broke that keystone at his place, his power over the town and us isn't anything like it was, right? So let's allow the universe to finish the job."

Mary-Jane was the first to reply. "That's why you're the leader, Shannon." She nodded. "So mote it be."

Libby crossed her arms over her chest. "I hope we don't regret this but... So mote it be, Shannon."

Robert stepped over to my side and rubbed his head along my thigh. When I looked down at him, he blinked slowly, dipping his head—his way of saying yes. That only left Cynthia.

There was an evil smirk on her lips as she stared down at Steve. "You wanted magic so bad, well, you're about to really experience the effects. Our hands are clean. Hell, I'll go get the ladder to get you out. Let the shitshow begin." She looked over at me. "So mote it be."

I faced Libby. "You're up, Libs. I think you're going to have to remove the silencing spell you put on him."

"This, I *gotta* see," Ray said as Libby stepped to the edge of the pit. His eyes darted from her to Steve, down in the pit.

Libby took a breath:

Your powers faded, a threat no more,

Have your say as you head out the
door.

Like a curious crow, Ray's head pivoted toward Steve, then back to Libby. "That's it?"

She shrugged. "My rhyming sucks, but my intent is pure."

Ray looked back down into the pit. "Is he able to talk now?"

"YOU FLAMING BITCHES! YOU RUINED EVERYTHING!" Steve bellowed.

"Guess it worked." Ray turned to us. "So now what?"

"I got the ladder, hon," Cynthia called, coming over from the shed.

"What?" Ray said. "You're not going to do some Jedi stuff and float him out of there??

I shook my head slowly. "I haven't ever even *tried* a levitation spell. I don't even know if there is one."

He chuckled. "I'll bet there is."

"Maybe, but I'd need to develop it, and then practice it with intent." Cynthia was standing by with the extension ladder. "This is a lot simpler, don't you think?" We got it extended and lowered it into the pit.

Steve scrambled up the ladder. He was a sight to behold. He was covered in mud stains all down his front, the crotch of his pants were wet from him peeing himself, and his eyes were wild with anger.

I felt an energy of decay, coupled with impotent rage, emit from him. It was like walking into an abandoned home—what once was would never be again. I figured once the anger passed, he would become a very sad man. To think he once fired up every single one of my erogenous zones with a look. I shuddered in disgust.

"You stupid, stupid bitches! We could have ruled this town! Shit! Probably the world! But noooo... you hadda do everything your way! You stupid, incompetent bitches!"

Ray sidled up next to him. "Watch your mouth."

"Screw you!"

And once again, a fully grown man flew across my yard to land on his ass. I barely saw Ray's hand move when he hit him square on the face; it was so fast!

"Whoa," I said.

Ray marched up to Steve, who scrabbled backward like a terrified crab, his eyes wide and blood seeping from his mouth and nose. "You hit me! I'm goin' to the cops!"

"You're damn well going somewhere, Murphy! Get on your feet and get the hell out of here before I lose my temper." Ray's voice was low, even, and dripping with hate. "Hurt *my* Mary-Jane? You cross my path, I'll goddamn kill you, I swear to God. And no jury would convict me."

Steve got to his feet. "This isn't over," he said. "Not by a long shot." His voice dripped menace, but again, I felt under it a sense of powerlessness from him. He *knew* his abilities were nothing like they had been. He knew it.

Cynthia looked over at me. "The keystone is neutralized, but he's being an ass right to the bitter end. Should I call the police and finish this? We've got enough on him that he could be put away. Attempted murder, assault. The magic he used on me was the equivalent of a roofie, but we won't be able to sell that."

My eyes met his full on now. The ebbing of his power was clear, and I could say what was on my mind without being influenced by him. In fact, covered in mud, he looked pretty pathetic. Was the memory spell even necessary? Nahhh, not at all.

Steve wasn't done yet. "You'll pay! You'll all pay!"

Robert let out a hiss and rushed at him. It was enough to stop the taunts and threats and replace them with a shriek when Steve spun around, sprinting up the drive.

"Robert! Leave him."

At my command, Robert stopped short. He turned and came to my side. I rubbed his ear as I watched Steve disappear from sight when he turned to follow the highway back to his house.

Ray faced all of us. "Hey, y'know something? He always was a miserable punk, wasn't he?" He looked up at the sky with a puzzled expression. "How come I forgot all about that?"

"Magic," MJ said, stepping over and putting her arms around her man's waist. "He put a glamour on the whole town."

"What's a glamour?"

"A spell. It makes people not see stuff that's there." She turned to me. "I think you made the right call, Shannon. Let him live his life as the universe allows."

I nodded. The feeling of peace that flooded through me was a sure sign that I'd made the right decision. And to have my friends agree was the icing on the cake. Again, Aunt Maeve's voice whispered to me:

"I'm proud of you, Shannon. This was hard for someone as headstrong and impatient as you are. But you'll see, sometimes stepping back and doing nothing is the best course of action. I would hate to be in his shoes."

I nodded. "And that's that," I said.

THIRTY SIX

Shannon

When we were all in my living room, having our second calm-down drink from the afternoon's events, my phone chirped with a series of text messages. I ignored them, figuring it was Steve ranting about one thing or another. So the hell with that. And... if it was Devon worried about me? Well—if he was only worried enough to send a text and not call. That said something, didn't it? To be perfectly honest. I was so damn worn out from this afternoon that I really didn't give much of a damn one way or another.

Libby wasn't worried about Stan's reaction to Steve's email; she felt he could either accept the truth or not. If he decided that her endeavors weren't for him, so be it.

Cynthia was completely blasé about how Eric would take it—she thought maybe the easiest way around it would be to just glamour his phone so the email wouldn't even register. "Or whatev. Maybe just let Steve take the weight," she said. "I might just shrug my shoulders and tell him I think Steve's got some loose screws." She snickered. "I won't lie to Eric, but I also don't think I need to answer it one way or the other outright." She gestured at MJ. "I mean... of all of us, only *one guy* cared enough to show up here and find out for himself, right?"

MJ said nothing, thank God. Instead of any kind of humble brag, she just squeezed into Ray, nodding. To be honest, I was envious. Not jealous, but yeah, envious.

Yeah, we were all beat to a snot. Everyone cleared out shortly after that.

"How about you and I Netflix and chill, Robert?" I grabbed the tray of munchies MJ had brought, and along with a Coke, headed into the living room. As I settled onto the couch, I realized I couldn't remember the last time I just sat around and watched TV!

Robert was fine with it too, hopping up on the couch beside me.

My phone chimed again, and again I ignored it.

A half hour later, I was watching a stand-up comedy special, and the sound of an SUV came skidding into my driveway.

Robert was up like a shot, standing on the arm of the couch with his back arched, hissing. But when the engine shut off, his nose twitched, and he relaxed.

"It's not Steve right?" He did his "Robert nod," slowly closing and opening his eyes. "Is it Devon?"

Yep.

"Shit. I don't think I can take any more drama today. And I was all comfy." I got up from the couch. "Maybe I'll just put him off till tomorrow. What do you think?"

I found out then that bobcats can shrug. Great.

Before I could get out of the living room, the knocking at my front door became louder and louder by the second. “Hang on! I’m coming!”

I flung the door open. “What’s the matter with you! Could you just give me a minute to get to the door?”

Devon let out a whoosh of air. “Oh man. Thank God, you’re okay!” He looked past me. “Is that asshole here?” Robert let out a small yowl. “Hey! Your cat came back! That’s great!”

He looked down at me. “So Murphy’s not here, right? Did you get an email from him? I think he’s losing his mind. Why didn’t you respond to any of my texts? What’s going on, Shannon?” He looked me up and down. “You going to ask me in?”

I stared at him and swung the door open. “I’m pretty beat, Devon. You could have called, you know.”

He snorted. “I tried, but for some stupid reason I could only get emails on my phone and send text messages. I couldn’t make any phone calls.”

I crossed my arms. “Yeah. Right.”

“Look, Shannon. I was seven miles up in the air.” He pointed a finger up toward the sky. “I was coming back from a meeting in Silicon Valley. We’re working on expanding our investor circle for my projects here in Wesley. I was probably over freaking Ohio or something when my cell dinged with that insane email from Steve Murphy.”

His eyebrow arched high when he shot me an incredulous look. “He was going on about how you guys had him trapped, and you thought you were witches or something. It was pretty weird. So I sent you a text asking what the hell was going on.” He paused. “Then I sent you another. And another. As soon as my flight touched down, I sent you a text telling you I was coming straight to your house.” His head tipped to the side. “Is your phone even working? What the hell’s happening?”

Jeezuz! Devon was going a mile a minute!

"And what's with the hole in the ground outside? Is your septic acting up again? Good grief. I leave for one lousy day, and things go nuts in town!"

"My septic's fine. Yes, I heard my phone alert. But you still could have phoned."

"Phoned."

"Yeah. You know..." I mimed holding a cell and punching buttons, and held my hand to my ear. "Hello, Shannon, it's Devon. Everything okay?"

"I'm standing right in front of you! That's the thanks I get for driving like a maniac from the airport? Forgive me for worrying about you."

"Well..." I held my hand up to make another point. And had nothing. Damn. Maybe, just maybe, I should have checked my text messages. Maybe. I put on a cheese grin. "Well, would you like a drink or something?" It was the least I could do.

"Sure." He walked past me into the foyer.

Robert had hopped off the couch and circled Devon's legs like a tabby cat. An overgrown tabby cat. But he was purring. Devon reached down and scratched him between the ears. "You okay, buddy? That son of a bitch tagged you, didn't he? He ran his hands down Robert's flanks. "You're kinda skinny. She feeding you okay?"

When Robert let out a series of low yowls, Devon laughed. "You would think he understands what I'm saying!" He looked over at me. "I think your cat here wants you to feed him more."

Robert blinked at me, gently rocking his head.

"Betcha you'd love a fresh fish, wouldn't ya, bud? Tell ya what. Next time I'm out, I'll make sure to bring you some fresh caught salmon, okay?" When Robert let out another bobcat *meow,* he laughed again. "Deal!"

I shot Robert a look. *Pretty slick move buster!* He just yawned and strutted away, leaving us alone. "Let's head into the kitchen," I said to Devon.

"What the hell is up with Murphy?"

As I reached for the bottle of Jack Daniels, I hesitated. "Steve is..." Finally, I settled for something vague. "He's not well, Devon."

"I could have told you that. But what's he doing? Is he dangerous now? To you, I mean?"

"Not anymore."

"That's good, but what happened? After that email he sent, he should be locked up in the looney bin."

I shook my head as I poured our drinks.

"And what's the deal with all this witch stuff he was raving about? That's some crazy shit going on there." He chuckled. "You'd think a guy Stevie Murphy's age would know better than to toss stupid kid stuff like that around."

"Well..." Damn it; I wish I had more time to have figured out what the hell to tell Devon. Part of me wanted to just dismiss Steve and everything that had happened, but another part of me wanted to come clean with him.

His eyes bored through me as he took the drink I handed to him. "Well, what, Shannon?"

So I told him. I skirted the subject of the well, telling him instead that I found things about witchcraft shortly after moving in here and that me, MJ, and Libby started messing with it. I told him how Cynthia is also a "practicing witch" and how she joined us. We learned that Steve Murphy was a practitioner of the dark side of magic, and he attempted to force us to bend to his will. There was a confrontation, and we sent Steve packing. I took a deep breath, glad to have it out in the open now.

He watched me with a steady gaze through my entire explanation. When I was done, he leaned in with narrowed eyes. "So you think you're a witch, Shannon?"

I shook my head. "No. I don't think it. I *am* a witch."

"Shannon... you really believe that you can do magical stuff? What do you do? Wave a wand? Or is it a broomstick? Come on. I thought we were past all this crazy stuff."

What the hell did I expect? I walked to the back patio door and crooked my finger at him. "Come here." When he joined me, I pushed the door open and stepped onto the deck. Pointing to my yard, I said, "See that? That hole in the ground? *I* did that."

"You did that." A smile teased at the corners of his mouth. "What—you waved your hands, and the earth 'magically' opened up?"

"Nope. I didn't have to wave my hands. I just got angry." I turned to him. "Don't make me angry. You wouldn't like me when I'm angry."

His face softened. "Shannon, come on..."

Damn it! Wait a second. "Follow me." I went back into the house.

I led the way to the dining room alter which I had set up. In addition to my Grimoire and herbs were a line of candles. I turned to Devon. "Watch." Gazing at the candles, I said a silent prayer to Mother Earth and the universe, stilling myself. Feeling the strong intent grow inside me, I said:

"Truths been told
I'm not to blame
Candles I ask, come aflame."

My hand waved over the candles. One by one, they lit up as my hand passed over them. My eyes popped wider as I watched the flame grow. "Holy shit!" I murmured. My first time trying that and it worked!

"Whoa!" Devon took a step back, gaping at the flames.

"Now do you believe me?"

His mouth fell open as he stared at the candles. "That is *some* trick, Shannon! How the hell'd you do it?"

"Magic!" I hopped up and down, clapping my hands. "Isn't it cool! I never tried to do that before! But I *really, really* wanted to show you it's true!"

He flipped his hand, like he was batting at a mosquito. "No, seriously now, Shannon. Granted, that trick was so damn cool! Great sleight of hand. How'd you do it?" He took my hands. "You don't have a cigarette lighter... or do you?" He looked over the surface of the altar. "Where'd you toss it?"

My heart sank, and I let out a sigh. "Fine."

"Wait. What? Don't say fine. I didn't mean to piss you off. I'm impressed by your talent. You're seriously good at this." He looked out the window at the pit in the yard. "When you used that line, 'You wouldn't like me when I'm angry...' I almost laughed out loud! Straight outta *The Incredible Hulk*! That was perfect!"

His mouth snapped shut when he noticed the *not good* look on my face. "Hey, c'mon, Shannon. I mean"—he gestured at the burning candles— "that's a really, really cool trick! It looked almost real!"

"ALMOST?" There was a short thud, and the house trembled. I hadn't even noticed that I'd stamped my foot until the vibrations tingled in my toes. I threw up my hands. "Fine!"

Devon's gaze darted around the living room. "Did you feel that?" He shook his head, grinning at me. "That was pretty cool too."

For a moment he was silent before he tapped his palm against his forehead. "Wait. This is all from the stuff you found, that your Aunt Maeve left, right?"

"What?" The level of exasperation at his reaction wasn't making me crazy enough? What the hell was he going on about now?

Smirking, he gaped at me. "Oh, come on. Lots of people in town knew about your aunt. There were rumors going around that she had told some people in town she was a witch. So she rigged some stuff up in this house or something, right? Fooling people at Halloween or something?"

Pointing at me, he continued, "You must have found them, and now you're doing something here with me. How come? Trying out your first rube or something?" He made a moue with his face. "Well, you did a good job, Shannon. You could have fooled me, for sure. Except..." He grimaced sheepishly. "Except there's no such thing as magic. Next thing I'll be seeing is ghosts, right?"

"He's gotten MY dander up too, Shannon!" Maeve's voice echoed in my mind. *"I only told Arthur Crenshaw! He didn't believe*

me either! And it was him who started those damn rumors back in '01! The bastard!"

"Take it easy, Maeve," I murmured.

"Oh my God, you're good!" Devon guffawed. "That's perfect!" He covered his mouth with his hands. "Perfect!"

Gazing around the room, he blurted. "Hi, Maeve! This is Devon Booker! Yooo hooo! Anybody there?" He turned in a circle, still grinning. "Anybody? Anyone?" Shooting a grin at me, he chuckled, "Your Aunt Maeve was a gracious lady, Shannon. A little eccentric, but okay for an old lady. I mean even discounting the purple bathrobe she wore everywhere, even grocery shopping."

My gaze swooped to my left when my aunt bellowed in my head:

"That wasn't a bathrobe! It was an over-sweater! It was all the rage for mature women in the 90s! I wasn't going around wearing a damn BATHROBE!"

It jogged a memory that flashed in my head. "I remember you wearing them, Aunt Maeve. But come to think of it, they did kind of look like a bathrobe...well, a vest that was really long..."

My gaze darted to Devon. "You're upsetting my aunt, Devon."

"Ooooh! Wouldn't want to upset ol' Auntie Beetlejuice!" He chortled as he stared at the ceiling. "Hey! If I say your name three times, will you show up? Whaddya say, Maeve? That's once! Maeve? That's—"

"IT WAS AN OVER-SWEATER, YOU BRATTY KID!" As bright as a strobe light, Maeve appeared right in front of Devon, glowing like a million suns.

Wearing a purple over-sweater.

"She's trying to tell you the truth, you idiot!" Aunt Maeve's voice was the screech of a banshee.

"AAAAAAAAAaaaaaaa!"

For the THIRD time today, a grown man flew through the air. Devon must have leaped back ten feet. He tripped over the end of the couch in the living room, bounced on his ass, and scrambled to his feet.

The whites of his eyes showed as he looked over at me. "You're completely out of your freaking mind, Shannon! This is insane!"

In a frazzle of pure panic, he flew to the front door. I watched him yank on the doorknob three times before remembering to turn the knob and throw the door wide open. His feet thundered across my verandah before I caught sight of him racing to his car.

Maeve's ghost and I stood there in shock, hearing his car start up, peel out of my driveway, and burn rubber down the road.

She turned to me, blinking slowly. *"Holy doodle. That didn't go well."*

"Ya think?"

THIRTY SEVEN

Shannon

After parking my car on the main street close to MJ's restaurant, I glanced at my watch. Perfect. The breakfast rush had finished, and we had over an hour to talk before she had to prep for the lunch crowd. As I headed down the main street, I slowed passing by Steve's hardware store. What the heck?

Plastered on the windows were large signs with Going Out Of Business and Everything Must Go-No Offer Refused. A veritable conga line of customers waited to get in while others trundled out carrying barbeques, gardening tools, woodworking tools and every sort of furnishing, geegaw and assorted stuff you'd find in a fair-sized hardware store.

When I entered MJ's place, she was in a booth toward the back, watching the door before she waved me over.

"What the hell's going on at Steve's place?" I asked, taking my seat.

Her eyes were wide. "The stuff I heard! You walk into that store, see a four-hundred-dollar table saw, offer him five bucks and bang! It's yours! Cash only, no credit cards, no holds, as is, and no returns. He's not ringing sales up, just stuffing the money in his pocket. Debbie went in as soon as the breakfast crowd thinned out about an hour ago and told me the store's almost empty already." She shook her head. "Word sure gets around fast, doesn't it?"

"What's he going to do?"

She shook her head. "I don't know, and I don't care. But"—she leaned across the table— "I'm pretty sure he's getting the hell out of Wesley as fast as he can!"

"How do you know that?"

"There's a For Sale sign up at his house! Didn't you see it when you headed in?"

My mouth became a firm line. "No. I didn't look at all toward his place." With a sharp nod, I added, "Well, if that's the case, good riddance." My heart went out to his son, Byron, though. I hoped he, at least, kept involved in the boy's life. But would it really be healthy for the lad to be in close and regular contact with that man?

I couldn't help but feel thankful that my own children would never have to deal with such a thing. There was a twisted, dark side to Steve that my own ex, Ass-hat that he is—never had. Yeah, he had his faults, for sure, but he wasn't a...a student of evil like Steve was. No, just a normal, run-of-the-mill Ass-hat.

In other words, it could be worse, for sure.

Pursing my lips, I changed the subject. "Devon stopped by my place after you guys cleared out last night."

"Oh?" Mary-Jane tilted her head at me with arched eyebrows.

"I...I tried to tell him the truth about us. I mean, he got the email that Steve sent, you know? So I figured if I was going to have anything to do with him in any general, long-term way, I had to tell him the truth." I looked down and fiddled with my coffee cup.

"Didn't go too well, huh?"

I shook my head. "Nope. Not. A. Bit." I let out a sigh. "Things went from bad to worse—Maeve even made an appearance, scaring the dickens out of him." I couldn't help but laugh. "He flew out of there soooo fast! Screaming, actually!"

"So he believes in magic now."

I looked up at MJ, and our eyes met. "Well, I'm not sure. I don't think so."

"What? Damn." Her eyes flicked over my shoulder to the front entrance as I heard the little bell at the entry dingle.

"You gotta go back to the kitchen?"

"Nope. Debbie's handling things there, and Sylvie's got the waitressing." She looked back at me. "So, Devon thinks you're crazy again, huh?"

I nodded. "Yeah. That idiot couldn't believe his own eyes! I showed him the pit I opened up in the yard, lit candles for him with just my finger...and *he saw a ghost!* A pretty pissed-off ghost, but a ghost. I don't blame him for being scared shitless, but to call me crazy? He saw it with his own eyes!"

"Maybe he needed time to process it, Shannon." When I shot her a look, she continued. "Devon's a good guy. He always had been. Even when most of the town thought he was a piece of shit, he still did the right thing, right?" I nodded. "I think he just needed to process it and maybe do some digging around on his own before coming to a conclusion. He was really, terrified when Maeve appeared!"

"Sure was! He fell over the couch and scrambled like Fred Flintstone trying to get out the door!" I laughed. Wait a minute... I peered at her. "How come you're so damn sure that Devon was really, terrified?"

"Because I told her, Shannon." Devon's voice came from behind me.

I didn't jump. I just dropped my head for a moment. "Hi, Devon."

MJ hopped to her feet. "He was waiting at the door to the restaurant when we showed up to prep for the breakfast crowd—"

"I spent the night in front of the place to make sure I didn't miss you guys," he said. I still didn't turn around. I was watching MJ.

"And...?" I asked.

She looked past me to where Devon stood behind my back. "And...well...I showed him I can read minds. It kind of opened you up to possibilities, didn't it, Devon?"

"Yeah," he said with a light laugh. "Something like that."

MJ chuckled too. "I'm envious you got to see Maeve's ghost, y'know."

"Don't be! She was pretty pissed off at me."

"I'll bet! And you had to do that *Beetlejuice* schtick?" She wrinkled her nose. "Not good."

I finally turned around. "It was more the bathrobe comment, Devon. That's what set her off."

"Sorry. I guess? I really thought it was a bathrobe." He held his hands up, palms out. "Whadda I know about women's fashion anyway?"

"Well..." MJ winked at me before she tapped the table with her knuckle. "I think you need to talk this out. I'll leave you two guys to it."

Devon slid into her seat in the booth across the table from me. He looked away for a moment before his eyes locked with mine. "I guess I ended it on an unpleasant note, didn't I?"

Instead of being pissed off at him, my chest melted as I gazed at him. Empathy? After all the rage I'd felt when me and my friends were subjected to Steve's attack, feeling the gentle emotion of empathy was welcomed like an old friend.

"We both overdid it a bit, I think. And Maeve losing her temper didn't help, did it?"

His eyes boggled at the memory. "Oh boy, you got that right." He paused for a second. "Let her know I apologized, would you? I mean, I don't want her coming to my place and...you know..."

"Haunting you? I think her dance card's full enough with her haunting me!" I laughed lightly. "I'll tell her." I leaned forward across the table. "But you ought to know she's pretty embarrassed herself for her outburst."

"Ghosts feel embarrassed?"

I nodded. "Holy doodle, yeah!"

It was again surprising how relaxed, how comfortable I felt. I sat back in my seat. "So you're telling me that you now believe in witchcraft and ghosts, huh?"

"Are there werewolves and vampires too?" he asked with a straight face. "Leprechauns and fairies?"

Hmmm.... "I honestly don't know. I haven't met any, if that means anything."

"Well, I haven't seen any so far, so I'll hold off any judgments, then."

"So you really believe me now."

He slid out of his seat and came over to my side of the table. I scootched over and he sat beside me. "It's a lot to take in, Shannon, which considering our history, shouldn't surprise me."

I nodded.

"How about I tell you what I *do* believe in."

I smiled at him. "G'head..."

His hand came up and cradled the back of my head, and he brought his mouth to mine and kissed me.

And it was a goooood one. Gentle, but firm, with lips slightly parted—our first real kiss.

Oh. GOD! It had been sooo long. Toooooo long since I had gotten a warm and wet one planted on me. I cupped the back of his head and pulled him closer, hungry for more. Oh, yeah. My hand came up and rubbed his chest over his polo shirt. He had great pecs; the muscle smooth under my fingers.

I pulled back, catching my breath. "Your place or mine?"

He was panting like he just ran a fifty-yard dash. Dayum! This girl still got it! "I have a different idea," he murmured.

"Oh?" I looked around the restaurant. "You don't mean here? We can't do that!" But it was empty, right? Maybe MJ had a storeroom? Oh my good goddess, listen to me! Shameless.

He held one of my hands in his, gazing into my eyes. "I just *had* to kiss you, Shannon—"

"I'm okay with it." I was still rubbing that solid chest with my free hand. Oh God, his pecs! Not man boobs—*pecs*! Pectorrrrallllsssssss!

"I'm so charged up right now..." he breathed. "Oh wow! Do you rock my world or what!"

Let's get to the what *part!* My insides went to jelly. Thank God we weren't standing because I think my knees would have given out.

He squeezed my fingers. "Listen. We're both super attracted to each other. And that kiss just proved that we're really simpatico."

Simpatico. I loved the way it caressed my ear. "Simpatico..." I purred.

"I want us to go slow."

WHAT?

He saw the look in my eyes and smiled. "Take a breath, Shannon. Over the course of the last six months—shit—almost a year! Since you moved in, you had a thing going with Steve Murphy, who turned out to be an even bigger douche than I thought he was. If Mary-Jane's story was true. On top of that, you and me, we were either hot to trot for each other or wanted to murder each other, and that was on the same day more than once, right?"

"Yeah, but. Yeah, but. Yeah, but..." Argh!

I took my hand off his chest and slapped the table. Dammit! "Dammit. I think you're right." When I looked at him, his eyes burned holes in me. The son of a gun was barely holding onto his self-control. I knew that if I took one of *his* hands and put it on *my* chest, the same way I had been playing with his chest...oh boyohboyohboy.

But I didn't. I watched him silently.

"Look," he said, "I think what we ought to do is take it slow. Let's go on...dates."

"Dates?"

"Yeah. Like when we were younger. The movies, dinner out, stuff like that. On the weekend, go to the lake..."

"I *live* on a lake, Devon."

"Okay! Okay! You know what I mean! Maybe go to Albany for a play or something? Syracuse for a festival? Day trips to the city kind of thing."

"Not New York City?"

He shook his head. "It's a three-hour drive, or more. We'd have to take a hotel room. And you know as well as me, that we'd be in bed in no time flat." He took my hand again. "Instead...let's get to know each other a lot more, okay? I'd love to see you do that candle thing again."

I laughed. "I'm so turned on now, a freaking bonfire wouldn't be a problem!"

"Just don't get angry, okay? I don't think I'd like you when you're angry." He shot me a cheesy grin.

I gave him a peck on the cheek. "Fair enough. So you're talking like real old-school kind of dating. Kissing but going slow, right?" It hit me. I was going to be "courted." Like in the old days! Shit, the last time a man courted me, I was standing before a judge listening to a divorce ruling. But this... was *right.* Right? "So, sir, you intend to court me, then?" I asked with my best Scarlett O'Hara voice.

"Yeah... well, just for a while, okay?"

"Why are you acting like a freaking Mormon right now? They're all pretty...you know... straight and narrow."

"So are the Catholics, you know. The one's that really buy into it, anyway."

"Whatever. How come?"

He took my hand again. "Because I want to do this right. I think that there's something really strong between us. And if we take our time, we'll strengthen it. At least that's how I want to play it."

I knew he was right, but that still didn't answer how I was going to manage it. I mean, he was hot as hell and it had been a very long time since... well, since I had sex. I took a deep breath. It wouldn't be easy, but then nothing worthwhile ever is. And Devon was totally worthwhile in my books.

He was watching me with a glint in his eye. "Whatcha thinking? Are we good?"

My hand cupped his cheek. "It won't be easy, but I guess we'll try to be 'good' or whatever. No promises, but we'll try to take it slow. It'll be a total change from our usual roller-coaster relationship, but maybe that's the only way things can work between us."

He kissed my fingers and grinned. "Not getting shot will be a bonus, but that problem has left town from what I hear." He sighed. "I hate to do this, but I have to run. I've got meetings all afternoon. I put them off this morning, but I really need to talk to these people. Some Wall Street investors are circling, and I got to fight them off."

"Wall Street? Isn't that a good thing? Stocks, bonds, and stuff?" I rubbed my fingers together. "Big bucks?"

He shook his head sharply. "No, not really. If they get their hooks in, they'll ruin it. I enjoy making a healthy profit, but these guys are vampire squids."

"Okay." I got out of the booth.

Standing, he took me in a hug and gave me another one of those Johnny Depp style kisses. Yep, I was right. My knees got weak for a bit. "I'll send a crew out to your place to fill that hole in. Don't kill 'em okay?" he said with a chuckle.

"I won't. I'll even make them coffee."

"Great. I'll phone you later. I'm going to ask you out legit. And I'll phone—no texts."

Fair enough.

And I kissed *him*. And felt *his* knees tremble.

So there.

***

Later that night I was sitting out in my yard on a cushioned bench. Naturally, Robert was curled up beside me, dozing. There was a small bonfire crackling (that I didn't need matches for, if you know what I mean... which is *really* cool) that warmed my legs as I sat gazing at the stars.

I'd stopped by to see Libby on the way home after leaving Devon. She was doing fine. Stan got the email, and when he asked her about it, she told him that the four of us were researching this sort of stuff. He took it with as much equanimity as if she'd told him we were doing a ceramics course together. As long as she was happy and safe, he was fine.

Steve Murphy was gone for good. He locked up his store and put a big sign on the window that said See Ya Wesley! Thanks for NOTHING! The lights in his house were all dark, and there was no vehicle in the driveway.

I wasn't too worried. I had Robert, and the girls told me they were going to stop by tomorrow to do a series of protection spells around my property. Cynthia lived in a pretty secure apartment in town; MJ had Ray at home, and Libby and Stan were pretty much inseparable. I was all alone out here.

Except I *did* have Robert, and that bobcat would die for me. He'd already proved it once, and if Steve ever showed up, Robert wouldn't give the man a chance. I was comfortable.

With my feet stretched out, wrapped up in one of Maeve's quilts. From the chill of the night air, it was very peaceful. My life felt damn good. That blowup with the ladies was like piercing a boil on my heart. Now that it had happened, I didn't feel any pressures or tension. I was able to just relax and *be* in the night. And it felt damn good.

I watched the stars above. There was something on the news about odd lights in the sky near Albany and the military base near Syracuse. With what had been all over the media lately, I was hoping I'd get a chance to see the dancing lights they were talking about.

And sure as shooting, two lights appeared in the sky above me. I watched them as they zipped along, glowing with a radiance like the moon. Except, instead of the white moonglow, they were yellowish to red. There were two of them. I'm not sure how high up they were, not as high as an airliner, but about as high as a propeller plane would be.

But they weren't planes. They would zip in one direction, then stop and hover, and then zip in the opposite direction. I didn't hear any engines or propellers; they flew around silently. Then, like two kids on Jet Skis, they wove over and under each other, making a spiral across the sky.

It was really cool to watch! Luke Skywalker and Han Solo out in their sky-buggies clowning around and having fun.

After a bit, they took off over the horizon, zigging and zagging between each other as they faded from sight. I smiled, and lifting a hand, bid them adieu.

It really is a wondrous universe.

The End

Author's Note:

I enjoyed creating and then spending time with Shannon through the course of these three books. When she first appeared in my mind, she was a woman coping with having her world ripped asunder through no fault of her own.

One thing I've learned in my life that I tried to get onto the pages of Hex After 40 is 'be careful what you wish for'! But when things go sideways, it's the measure of the quality of a person's character in how they cope with unforeseen and unwanted fallout.

Shannon, Mary-Jane, Libby and Cynthia are dog tired right now. They need some serious down time to just relax. The sisterhood of their coven is stronger than ever, but each of them has things to process.

I wanted to close the book on 'The Witches Of Wesley' before it became a job for me. Finishing up at three books has left me feeling energized and happy. I hope you feel the same way too!

I'm not going to commit to further writing about their adventures.

But I'm also not going to say that there's nothing left for them!

Currently, I'm developing a new series of paranormal women's fantasy (new characters and a *waaay* different take) and I'm really having a good time! I'm so new at this series I can't even give you a title right now! Talk about fresh, huh? LOL

If you'd like to keep up with my own shenanigans, just join my readers group!

Just fire off an email: to michelle@michelledorey.com and I'll add you to the group! I'd love to let you know when my latest releases are up!

ABOUT THE AUTHOR

Michelle Dorey, writing as 'Shelley Dorey' is the author of more than a dozen spine-chilling novels featuring ghosts, haunted houses and the supernatural. She has been on the Amazon best seller list many times throughout her career.

A voracious reader of the masters like Stephen King and Dean Koontz, she decided to try her hand at writing after going on a Ghost Walk in the enigmatic city of Kingston, Ontario, Canada where she lives. Her first book, Crawley House was inspired by a true tale of a family's nightmare, living in a home owned by Queen's University.

"Expect the supernatural when the bedrock of a city is limestone. Throw in the fact it is bordered on three sides by the mighty St. Lawrence River, The Rideau River and Lake Ontario and you are in for some thrills and chills of the paranormal variety--which of course is my cup of tea."

Does she love Kingston? You bet! Her husband Jim, a transplanted native New Yorker born and raised in the Bronx, agrees. Michelle and Jim like nothing better than spoiling their two pugs with treats and long walks in their neighborhood. Funny, but the slightly neurotic dogs always refuse to go for a stroll in the cemetery nearby.

OTHER WORKS

All of Michelle Dorey and Shelley Dorey books are exclusively available on Amazon

Women's Paranormal Fantasy By Shelley Dorey

The Mystical Veil Series
Hex After 40 Series
Celtic Knot Series

Ghosts And Hauntings By Michelle Dorey

The Hauntings Of Kingston Series
The Haunted Ones Series
The Haunted Cabin

Printed in Dunstable, United Kingdom

70891368R00147